ır
RE

(
)
SCEPTRE

An Act of Worship

KATE THOMPSON

SCEPTRE
Hodder & Stoughton

Copyright © 2000 by Kate Thompson

First published in 2000 by Hodder and Stoughton
A division of Hodder Headline
A Sceptre Lir book

The right of Kate Thompson to be identified as the Author of the Work has been asserted by her in accordance with the Copyright, Designs and Patents Act 1988.

10 9 8 7 6 5 4 3 2 1

All characters in this publication are fictitious and any resemblance to real persons, living or dead, is purely coincidental.

A CIP catalogue record for this title is available from the British Library

ISBN 0 340 73959 2

Typeset by Palimpsest Book Production Limited,
Polmont, Stirlingshire
Printed and bound in Great Britain
by Clays Ltd, St Ives plc.

Hodder and Stoughton
A division of Hodder Headline
338 Euston Road
London NW1 3BH

My thanks to Tara Godfrey, Declan Bowes, Danny Duffy, Gerard Ruane and Niall Fallon, who all helped me with research for this book.

Prologue ∫

I was about three years old when I first saw the games a cat plays with a mouse. I crept underneath the kitchen table and watched. The mouse was paralysed with terror, and the cat was teasing it; batting at it with soft paws, then pretending to ignore it, turning its hard, yellow gaze away. But when the mouse thought it had a chance and tried to make a run for it, the cat would spring up and start cuffing it again.

It was quite clear that the mouse was taking no pleasure from the game. My sympathies were with it throughout, especially when it stood on its hind legs and raised it paws to the cat, as though it were pleading for its life. When my mother came in and saw what was going on, she tried to distract me and lead me away, but I couldn't be persuaded to leave until the mouse died and the cat, realising there was no sport left in it, began to eat it.

I don't remember being particularly upset, but my mother wrapped me in her arms in a comforting kind of way.

'The cat has to kill the little mice,' she said. 'That's the cat's job.'

There are definite advantages to being born in western Europe, even if we are, as my mother says, in the last stages of eating the goose that laid the golden eggs. Murder

1 •

and torture are comparatively rare and life is, on the whole, peaceful. Provided, of course, that you have the good sense to be a human being.

When I was born, I wasn't torn from my mother's body with the help of a winch, and I wasn't separated from her during my first days on earth. Nor, for a finish, did I end up in the hands of my father.

ʃ

Above the dump, a motley flock of birds was circling in a haphazard holding pattern. There were herring gulls, hooded crows, starlings, a few shabby pigeons. All the scavengers; the flying rats, blowing around like smutty ashes from a chimney. Waiting.

It was early. The tip-head wasn't open for business, yet. There had been a time when the gates were closed at night, but people had piled their rubbish outside them and caused trouble for Jimmy Kelly, who was the dump manager. Now the gates were open twenty-four hours a day. Green fields, swampy and rank, stretched away for miles in all directions. Apart from a few despondent cattle, they were empty. But still the birds were wary.

They began to drop carefully from the skies, one at a time, watching the wind, watching each other. There was no one around, but there was something moving on the edge of the level plateau, at the drop-off point. Something was alive that shouldn't have been. It shouldn't have been there at all.

Up among the birds I was watching as well; hanging in the ether, waiting. Their wings passed through me but did not touch me. We shared neither space nor concerns. They were waiting for the opportunity to scavenge, but I had no belly to fill. My hunger was of a different nature. I was waiting to be born.

A crow alighted near the tiny calf, pushing its courage, determined to have the eyes. The breeze blew thin smoke around it, reeking of burning offal and sludge. Closer and closer it edged until the calf saw it, discerned its intentions, and thrashed around in feeble protest. The crow lifted off and dislodged a young gull from its observation post on a disembowelled television. There it waited. It knew the calf couldn't hold out for much longer.

Jimmy Kelly arrived and opened up the rusty Portakabin that was the tip-head's office. A blizzard of birds rose, flurried around in the breeze for a while, then began to settle again. Jimmy looked at the bulldozer and wondered whether it would start today. He didn't even see the scavengers. He was used to them. Their behaviour was of no interest to him whatsoever.

But he decided to take a look around before he started work. It wouldn't be long before the Traveller lads arrived, and once that happened there would be no pickings to be had. They would waylay drivers as they arrived, unload their car boots or trailers for them, trawling through the rubbish for the things they valued – scrap metals, copper wire, anything saleable or salvageable or unusual. But this shift, the first of the morning, was his alone.

Last week someone had dumped a perfectly good steel-legged table, and a small gas cooker that still had two rings working. Jimmy had set them both up in the office, and they made the place quite homely, but he didn't really use them. He would probably try and sell them sooner or later.

No one had left anything remotely valuable that morning. There was, however, another carcass. The rules, posted on the chain-link fence beside the gates, stated that the dumping of carcasses or offal was prohibited by law. They were consistently ignored. The place stank like the cesspits of hell. People who came to drop rubbish tiptoed through the slime, their faces stiff with displeasure. Jimmy stank when he got home. It was, perhaps, just as well that there was no one there to greet him.

The crow hopped nearer to the calf's head and peered very closely into its eyes. It was a polite enough gesture, a desire to know whether or not it was finished with them, yet. But, weak and exhausted though it was, the calf wasn't, not quite. It drew on the last of its strength and rolled wildly, desperate to find its feet. Jimmy nearly jumped out of his skin. The crow departed, offended, and rejoined the complex manoeuvres in the skies.

Keeping his distance, a bit like the crow in his tattered black raincoat and soft hat, Jimmy edged up to the struggling beast. It was very young, and the few areas of its coat that weren't plastered with dung or dump slime were brilliant white and glossy black, as clean as only the newly born could ever be. There was no tag in either of its small ears.

Jimmy sighed. The calf had an empty look, as though it had never known nourishment. Its eyes were dull. It was definitely on its way out; there was no doubt about that. But it wasn't necessarily hopeless. Jimmy had seen amazing recoveries by young creatures. Once, when he was a child, he had discovered a sack full of abandoned kittens. They were cold and limp, but one of them had opened its mouth in a silent cry, and Jimmy had taken them all home. His mother had put them in a box above the range, and within a few hours they were all wriggling and mewling. Jimmy was thrilled, but his father wasn't. When he came home he took the kittens outside and drowned them all.

It was a lesson Jimmy had never forgotten. This calf might be revived, but if anyone in the county had any use for it, it wouldn't have been there in the first place.

Jimmy sighed again and wandered away. Above all, the calf was an inconvenience to him, and he wasn't ready yet to make a decision about it. He had learned, long ago, that decisions tended to make themselves, if you gave them enough time.

2 ∫

Sarah opened the back door and kicked her sister's idle dogs out into the damp street, where they yawned and stretched and sat down again. Beyond the roofs of the town the green-black mountain rose, darkened by the motionless clouds sitting inches above its head. It was not the day to climb it. Sarah was beginning to wonder if that day would ever come.

The butcher's van pulled up at the kerb a few feet away, and Sarah averted her eyes. She still hadn't got used to the idea that her sister's wholefood business was right next door to that Bluebeard's lair. She wasn't at all sure that she would have agreed to come and stay if she had realised. The smell of blood was in her nostrils all day, barely masked by the purifying incense cloud inside the wholefood shop. It seemed to her that every time a customer came through the door, they were greeted by the sound of cleaving bone or mincing flesh from next door. But if anyone noticed besides her, they were too polite to mention it.

The delivery man jumped out of his van. The dogs shifted themselves to greet him. He spoke to them and rubbed their ears, and nodded stiffly at Sarah.

'How's it going?' he said.

Sarah turned a tight-lipped grin on him, and nodded back.

'Soft day.' He unlocked the back door of the shop, then slid open the side door of the van and heaved a haunch of beef on to his shoulder. Sarah turned away and went back inside, to the safe, dusty silence of lentils and beans.

The vet, Gerry Fitz, was sleeping deeply. His clothes, stiff with blood and shit, lay in a heap at his side. He was dreaming of his wife and their fourth child, which was due any day now. The baby was refusing to be born, and a long discussion with it revealed that it had made a mistake, and had no desire to emerge into the bleak and rainswept future that awaited it. But one of the farmers said that it oughtn't to be given the choice, and the calving-jack was brought in.

'It'll never work,' his wife was saying. 'The father was a Belgian.'

Lights began to flash, and a dreadful siren erupted into the air all around. Gerry opened his eyes, his heart racing. The phone was ringing in the office next door. Barely conscious, Gerry heard the answerphone take the call and went back to sleep.

Sarah opened the shop, even though it was half an hour too early. She didn't understand how Mairead could stand this life. It was a noble idea, but there were far more exciting ways to give effect to your beliefs. Sarah knew that. She had spent the last ten years of her life proving it.

There were shelves to be restocked; bags of rice and millet and spices to be filled and taped and priced and laid out. There were books to be kept and orders to be placed and general tidying to be done. All these things, it turned out, took up far more time than serving the customers who called. They were few. Three years after Mairead had opened the shop, she was still barely breaking even. Sarah had begun to suspect that she would not even be achieving that if it were not for a few stalwarts who seemed to have taken it upon themselves as a charitable mission to keep her in business.

In the week that Sarah had been keeping the shop for her sister she had learned a few interesting things. One of them was that the more obsessed people were about what they ate, the more haggard and unhealthy they appeared to be. There were people who knew more about the stock than she did, who were on wheat-free, or dairy-free, or pleasure-free diets. There were yoga teachers and homeopaths and acupuncturists, all of whom had long and despotic theories about diet and health, all of whom seemed to spend a good deal of time in the shop consulting each other about various ailments and passing clients backwards and forwards. There were people who swore by one thing and one thing alone. Paprika was one woman's cure-all; prunes another's. As day followed day Sarah wished that she had never left the tree camp in the Glen of the Downs, or that she had stowed away aboard the *Rainbow Warrior*. Anything but this.

Jimmy hoped the calf would die before he got to it with the bulldozer. It would have been a perfect solution. But every time he thought it had finally expired, something would start it up again, and it would thrash and bleat pathetically, sending a renewed tide of anxiety through Jimmy's hard old arteries.

It wasn't right. Someone ought to be told.

By the time he got his moped going, it was raining. The lads still hadn't arrived and the dump was quiet again; empty apart from the dying calf and the birds, who settled around it now. They picked nonchalantly among the debris, pretending they hadn't noticed it was there, still watching them through those dim, desirable eyes.

*   *   *

In Gerry Fitz's reeking jacket, his mobile was ringing. His limbs were stiff with tension and he was glad to have been woken from another, even worse dream. But it didn't mean he was ready to face the day.

The job was getting to him. He hadn't become a vet to spend his life doing TB tests and delivering undeliverable, unwanted calves. It was always raining here, always muddy. The partnership he worked for was overstretched, even when everyone was at their post. The farmers were as disillusioned as their sad cattle; every year that passed was worse for them than the last, and Gerry was tired of listening to their continuous laments.

He had wanted to work with horses. It was his life's ambition. Racehorses, on the Curragh; that was the way it was supposed to have been. He had pictured himself feeling their delicate legs and listening to their powerful hearts, curing where no vet before him had cured, watching the recipients of his tender attentions forge ahead to victory. He should have been having drinks with politicians, rubbing shoulders with Arab millionaires and business prodigies. Instead, the shoulders of his jacket bore the stinking stains of all he had been rubbing up against recently.

And another baby on the way. As if there weren't enough intrusions on his precious sleep already.

By the time he became aware of the mobile again and began to wonder whether he should answer it, it had stopped ringing.

When Sarah remembered to put out the sandwich board the local guard was standing outside the butcher's shop, talking to the man who had delivered the beef and a smaller man in a tattered black raincoat. The smell from the little man was appalling, and Sarah assumed he must have something to do with the slaughterhouse. She waited, despite the rain, to hear what was going on.

The guard looked around and Sarah caught the dismissive expression in his eyes. She knew what it meant. Mind your own business. She ignored it, and continued to fuss about with the sandwich board, even though it was perfectly level and firm.

The guard turned his back on Sarah and lowered his voice. She didn't hear much. Something about the local dump. It wasn't, she decided, worth getting wet for, and she went back inside.

Garda Raymond Murray parked the car in the middle of the tip-head. Jimmy Kelly and the butcher, Malachy Glynn, were with him. Jimmy was no longer hoping that the calf would be dead, in case the others didn't believe that it had been alive at all. He wasn't sure enough himself any more about what was real and what wasn't, especially after the nights when he got his wages. People could convince him of anything, these days.

As the three men got out of the car, the pied flock exploded and dispersed into the wet air. Only the hoodie remained, hopping reluctantly away at the last minute. The calf was still alive, just barely. With every breath its sides heaved painfully. The butcher shook his head in disbelief. The guard took out a notebook and checked the time on his watch.

'I never had a live one before,' said Jimmy. 'Plenty of dead ones, mind.'

Raymond took a photograph with a disposable camera, then wrote something in his notebook.

'Any idea who might have dumped him?' he asked.

'I didn't see anyone,' said Jimmy.

'Could be anybody's,' said Malachy. 'Anyone with a dairy herd.'

The Traveller lads arrived and joined the party.

'Clear off, now,' said Raymond. 'This is a garda enquiry.'

The boys ignored him, crowding around the calf and asking questions. Malachy answered them. Raymond scuffed around in the muck, as though the calf might have been just one item in a heap of domestic rubbish, and some incriminating clue might have been left behind. But the spot where the calf had been discarded was otherwise quite clear. There were tractor-tyre marks, but the sludge was too soft to have held a firm imprint.

'There's no saving him, anyway,' said the butcher. 'Isn't that right, Jimmy?'

'I suppose,' said Jimmy.

The butcher went to the garda car and returned with the captive-bolt pistol and the knife that he had collected from the slaughterhouse on the way. The lads reached out for them in urgent curiosity, but Malachy shook his head and kneeled beside the calf.

There was a sharp report on the earth and a sudden jolt in the ether, which made me wonder if a new life down there was such an attractive proposition after all. The calf's blood left his throat. But as he waned below, he waxed above. The desperation of dying faded into exquisite expansion, and the peace of the young creature's passing was so evident that even the feeble senses of the human beings appeared to perceive it.

For a moment there was silence. Then the boys began to pester Malachy for a look at the gun, and he went over to the car to put it away.

'Leave him there for the moment,' said Raymond, 'till we make a few more enquiries. Don't be messing with him, lads.'

Raymond and Malachy left. The boys stood over the warm carcass for a few moments, then set out on a tour of the dump. The hoodie took their place. His vigilance had, at last, paid off.

3

The dogs were damp and fed up. They made their way round to the front of the shop and scratched on the door. Sarah opened it and they swarmed in, shook themselves hard, and gazed at her reproachfully. She had no time for their self-pity. The dogs at the tree camp were out in all kinds of weather, and never complained. These ones were spoiled. They represented, she decided, some of the worst aspects of her sister.

Behind them, the garda car pulled up and the man from the butcher's van got out. He was, Sarah noticed, good-looking in a rustic, windblown sort of way. When he glanced up towards her she could see that he was disquieted. Their eyes met and, in the moment before Sarah dropped her gaze from his, some current of energy passed between them.

They didn't know it, but they had been touched by my influence. I was on the point of becoming a gleam in my father's eye. And my mother's, too.

Shocked, she turned away and closed the door. It was all a mistake of some kind. Handsome is as handsome does, and what he did wasn't. For a moment longer, Sarah stood still, registering the shock, looking down at the offended dogs. Then Duncan was there, holding her in his cold embrace and erasing her lingering confusion.

*   *   *

I hadn't been aware of Duncan before, but now I felt his presence. I averted my attention from the glorious particle-dance around me, and observed him. He was a retrograde force, not free yet of his previous earthly existence. I couldn't tell whether it was his own will that caused this retrospective inclination, or whether it was Sarah who couldn't allow him to be free. It made little difference; the effect was the same. Their spirits were strongly linked. It was not a healthy state of affairs for either of them. Nor was it particularly helpful to me.

Soon afterwards the news began to trickle in. Eileen Kilroy was the first to mention it, arriving at the counter with her packets.

'Baking again?' said Sarah.

The sultanas and raisins were plumper than the ones she had been buying in the supermarkets, or so she had informed Sarah the first time they met. They made much better boiled cakes.

'I am,' she said. 'There's a cake sale for the community centre on Friday.'

Sarah rang up the total on the ancient till and rummaged for change.

'Terrible, isn't it?' said Eileen.

'What?'

'That calf on the dump.'

'Calf?'

'Still alive, it was. Awful times for farming.'

Sarah prised the story out of Eileen, and the shock accumulated in her veins like a toxin. While they were speaking, Daniel O'Dea came in to get his daily diabetic sweets.

'You can hardly blame the farmer, though, can you?' he said, entering the conversation seamlessly.

'I certainly can,' said Sarah. 'How could there be any excuse for doing that?'

'You can't keep cattle these days,' said Daniel. 'There's no market. By the time you come to sell them they're worth less than it cost you to feed them. This calf on the dump is a kind of a statement as far as I can see. A cry for help.'

'A what?' said Sarah.

'True enough for you,' said Eileen. 'There's no value in calves these days. You can't give them away.'

'And if you get the lorry to take them, you'll have to pay him,' said Daniel. 'The state that farming's in. It's a crime.'

'It's a crime to leave a live animal on the dump,' said Sarah.

Daniel and Eileen left the shop. Sarah knew that she hadn't said the right thing. She could hear Mairead placating and understanding, keeping her feelings to herself; keeping her customers happy. Small-town existence was delicate, she had warned Sarah. You had to walk on eggs if you wanted to stay in business.

'It's just another sell-out,' said Duncan. 'A thing can't be worth doing if you have to compromise your principles.'

Sarah nodded and felt justified. But she couldn't so easily shake off the heavy mood that was beginning to drag her down. She moved into the back room of the shop and, guiltily, rolled a cigarette. Mairead would kill her if she knew. The smell of roll-ups was a pollutant; it would contaminate the food; it would put customers off. But Sarah needed it. The pathetic image of brutalised innocence had brought her to a dead-end.

For some days now, she had been having grave doubts about the direction she was taking. Since Duncan had died three years before, he had guided her unerringly in all she did. She had stayed at the coastal protest where he met his death until the group was defeated and the new golf course was built. Then she had joined some friends in their London squat and helped with fund-raising for the McLibel campaign and with organising one of the anti-capitalist demos. But she had begun to feel that London wasn't good for her, and Duncan had confirmed it.

'You need to get back into contact with the earth,' he had told her. So she had gone on a weekend excursion to join a group of activists laying waste to a field of GM crops in Oxfordshire, and there she had met Theresa. They had shared a cell together after they were all arrested, and had become good friends. Theresa had suggested that Sarah come back to Ireland and stay for a while with her and her partner, Mike, on their organic vegetable farm in Carlow. Sarah had agreed to give it a try.

She had stayed there for more than a year. She abandoned, for the time being, her struggles against individuals and ideologies, and plunged with her habitual energy into new battles: against leatherjackets, scutch grass, creeping buttercup. In return she was supplied with a warm bed, food, and enough pocket money to keep her in tobacco and tampons. That was all, apart from her ideals, that she required. She might have stayed longer had it not been for the Glen of the Downs tree crisis.

Another road, another senseless tree slaughter. Duncan's voice came to her in a dream. 'If they spent half the money on a decent public transport system, there'd be no need for it.'

Two days later she went to join the small band of warriors who had made their homes, like elves, among the ancient oaks. Theresa and Mike visited from time to time, bringing much-appreciated supplies and equipment. But they couldn't stay. The farm wouldn't run on its own. Sarah missed them, but not for long. The tree people were like family. Throughout the summer months their life was an extraordinary idyll of leaf-filtered sunshine and midnight campfires, and the following winter, though it was less comfortable, the warrior spirit kept them alive and hopeful.

Then Mairead had tracked her down. She sent a letter, via a mutual friend.

'You have abandoned your family and your responsibilities,' it read. 'Mum and Dad are getting on. They don't even know where you are. If you don't want to see them, you could at least take over the shop for a while and let me pay them a visit.'

Sarah committed the letter to the campfire. But on a stormy night soon afterwards she dreamed that her father was dying, and when she tried to get to him, an ancient oak was felled across his bedroom door, blocking her entry.

She hitched over to Galway, where her father was far from dying and her mother had taken on a new and vigorous identity as a student of psychology. She stayed in their comfortable house for three gluttonous weeks, sleeping beneath a feather duvet and guiltily enjoying three pulpy meals a day. She might have stayed for longer, if her mother had not been so determined to analyse all the family relationships and take responsibility for the state of estrangement in which the children had existed for most of their adult lives. Galvanised by the outrageous possibility of total healing, Sarah took the first escape route that offered itself, willingly changing places with Mairead for a couple of weeks.

But as soon as she arrived in Kilbracken Sarah had begun to feel that somewhere along the line she had taken a wrong turn. Duncan seemed distant and vague, not at all his usual, helpful self. Somehow, unaccountably, Sarah had departed from the Way.

She had felt it in every bone and sinew, in every beat of her heavy heart. The rain in Clare had a different quality to that which leaked into her tree-house in Wicklow.

It did not cleanse or refresh, it could not be kept out of her bones by prayer or camaraderie. Even inside the house her joints ached and she had been tempted several times to use the electric blanket that Mairead kept on her bed.

She had thought she understood the reasons. The food she had eaten in her parents' house was tainted by chemical pollutants and over-refinement. It had sludged up her workings and drugged her mind. Praising the force for allowing her to escape in time, she had embarked upon a strict diet of purification, and purged her system with organic castor-oil until she was as thin and as dry as a Bombay duck. She had put the dogs on a diet as well. Mairead spoiled them. They were fat and lazy. But the energy and gratitude that she had expected them to express was not forthcoming. Instead they followed her around incessantly with mournful expressions until, eventually, the pressure forced her to absolve herself of responsibility for their spiritual health.

'You're pigs, not dogs,' she said, as she poured a mountain of vegetarian dog slush into their bowls. 'You have pig souls.'

They wagged their tails ecstatically and ploughed into the trough.

The purification regime hadn't worked for Sarah, either. She fretted endlessly, amazed at her discontent, unable to account for her loss of direction, her failure to find her soul's path and the meaning that ought to be apparent in every moment of existence. But as soon as Daniel O'Dea and Eileen left Mairead's shop that morning, Sarah found herself back on track again. Not only that, but she knew she had never gone wrong in the first place.

'Who owned that calf?' Duncan was asking her. 'Where is it now? What happened to it?'

'How should I know?' she asked him, glad that he was

back in possession of her, but a bit irritated by the questions.

'Find out,' he said. 'This is big.'

And, suddenly, Sarah understood. She had served her apprenticeship on the streets of London, in the soggy fields of Carlow and the scant shelter of the Wicklow oaks. She had experienced the rawest of raw edges, and knew about reality. Not the reality the politicians talked about: the reality of economics and armaments and the sad but noble necessity of killing some people for the sake of humanity and exploiting others in the name of free trade. She knew the truth that existed beyond the cloud-castle comforts of modern life. She knew what would be there waiting for everyone when the bubble burst and the earth cried, 'Halt!'

Sarah had believed that all she needed to do was to learn and be ready. But now she saw that there was more required of her than that. She was to be a researcher, a student of the human condition. She was to report to the world on what she had discovered.

The calf on the dump would be her first assignment. A perfect example of the horrors spawned by the European Economic Plutocracy and its Common Agricultural Psychosis. The time was ripe; there were journals all over Europe waiting for this kind of reporting.

'Go for it, Sal!' said Duncan. Her heart soared. He was so close that if she closed her eyes she could feel him in her arms. There had been no diversion from her path in life. She had experienced a temporary failure of faith, that was all.

She grabbed her trusty oilskin from the hook in the hall, shut the dogs in the back room and chose one of the assortment of signs to hang inside the door.

BACK IN FIVE MINUTES, it read.

4 ∫

Eileen Kilroy got a lift home with Daniel O'Dea. He was a good neighbour, God bless him. Went out of his way to bring her to the door and keep her dry. More than her own man would do.

John was up and about, eating cereals at the kitchen table. Eileen's heart swelled with pride at the sight of him.

'Would you not have a fry?' she said. 'I'll put it on for you.'

'I'm all right, Mam,' he said. So gentle, so undemanding.

'Sure, I'll put it on for you anyway.' He needed feeding up. The other boys had all grown like nettles on a muck heap, but for some reason John had lagged behind them; small and skinny.

'Why didn't you wait till I got up to go shopping?' he said. 'I would have given you a lift in.'

'Are you going into town?'

'No. But I would have given you a lift in.'

He might be the runt of the family, but he had done better than any of them so far. PJ was working on a FAS scheme in Limerick, and Liam was off in Ballinasloe, living with some strange people and drawing the dole. Only John had a decent job, up there in Athlone. But he never bragged about it. Just quietly arrived home from time to time, always with a present for her.

'You should learn to drive, Mam,' he said. 'Specially now that you've got the new car.'

'Ah, why would I bother?'

'You could get out of here whenever you wanted. Be your own boss.'

The rashers were swimming in salty water. They had never done that in the old days. Eileen left them to simmer and washed a couple of eggs under the tap.

'Where did the money come from, anyway?' John went on. 'Did you win the Lotto, or what?'

Eileen gave him a conspiratorial wink, but it didn't quite hit the mark. There was too much unease behind it.

John put his cereal dish on the draining board and swigged the last of his tea. 'I don't want the fry, Mam. You'll have to eat it yourself.'

'It'll do you good,' said his mother.

He didn't answer, and when she turned round to see why, he had gone.

The rain seemed to be blowing into Sarah's face whichever way the narrow road turned. Behind the thick, black hedges, wet cattle ate wet grass in boggy fields which ranged in colour from electric green to dull, marshy red. Here and there Sitka spruce trees stood in dark, military precision across hillsides which had once been bare. Where the plantations came close to the road, Sarah peered into their gloomy interiors and shuddered. She knew about trees. These young forests did not welcome people.

She smelled the putrid stench and saw the flocking birds long before she arrived at the dump. The last, straight half-mile of the approach road was littered with plastic bags and papers, blown from the tip by the strong westerlies, wrapped around every bush and fence-post like markers along the way to Armageddon. As Sarah drew closer, the birds swirled above her head. How would she describe them in her article? Were they traitors to their species; selling out for the luxury of easy pickings? Or were they victims; feathered casualties of consumerism?

The Traveller lads were swarming around a pick-up truck. Sarah left the bicycle leaning against the chain link and walked in. As she did so, she realised that she hadn't brought a pencil or paper. Or a camera, for that matter. She would have to remember everything.

Lesson number one. Be prepared.

She recognised Jimmy from that morning, and went over to speak to him. Stinking black slime oozed around her shoes and found its way in through the holes.

Lesson number two. Be prepared.

Jimmy was standing back from the fray, leaning against the Portakabin. Drips were gathering on the brim of his hat and falling down in front of his face.

'I hear there was a calf found here this morning?' she asked him.

Jimmy's eyes widened with shock, and he looked away, intent, it seemed, on what was happening at the tip-head. Sarah followed his gaze. The truck was almost empty and the boys were in a kind of feeding frenzy, scattering rubbish around them. One of them was dragging at a broken box with wires hanging out of it. Another was accumulating bits of copper pipe from the bed of the pick-up. The driver jumped out, took them off him and threw them back in. The boy shrugged and turned to examine a heap of bulging fertiliser bags.

'Is it still here?' said Sarah.

Jimmy began to walk away, towards the bulldozer.

'Excuse me,' said Sarah. 'Would you mind if I asked you a few questions?'

'Ask away,' said Jimmy, climbing into the machine and starting the engine.

'Fuck!' said Sarah.

The pick-up started, spun round in a tight circle and sped out of the gates. The boys pulled and kicked at the remaining rubbish. Sarah walked over towards them, then spotted the calf at the edge of the plateau.

It wasn't alive now; that much was certain. As she came closer to it, Sarah realised with a shock that its eye sockets were hollow. She wondered if it had been born like that, or whether some satanic monster had gouged out the eyes in a fit of rage.

One of the boys called across to her. 'Want to buy some wellies, missus?'

'How much?' she called back.

The boy stood stunned for a moment, then rummaged in a bag at his side.

Sarah returned her attention to the calf. She saw the red gash at its throat and shuddered. Even without its eyes it was beautiful; so perfect and fragile.

'There you are, missus,' said the boy, arriving at her side with a pair of ancient, green wellingtons. 'A fiver.'

Sarah inspected the boots.

'That one has a hole in it,' she said.

'Four quid, then,' said the boy.

'I don't want boots with holes in them.'

'Two quid.'

'Did you see this?' said Sarah, indicating the calf.

'Sure, there's always a few of them here,' said the boy.

'Is there?'

'Most days.'

'But this one was alive.'

'They all were. Before they were dead.'

'But this one was still alive when it was left here. Did you see it?'

The boy shrugged. 'What if I did? Give us a quid for them, then. Can't say fairer than that.'

'I don't want them,' said Sarah. 'Did you see anyone else here? Did you see who killed it?'

'Give us a quid for the wellies and I'll tell you,' said the boy.

Sarah felt in her pocket. Mairead let her keep ten per cent of the takings from the shop, and she was richer than she had been for years. She gave the boy a pound.

'I don't want the boots,' she said.

The boy tossed them aside, back with the rest of the rubbish.

'Malachy Glynn did away with it,' he said.

'Malachy Glynn?'

'The butcher.'

The boy walked away, and Sarah turned back to the calf. It had, she noticed, a small rusty mark between its empty eye sockets.

John, as he had told his mother, wasn't going into town. He was cruising the winding lanes, driving slowly and carefully, peering over the hedges and through the gates into the fields beyond. Sometimes he would pull into a gap and examine a herd of cattle. Once he got out of the car and leaned on a gate, scanning a distant scattering of bullocks on a hillside. They didn't please him, and he got back into the car and drove on.

Above him the clouds were being blown eastward, chucking their rain as they went. The whole sky was muddy and drab, like the wet roads and the dismal land on either side. But the car was warm and dry, and sweet music played softly on the stereo. And when, suddenly, he found what he was looking for, it was almost a disappointment. It was too easy. His objective was actually advertised for him, by a sign on a five-bar gate.

Beware of the Bull.

He stopped again and got out. The cattle were bunched

together, standing in the shelter of a high hawthorn hedge. The bull was a little apart from the cows and heifers, standing aloof. Lonely, John thought. A sad, heavy, cumbersome creature, bred for meat, not speed or grace. It was in no way ideal for his purpose, but John knew that he was unlikely to find anything better. It would have to do.

5

It was years since Sarah had been in a butcher's shop. She couldn't even remember the last time it had happened. When she was a child, possibly; one of those traumatic experiences her mother was so keen to resurrect. She had bought meat for a year or two when she first left home, and was working in the motor tax office in Galway. She had been living with a flatmate and they had taken it in turns to cook: week on, week off. Sarah's skills had never brought her much further than toad-in-the-hole and Irish stew, and she bought everything she needed in the supermarket, where the food was so processed and packaged it wasn't easy to see where any of it had originated. After she met Duncan, the only time she went near a supermarket was to picket it, and she had never eaten meat since.

Now, as she stood on the street between Mairead's shopfront and the butcher's, she tried to imagine what lay ahead of her. She was not going to get in and out of that shop without seeing the carnage on display. Vivid images of splattered blood and jagged hunks of dripping flesh passed across her mind. A lean bitch and her doddery, undernourished pup nosed at the bottom of the door, adding fuel to the images of recent slaughter. Sarah took a step closer, crossing the halfway point between the two shops. She had brought her notebook with her this time, and the first few lines of her article were scribbled on the first page. 'On Wednesday, 14 July, a newborn calf was found on Kilbracken dump. According to local residents, this is not the first time such a thing has happened, but in this case there was one crucial difference. The little Friesian bull calf was, when it was discovered by tip-head workers, still alive. Mr Jimmy Kelly, manager of the dump, declined to make any comment.'

The street was quiet. Apart from the slow traffic and the stray dogs, nothing was moving. Sarah knew that she would have to make her move soon, before another wave of shoppers arrived at the butcher's. It was seldom so empty. As well as that, her imaginings of what lay inside were beginning to grow fantastic, and they could only get worse. Taking a firmer grip on her notebook, she stepped forward and pushed open the door.

It was darker inside than out, and Sarah experienced a momentary panic. Then, as her eyes adjusted, she saw the displayed cuts, the slabs and blocks and mincers, the hooks and dangling joints, the knives and cleavers hanging neatly on the wall.

'Not a bad morning,' said the grey-haired man who stood behind the counter.

'I was looking for the butcher,' she said.

'You found him,' said the grey-haired man. 'Oliver Mulligan is my name.'

Sarah hesitated. 'Oh. You're not Mr Glynn?'

The man looked at her more closely. 'Is it himself you're looking for?'

'It is,' said Sarah.

'He isn't usually in the shop much. But I can give him a message for you if you like. Who shall I say?'

'I'm Sarah, from next door.'

'Mairead's sister, is it?'

'That's right.'

'I know Mairead well. You're welcome to Kilbracken.' He held out a sparklingly clean, pink hand, but Sarah didn't take it.

'Can you tell me where I might find Mr Glynn?'

Oliver dropped the rejected hand on to the counter. 'He'd be out around the farm at the moment, I'd say. Attending to the beasts.'

Surrounded as she was by so much raw flesh, the word gave Sarah the creeps, conjuring images of slavering jaws filled with rows of razor-sharp teeth.

'Beasts?' she said.

'I just work in the shop,' Oliver said. 'Malachy finishes the cattle himself, on his own land.'

'Finishes them?' Sarah sent out an urgent summons to Duncan, but if he was around, he didn't seem to hear.

'Fattens them, you know. We can't call them organic because we don't breed them ourselves, but we finish them organically. They're chemical-free when they're killed.' Oliver seemed to glow as he spoke. 'Sure we're famous throughout the county. Everyone who's anyone comes here for their meat.'

'Oh,' said Sarah. And then, remembering herself, she added, 'I'm a vegetarian myself.'

'Me too,' said the assistant. 'On account of my dicky ticker.'

'So where is this farm, then?'

'You might be best to try the house.'

'Where is it?' said Sarah.

She took down the directions in her notebook, feeling efficient. As she turned to leave, the butcher said, 'We have a special on fillet steak this week. Best in Ireland.'

'I'm a vegetarian,' Sarah repeated.

'Me too,' said the assistant. 'But a small bit now and then never did anyone any harm, sure it didn't?'

*　　*　　*

John drove around for a while before he went home. He wasn't looking for anything now, and the roads of his childhood were as familiar to him as the dreary house he shared with three other guys in Athlone. But he liked driving, and it was still a novelty to be at the wheel of his own car. It wasn't flash and new like the one his parents had just bought, but it was the first one he had ever owned, and he loved every inch of it. Being in it was nearly enough for him. He kept the radio turned down low, and took his time on the blind bends. Accidents were common enough on these roads, and he didn't want to draw anyone's attention to the fact that he had no licence or tax or insurance.

John hated his job with every passion that lurked in his dark and secretive soul. It was a torment to be endured, a mistake he had made that he couldn't see how to unmake. Getting out of bed in the mornings was a major ordeal.

The other men who worked with him seemed to be able to handle it. They made a great show of their bravado, as though there were something courageous and manly about what they did every day. But there wasn't. What they did for a living was cowardly, cruel and mind-numbingly boring.

John had passed the tests of manhood that were inevitably imposed upon every new recruit. Afterwards he had done his best to join the macho camaraderie that echoed around the tense yards and buildings. But it wasn't in him. Gradually he had withdrawn; entered a quiet, efficient place within himself where he could work with some measure of detachment and make some effort to face up to the realities of what he was doing. And, despite the fact that his silence made him unpopular among the others, he had reached some conclusions. What he did lacked dignity. More than that, it imposed a lack of dignity on those who, in their final minutes, were given into his care.

He had come home to find redemption.

*   *   *

The butcher's house was not at all as Sarah had expected. She couldn't, however, have told anyone what kind of house she would have expected him to live in. She knew nothing of butchers or their lifestyles and habits.

First of all, she had to cycle down a long, long driveway. Not a farm track, but a real driveway. It was covered with loose gravel now, and pitted with potholes full of muddy water, but it was clear that it had once been properly metalled, and there were broken walls and tall old trees on either side.

'Go down to the end,' Oliver had said. 'It's the only house down there.'

But he hadn't said how far away the end was. Mairead's bicycle had no rear mudguard, and by the time she finally got there, Sarah's legs and backside were drenched.

She had assumed that the butcher would be at home, simply because she wanted to find him there and because the great guiding spirits, Duncan included, were on her side. But the butcher seemed not to have heard their summons. Or if he had, he had not obeyed. The tiny bungalow was dark and empty. From outside the front door she could smell the burned grease of a late breakfast or early lunch. He couldn't be far away.

Beyond the bungalow was another stand of mature deciduous trees. A continuation of the drive led among them, and Sarah left the bicycle propped against the wall of the house and walked along it. The breeze was light but consistent, and the leaves above her were speaking to it, in a voice that she had learned to understand in the tree camp. The wind was welcome, and carried news from sister trees in other parts of the island. If she stopped and listened for long enough, she could tune in to their vibrations and learn a lot about their conditions, but for the moment, at least, Sarah was too cold and too distracted to stay. She became aware that this new calling could bring her into contact with all kinds of pernicious influences, which might diminish her capabilities and weaken her links with the divine. She would have to be careful. But she was glad to have found these trees. There were few enough of their age and stature in this barren county.

On the other side of the copse stood the gaunt, cavernous remains of an enormous stately home. Sarah ought to have anticipated it, given the nature of the driveway, the high walls and the trees. But she hadn't, and it gave her the creeps. The roof was long gone. The door and window frames gaped like the empty eye sockets of the dead calf. Brambles and elder had taken up residence and peered out through the crumbling masonry like uneasy squatters. The edifice seemed to be burdened by some grisly history which induced Sarah to turn away, protecting her psychic boundaries from invasion by its acrimonious resonances.

Another track led on. This one was muddier but still passable. Sarah could make out the tyre-prints of the butcher's van, and wondered if he was down there. More trees stood on either side, concealing for a while the range of buildings that lay at the end. As they came into view, the hairs on the back of Sarah's neck began to stand up.

'Finish them,' Oliver Mulligan had said. What if it was happening now?

The buildings were a mixture of old and new. From the track, Sarah could see a long, two-storey block built from cut stone, and a row of loose boxes which opened on to a cobbled yard. Beyond them, at the end of a railed, concrete roadway, was a range of modern buildings with breeze-block sides and green, box-profile roofs. There was no sign of the van anywhere and, her heart in her mouth, Sarah walked on and opened the gate into the yard.

'Hello?' she called. Her voice was a wan little whimper,

swallowed up by the enormous silence of the buildings. 'Anybody there?'

Inside the long stone block, something was moving. Sarah wandered across to the double doors in the middle of it and peered into the darkness.

'Hello?'

She was answered by a bellow which sent stinging currents through her bloodstream and, for some reason, caused her to make a grab for a pitchfork which leaned against the wall. She practised her pranic breathing.

'You're all right, Sal,' said Duncan, calm and powerful. 'It's a cow.'

'Dying?' she asked.

'Go and see.'

Sarah's spirit flagged, but she remembered her new purpose and, putting down the pitchfork, stepped into the gloom.

The building was an old coach-house, one half open for the vehicles, the other half divided into boxes for the horses. The open side was occupied by a dozen yearling bullocks, who were crowding up against a pair of wide aluminium gates, clearly not part of the original design. It was one of them who had bellowed at the sound of her voice, and now they all seemed eager to meet her, and leaned forward, shouldering each other aside and huffing the damp air. Sarah edged past them. She was fond of telling people how much she loved cows. They were gentle creatures, she said. The BSE cull was the worst slaughter of innocents that Britain had ever seen. The karma of such an act would surely rebound upon its perpetrators. A great conflagration would ensue. It was all true, she was sure of it. But the bit about loving cows was now being put to the test. At this distance, they looked extremely large and pushy.

Sarah began to creep forward, but she was looking more closely at the ropes that held the gates in place than she was

at the bullocks. One step. Two. So far so good. She reached
out a cautious hand, and to her amazement the creatures
shrank back, blowing warily, jostling each other now to get
away. It gave Sarah confidence. All she needed to do was to
tune in to their gentle souls. They were sure to understand
that she was an ally, not an enemy. She took another tiny
step, her hand held out palm upwards, as though she were
trying to catch a nervous pony.

'All right?' said a voice behind her.

Sarah, already brittle with tension, nearly shattered with
the shock. She swung round. The butcher, the man she had
taken for the delivery boy, was standing in the doorway,
blocking her only escape route. He was wearing mud-
encrusted jeans and a sloppy anorak that was shiny with
age and grime. He took a step forward and stretched out
a hand; her negative animus in all his terrifying glory.
'Malachy Glynn,' he said.

Sarah ignored the hand. It might not look bloodstained,
but it was.

'Sarah, isn't it?' said Malachy. 'You're Mairead's sister.'

'Yes. I was just . . .'

The butcher walked by her and stood at the gates. 'Nice
lot of bullocks, aren't they?'

'Very nice,' said Sarah.

'They're getting quiet, bit by bit.' The cattle were inching
closer again, and Sarah was surprised to discover that
they were a good deal more comfortable in the butcher's
presence than they were in hers. They came up quite
confidently now, blowing Malachy's hair with their blustery
breath, reaching towards his hand with their dripping noses
and long, coarse tongues.

Which would end up jellied on somebody's sideboard.

Sarah's courage returned. 'I wanted to ask you about the
calf on the dump,' she said.

Malachy shook his head wistfully. 'Terrible business.'

'Were you there?'

The butcher moved away from the bullocks, who crowded around the gates, causing them to bend outwards and creak alarmingly. He pulled a bale of sweet hay from a high stack which stood opposite the double doors, broke it open and tossed the flakes into the enclosure. The bullocks swung around in pursuit and began to tear at them.

'Somebody said you were out there,' Sarah went on.

Malachy walked along the passage between the loose boxes. The partitions were made of solid timber to about shoulder height, and above that steel bars stretched up to the ceiling, allowing the horses they had been built for to see each other but not to fraternise too closely.

'I was,' said the butcher, opening the first of the sliding doors. 'Stand back, now.'

A huge, hefty bullock lunged out and set off down the passage, towards another, narrower door which stood open at the end.

Sarah followed as Malachy continued down the passage-way, releasing more bullocks, one by one.

'I'm writing an article about it,' she said.

'For who?'

She hadn't exactly thought that far. 'For . . . I'm working freelance. I'll syndicate it.'

'Big audience for that kind of story, is there?'

'You can be sure of it,' said Sarah.

The butcher opened the last of the cage boxes and followed the hurrying bullock out into the yard. The others had gathered at the gate to the concrete road which led to the newer buildings.

'So,' Sarah went on. 'Maybe you wouldn't mind just answering a few questions for me?'

Malachy opened the gate and watched the bullocks as they hurried through. Then he turned and met her eye.

Sarah felt something tug at her solar plexus. She tried to ignore it.

'I'm very busy just now,' said the butcher. 'Perhaps we could meet later on?'

Sarah nodded. She watched the bullocks running along the roadway. 'Where are they going?'

Malachy grinned. 'That's the slaughterhouse, down there.'

'You're going to kill them?'

'Not today. I'll kill one of them tomorrow.'

'But why are they in such a hurry to get there?'

'They're hungry,' said Malachy.

'You feed them in the slaughterhouse?'

'I do. It means they're not afraid, you see. When their turn comes. They're used to the place. They're not expecting to die.'

Sarah's stomach turned. 'Oh my God.'

Malachy closed the gate between them. 'If you'll meet me in Reagan's tonight I'll buy you a pint and tell you whatever you want to hear. About the calf.'

Sarah's heart lurched between excitement and horror. But she knew that even the most high-profile journalists had to make deals.

'I suppose so,' she said.

'I'll call for you,' said Malachy.

6

John helped his father exercise the greyhounds, then gave him a hand around the farm. He spent two hours carrying newly baled silage from one of the low-lying fields, putting the new tractor through its paces; delighted by the unaccustomed efficiency. With equipment like this, farming didn't seem so bad. If the place was making money at last, maybe he would consider coming home and helping out. It had to be better than the factory.

The vet was due to call after dinner for a TB test on all the cattle. They were already penned in the small field at the side of the house where the crush was, waiting. After dinner could mean any time between two o'clock in the afternoon and next Tuesday evening. Mr Leary, the senior partner in the veterinary practice, still hadn't returned from the Canaries, and everyone knew that Gerry Fitz had problems. They were beginning to show in his face and in his drinking habits and in the endlessly unanswered ringing of all the practice phones.

'They ought to have a secretary,' said Eileen. 'At least that way you'd know he wasn't coming.'

'You'll be around to give us a hand,' said Matty.

'No. Sorry, Dad,' said John. 'I have to go into Limerick to get a part for the car.'

'Part for the car my arse,' said Matty. 'You were always

afraid of the cattle since you got knocked by that heifer when you were a small lad.'

'Afraid!' he said. 'Don't you know what I do for a living?'

'That's different,' said Matty. 'There's hardly any room for argument once they get to your doorstep.'

John said nothing, but his mind was full of silent rage as he got into the car and drove away. It wasn't until he was well clear of the farm that the memory came pouring back, so vividly that he could smell the sour earth and see the brilliant green of the short grass in the field. It was a child's vision of the world. He had been seven years old when it happened.

He had often driven cattle along the roads with his father, swinging his piece of black water-pipe behind them or standing at a junction to guide them in the right direction. He understood cattle to be stupid, timid creatures whose only desires were to eat and avoid trouble. But he had never been required to help in a situation that turned out to be so difficult and dangerous.

They were loading two heifers into a borrowed lorry, heading for the mart. The first of them, seeing no alternative, had clattered up the steep ramp obligingly, but the second had other ideas. The lorry had been reversed into the field, and its wooden ramp gates opened wide to create a funnel. Matty and the two older boys were behind the cattle. John was out of the way, minding the narrow gap between the wall and the edge of the nearest ramp gate. He was too small to be seen as a deterrent to the terrified heifer, and it had plunged straight at him, knocking him down. It all happened too quickly for him to react, and he fell on his face among the stones and brambles. The heifer's front feet came down on either side of his head; huge and heavy. The one he could see appeared to rest in the earth for an age, and he watched it press down into the wet ground, pushing muddy water up around itself before it finally heaved free again, leaving a neat imprint behind. Then the pain had come. The beast's hind feet had not cleared him, and one of them landed in his back, the other on his elbow, bending it the wrong way, making a horribly gristly crunch. Then the heifer was gone. The other one charged back out of the lorry and everyone was shouting. His brothers lit off after the bolting cattle, but his father dragged him up from the ground, turned him around, and ate the head off him for letting the heifer through. John had been so shocked and terrified that he hadn't dared to mention the pain in his arm, and it wasn't until some time later that one of his brothers had noticed it hanging uselessly by his side, and brought it to their father's attention.

The heifers and the market had been forgotten for the day, and John had been delivered to the casualty ward of Ennis hospital in the lorry. After that, it was true, he had been reluctant to help with anything that involved manoeuvring cattle in small spaces. That was one of the reasons he had moved from the slaughter hall to the holding pens, where he was responsible for prodding the terrified cattle into the slaughter crush. He was facing his anxiety every day, and keeping it under control. But he had to admit, to himself at least, that he wasn't entirely cured.

Sarah sat over a sandwich of rennet-free cheese and stale bread. She wondered whether it wouldn't be more ethical to be a vegan. After all, to get milk you had to get calves, and if no one wanted calves, or only wanted them to eat, wouldn't it be better not to use dairy products at all?

But then there wouldn't be any cattle. No warm, doe-eyed creatures grazing the pastures of Ireland. She remembered the bullocks; their smell and their enormous weight, their restrained power. She wasn't sure whether she had been really frightened of them or not. She preferred to believe that it hadn't been her own fear that had made her so hesitant, but theirs.

'You fancy him, don't you?' said Duncan.

'No.'

'You do. I could tell.'

'How could I possibly fancy someone who does what he does?'

'That's what I'd like to know.'

'Oh, Duncan. There will never be anybody else. How many times do I have to tell you?'

'Don't go, then. Don't meet him. Go and find the guard and quiz him about the calf. What can the butcher tell you anyway? He did away with it. So what?'

Sarah realised she was looking forward to the pint that evening. She hadn't been out since she arrived. She was bored, and the prospect of spending yet another evening in the company of Mairead's sulking dogs was stultifying.

'You'll just have to trust me, that's all,' she said.

'Do you trust yourself?'

'To keep clear of entanglements with the enemy? What do you think?'

'I think,' said Duncan, 'that I would like to hold you.'

Sarah closed her eyes and moulded herself into his arms. No matter how much time elapsed, she could always feel his embrace as though it were really happening. And she was surprised, now, at how sensual she felt. She had been cycling around for hours. A short nap wouldn't do her any harm.

Above the shop, in Mairead's double bed, Sarah relaxed in the golden arms of her numinous warrior lover. For half an hour or more, her life seemed totally perfect.

John took the back roads to Limerick and parked the car among the shabby, neglected outskirts. 'Stab City', some people called the place, because of its reputation for brawls and knife-fights. He ought to be able to get what he was looking for here, if anywhere.

The wind had dropped, and the clouds sat on the city as though they were trying to hatch something out of it. John couldn't remember ever having been in Limerick when it wasn't raining. Maybe it was just the greyness of the place that gave him that impression. The shoppers in the main street seemed dogged and purposeful, as though they couldn't wait to be finished with their business and out of there.

Somehow, John had expected to find what he wanted immediately. A row of shops, perhaps; Butcher's Alley, with large display windows offering every conceivable variation in knives and cleavers. He wished he had taken the opportunity to stock up when he was still working inside the slaughter hall of the factory. It would have been easy, then, to slip a knife into his pocket, and another one a few days later. No one ever checked. But where he worked now, in the holding pens, the only tool he used was an electric cattle prod.

In the end he had to make do with a hardware shop, even less well stocked than his father's regular one in Ennis. When he lined up his purchases at the counter, the assistant gave him an odd look.

'Wedding present,' he said. 'My sister's getting married.'

Sarah felt compelled to stay in the shop for the rest of the afternoon. She got some first-hand news of the Glen of the Downs camp from a couple who had called in there the previous day. Things weren't going well. The activists had been given their marching orders. They were trying to dig tunnels, she learned, but the roots of the oaks were getting in the way, and there were long debates about the ethics of cutting through them. Heavy rains were dampening everyone's spirits, but there were a few staunch individuals who were determined to stay on and make a fight of it.

The news made Sarah feel guilty. She wished she was with her friends, but she was also relieved that she wasn't. There would, inevitably, be scuffles with the police. There would be arrests, probably stretches in jail. Sarah had been through all that before, and had no desire to repeat the experience.

The couple piled up a box-load of groceries on the counter, and Sarah had already packed everything before she realised they intended to pay by a debit card for which Mairead had no terminal. They had no cash, and were unwilling to go to the bank and get it, so the best single sale of the day was lost. Sarah had to unpack everything again and put it back on the shelves.

During the quiet spell that followed she tried to phone the local guard, but got no reply. The station in Ennis said they had no record of the incident, and couldn't comment. She tried the vet, to get his views, but both numbers in the book rang out. The rain fell interminably. She smoked several cigarettes in the back room and once, by mistake, carried one through to the shop with her when she went in to attend to a customer. After that she was beyond caring, and smoked when and where she pleased. If anyone noticed, they didn't comment.

Mairead rang as Sarah was closing the shop for the day. She had been through enough of their mother's de-conditioning and was ready to come home. Would Sarah mind?

'Of course not,' said Sarah. In her mind's eye she had already become a roving reporter and was ready to follow the next story as soon as this one was wrapped up and sold. But when Mairead rang off, Sarah realised she hadn't yet decided where she would sell it. She lit a fire in the tiny grate in Mairead's boxy little sitting-room. In the corner, at the bottom of a set of bright yellow bookshelves, was a stack of alternative magazines that Mairead had clearly been collecting for years. Sarah picked up a handful and leafed through them. It didn't, she had to admit, look terribly hopeful. Most of them were monthlies and didn't carry any sort of live news. She would have to build the article into a much bigger and more in-depth piece if she was going to interest any of them, and the prospect of the research that would be involved in doing that was daunting. What was the Common Agricultural Policy anyway? Why had it led to calves being discarded like the by-products of some egregious industrial process? What had it done to the common decency of farmers? She had hoped that she could end the article with these questions, not begin it with them.

Despondently, she dropped the periodicals back on to the stack and set about making some dinner.

John had just finished his. He helped his mother clear the table. She was pleased and embarrassed at the same time.

'Get away out of that,' she said, but she was glad when he didn't.

'I do it in Athlone, Mam. I cook as well.'

'God help us,' said Matty.

'Times are changing,' said Eileen. 'The lads are expected to do that kind of thing these days.'

'By who?' said Matty.

'Have you got a girlfriend, then?' Eileen asked.

'If I had I wouldn't tell you,' said John.

'Why not?'

'You'd only be nosing.'

'She would too,' said Matty.

'Why wouldn't I?' said Eileen. 'What's she like?'

John stacked the dishes on the draining board. 'Will I feed the hens for you?' he said.

Eileen kept geese as well as hens, and a pair of elderly
ducks who only laid about six eggs every year but were too
old to eat. As John ladled out the mash they turned their
heads sideways and looked up at him with their warm,
brown eyes, and he said, 'Hey, Wacky. Hey, Peeps. How're
you doing?'

The hens were less likeable. Their eyes were hard and cold
and full of disdain. There were a few young cockerels among
them, he noticed, from an early brood of chicks. They would
soon be ready for the table. He hoped his mother would
roast one before he went back to Athlone. It was a long
time since he had tasted a home-reared bird.

How old had he been when he had first been given the
job of killing them? Ten? Twelve? All he could remember
was the terror of it. He would wait outside the hen-house
for the chosen victim to emerge, blinking, into the daylight.
Once, not the first time, his heart had hammered so hard
that he had closed the tiny door again and walked around
for several minutes to calm himself. It wasn't the cockerels
that frightened him, even though they flapped and clawed
with surprising strength and stared at him with ferocious
accusation. It wasn't even the screeching that some of them
uttered when he carried them into the dark feed-shed. It
was their deaths that had drained his courage; the leaking
away of their proud strength once their necks had been
wrung. The first time, he had dropped the bird as soon as
he heard its neck bones snap, and it had thrashed around
the confines of the shed for nearly a minute before finally
collapsing at his feet in a ragged heap. After that he always
held them tightly beneath his arm, feeling their strong
wings struggling for the air, then twitching, then becoming
finally, utterly still.

He looked towards the horizon. A heavy mist was descend-
ing, smothering the mountain. He had got all he needed
in Limerick, but unless the weather changed very rapidly

there would be no chance of going into action that night. He would need to work in darkness, but not the kind of blind darkness that would be likely to fall upon a day like this one. He would have to wait and hope for a clear night and a moon. It was summer, after all. He had every right to expect it.

The birds crowded around his feet, completely at ease and trusting. He could set down the bucket, quietly reach out for the plumpest of the cockerels, tuck it snugly under his arm and dispatch it without any of the others even knowing it was happening. It seemed so simple to him now, and so kind compared to the fluttering, screeching panic he had caused in the past. As he emptied the bucket and turned back towards the house, he wondered why he had never thought of it before.

Sarah washed the few dishes and returned to the fireside. She felt guilty about burning the earth's precious resources in the middle of summer, but the damp in this place was getting into her bones. The dogs must have been suffering from the same complaint, because they were so close to the fire they were almost in it. Sarah rolled another cigarette and took out her notebook.

'Not much more than a generation ago,' she wrote, 'the cow was a cherished extension of the Irish smallholder's family unit. She was docile and calm, knowing she was loved and needed, and her welfare would have been held on a level second only to the human members of the household. When her time came to calve, she would have been watched as closely as any expectant mother, and her newborn offspring would have been cosseted as carefully as any infant. But look at her now. Look at her calf, dying a long, slow, painful death on a rural tip-head in County Clare.'

Sarah sat back. It wasn't bad. One of the animal rights

organisations might be interested. She wondered whether they paid. If she got the tone right, she could try the national dailies or the local weeklies. Maybe she would make her fortune and find herself in demand. The vision of a large cheque swam into her mind's eye, and hot on its heels came scenes of comfort and content. A snug little cottage somewhere, warm and dry. A washing-machine, rumbling gently in the corner. Clean, new clothes. Food that tasted good and didn't give her indigestion.

She was slipping, she knew. She could sense Duncan's disgust as he tuned in to her thoughts.

, 'It's a fantasy,' she told him. 'People are allowed to fantasise about whatever they want.'

'Greed is the cause of all human misery,' he said. 'Once desire wheedles its way into your heart there's no getting rid of it.'

'I wasn't desiring. Just dreaming.'

'You were wanting. Almost everyone in the world believes that if they just had twenty-five per cent more than they have, they would be happy. From people on the dole queue to millionaires. It's a slippery slope, Sarah.'

'I know. Better to have nothing and want nothing.'

'When you ain't got nothing you got nothing to lose.'

'I lost you, Duncan.'

He vanished, leaving the familiar pain. Sarah relit her roll-up. Were her motives pure, in this new ambition? Did she really want to tell the world what was happening, or did she merely want to get paid for it?

She could give the story away, of course. Present it to the papers and decline any payment. But then how would she live? A person had to live.

Other worries began to intrude. Would she need a journalists' union card? How did you get one? Inspiration was one thing. Implementation, it seemed, was a completely different ball-game.

There was a knock on the back door and the dogs barked, reminding Sarah that she still hadn't fed them. They preceded her down the narrow stairs, trying to keep their minds on the job but managing, somehow, to arrive hopefully at their bowls and not at the back door.

'I'll feed you in a minute,' said Sarah, and opened the door. Outside in the misty damp stood Malachy Glynn.

7

His appearance surprised Sarah.

He was wearing a canvas bomber-jacket which fitted tight at the waist, and well-cut jeans which looked warm and comfortable. His hair was spangled with drops of mist, which gave Sarah the brief but distinct impression that he was lit from within. He had a tight, anxious smile, which made a late refusal difficult. Impossible, actually.

'I just have to feed the dogs,' said Sarah.

'Oh yes, the dogs,' said Malachy. 'Has Oliver been giving you some bones?'

'Do they get bones?'

'Mairead usually drops over for a few, now and then.'

'She didn't tell me that,' said Sarah, and wondered why. The idea that Mairead, who was also a vegetarian, didn't share her disgust of the shop next door hadn't occurred to her.

They left the dogs bolting down their Vegi-Pooch and crossed the street to Reagan's. It was still early and the day, despite its cloud and rain, was considerably brighter than the dim interior. Sarah stood inside the door, experiencing a momentary flashback to the coach-house earlier that day. Was this another place where unknown terrors lurked, waiting for her eyes to adjust to them?

Malachy stepped around her and led the way to an empty table in the corner. 'What'll you have?'

Sarah tried to get her bearings; not only in the gloomy pub but in her life's story.

'I'll get them.' It was her gig, after all. She was the reporter.

She wasn't accustomed to carrying money and for a moment she nearly succeeded in convincing herself that she hadn't brought any. But there were a few coins and a damp, soft fiver in the pocket of her jeans, which she produced with relief and pride.

'I'll have a pint, so,' said Malachy.

Sarah ordered the same for herself and rejoined the butcher at the table while she waited for their drinks to be pulled. There was a sparse gathering of customers, most of them leaning against the dark, shining counter of the bar; all of them sneaking gossip-hungry glances at Sarah and Malachy.

'This'll give them something to talk about, anyway,' said Malachy.

'I hope they don't get the wrong idea,' said Sarah.

Malachy coloured and looked into his lap. 'Would that be so terrible?'

Sarah was struck with an inexplicable desire to laugh. The response confused her, and she could tell that the stony expression she was attempting to maintain was failing. To conceal her bubbling emotions, she returned to the bar, even though the pints were still settling and would be settling for a good few minutes more. There was something about the butcher that she liked, despite herself. He was, she decided, surprisingly human for someone who lived such an atavistic existence. He seemed to lack the belligerent machismo that she would have expected from someone who pursued such a pariah profession. If anything, he gave her the impression of being a somewhat shy and sensitive soul.

'Watch yourself, Sarah,' said Duncan, muscling in on the act. 'Don't allow yourself to be deceived.'

The barman topped off the black pints, and Sarah was shocked to discover that her fiver barely covered the cost of them. She was going to have to get more familiar with this money business if she was going to start earning it.

'So,' she said, as she set the slopping glasses on to a pair of beer-mats. 'Let's get down to business, shall we?'

The butcher took a long pull at his pint, then put it down. 'Fine. Have you been freelancing long?'

'Oh. Just . . . Not long, actually.'

'Who were you working for before that?'

'Is this an inquisition or what?' said Sarah. 'Do you want me to show you my ID or something?'

'No, no,' said Malachy, recoiling from her sharpness. 'Just interested, that's all.'

'I've done a lot of things,' said Sarah. 'Journalism is just one of the strings to my bow.'

'Yes. Mairead said you were a bit of an idealist. Living in trees and such-like.'

He wasn't, to Sarah's surprise, laughing at her. Or at least, he didn't appear to be.

'So what if I have?'

'I'd like to hear about it. That's all.'

By the time Malachy went to order a second round of drinks, they were still talking about the destruction of the environment and what could or couldn't be done about it. But while he was away, Duncan came and took his place at Sarah's side.

'He's humouring you, Sal,' he said. 'He doesn't really agree with you. He's coming the caring, interested male, and you're falling for it at every step of the way.'

Sarah's spirits sank.

'Do you really believe he could be interested in anything more than a quick conquest?' Duncan went on. 'I mean, look at him! Look at his blood-fed cheeks. Look at the muscles bursting out all over the place. Mr Illegal Hormone Man himself.'

'I'm not falling for anything,' Sarah said, defensively. 'I'm just softening him up. To get at the inside story. I know what I'm doing.'

'I hope so,' said Duncan. 'Because I can see straight through him, you know? I can read his mind. A beautiful, vulnerable stranger in town. No morality, these hippy types. Easy pickings.'

'I'm no one's pickings,' said Sarah.

'Who're you talking to?' asked Malachy, returning to the table with the fresh pints.

'No one,' said Sarah. 'Myself.'

'Do you often do that?'

'I wasn't really talking, was I?'

'Your lips were moving.'

'I was saying the Hail Mary,' said Sarah.

Malachy laughed, and Sarah clamped down hard on her eagerness to laugh with him. To be happy.

'So you don't think I'm nuts, then?' she asked, truculently. 'Living in the trees? Having a conscience?'

'I think you're great,' said Malachy. 'Standing up for what you believe in. I wish more people could be like that.'

Duncan was right. 'They can,' said Sarah. 'I might go back there in a while. Why don't you join me?'

'I'm a butcher,' said Malachy. 'That's what I do.'

'Why?'

'Why what?'

'Why are you a butcher?'

Malachy sighed and drank from his glass. 'Do you want the long version or the short version?'

'The shorter the better,' said Sarah, feeling in command again, freed from the trap.

'All right,' said Malachy. 'I'm a butcher because my father was a butcher.'

'Ah,' said Sarah. 'That's profound. And will your son be a butcher as well?'

'That will be up to him,' said Malachy. 'If it should happen that I ever have a son.'

'You're not married, then?' Sarah didn't know where that came from. She would have hoiked it out of the air between them if she could.

Malachy shook his head. 'Nor ever will be, by the looks of things.'

'Why not?'

'It's not every day a man meets someone who understands him.' He looked closely at Sarah as he spoke, but it was an old hook and she wasn't going anywhere near that one.

'Tell me about the calf,' she said. 'That's what we came here to discuss.'

'There's not much to tell,' said Malachy. 'The vet wasn't available. They called me out to put the poor creature out of its misery.'

'And did you?'

'I did.'

'Who put it there?'

Malachy shrugged. 'Could have been any one of a hundred hard-pressed farmers.'

'Do you think it was justified?' said Sarah. 'Do you see it as a cry for help?'

'No,' said Malachy. 'I see it as a crime.'

'Then why did you take part in it?'

'Take part in it?'

'It was a cover-up, basically, wasn't it? Get rid of the evidence.'

'What should I have done, then? According to your exalted conscience?'

Sarah could tell that she had touched on a nerve, but she wasn't so sure it was the one she had been aiming at. She didn't have an answer to his question.

Malachy drained his glass and put it down. He didn't offer another one, and Sarah hadn't enough money to buy him one. She wasn't sure whether she would have done anyway. Nor was she sure that she wouldn't.

He reached for his jacket. 'You should come and have a look at my set-up some time,' he said. 'You might learn something.'

'About how to kill things?'

'Exactly,' said Malachy. 'About how to kill things.'

'No thanks,' said Sarah.

'Fine,' said the butcher. He put on his jacket and seemed about to leave, but he didn't. They sat together in awkward silence until she realised that he was waiting for her to finish her drink. The pub was filling up and had become, without Sarah noticing it, quite noisy. She had no desire to stay there on her own.

'I don't really want it,' she said at last. 'Would you like it?'

'I'll share it with you,' said Malachy. Their eyes met above the glass. To her amazement, and Duncan's horror, Sarah realised that she was quite willing to drink from the same glass as the butcher.

John nodded to Malachy Glynn as they passed each other in the doorway of the pub.

'Not like Malachy,' said his brother, Liam, who had come home from Ballinasloe to help him spend his wages. 'Who's your woman, anyway?'

'No idea,' said John.

'Wo ho,' said Liam. 'You think he's getting his leg over at last?'

John ignored him and wriggled his way over to the bar. It had occurred to him as he was driving his brother into town that it might be useful to have someone else along on his jaunt; a picador perhaps, or simply an audience. But Liam wasn't the man. He was just like the other lads in the job, coarse and shallow and brutal. He wouldn't understand the value of what John was proposing to do.

Sarah and Malachy walked together to the back of the adjoining shops.

'Wait here a moment,' said Malachy. He unlocked his door and went inside for a few minutes. Sarah could hear the river a few streets away, barging its way through the salmon weir. The rain no longer seemed odious, and for the first time she understood the local expression for this kind of weather. It was a soft evening. Soft and sweet. Whether she liked it or not, something new had begun to happen in her life. All her pores were open and beckoning to the soft rain and to the unexpected newness of everything.

Inside the shop doors opened and closed. Eventually the butcher returned with a bagful of bones. He threw the choicest ones to the skinny bitch and her pup, who were cowering in a dark corner on the other side of the street. The others he offered to Sarah.

She took a step back. 'Perhaps you'd bring them in,' she said. And then, realising how it might sound, she added, 'I mean, just drop them inside the door. The dogs will find them.'

Malachy laughed again, and this time, in spite of herself, Sarah laughed as well.

8 ♪

When John and Liam were about halfway down their second pint, the musicians started to play. They were local men and women, no big names among them, but they knew their stuff and people came from all over the area to hear them.

'I told you we shouldn't have come in here,' said Liam, over the heads of the other drinkers. 'There's a half-decent band playing in the Weir. Will we go down there?'

The Weir had a nightclub, John knew. He hadn't intended to get involved in that. But he couldn't think of an excuse to stay where he was, so they drained their glasses and left.

Sarah could hear the faint strains of the fiddles and boxes from the sitting-room. She had taken out her notebook when she got in, and jotted down a few lines about the butcher. She wondered whether she should mention him by name. He hadn't said she couldn't. And it was, she thought now, such a nice name. Malachy Glynn. Malachy Glynn.

'Are you losing your mind?' said Duncan.

'You might have liked him, Dunc,' she said.

'You can't be serious?'

'I know he's a butcher and all. But . . .'

'But what? Next you'll be sucking up to some military

type. He's a five-star general with a senior position in NATO, but he's rather sweet all the same.'

'Don't be ridiculous.'

'He's only a land developer. He's only a hamburger magnate. He's only an old man called Pinochet.'

'Duncan . . .'

'You're losing it, Sarah. You're being tempted.'

'I don't believe you're saying this to me.'

There was a silence inside her mind, and she could hear the music again. She wished she hadn't messed it up with Malachy. She wished she was still there, listening, sharing another pint. Whatever it was that had begun to happen was still happening.

'I believe in you, Duncan,' Sarah said. 'I believe in all you stood for and all I still stand for. I believe that there's an alternative to the madness that is destroying the planet. It's my mission in life to preserve what's left. That hasn't changed. It won't change. But . . .'

'No buts, Sarah. There can never be any buts. Not even the smallest but.'

One of the dogs crept up close to her legs, and she reached out to stroke its head without even thinking. 'Why does it always have to be so grim? Why does it always have to be heads down; hard slog?'

'Joy is in right living, Sarah.'

'But it isn't. Not since you died.'

The dog was trying to climb on to her lap, but Sarah wasn't even aware of it. She wasn't prepared for the thought that followed, and it sent a wave of dread through her. It was a treacherous thought.

'Not when you were alive, either.'

She could feel Duncan's disgust. His spirit turned away from her. But it was true. There had been passion and adoration and intensity. But no joy.

'I only have one life,' said Sarah. 'Can't I enjoy it a bit?'

'He's a butcher, Sarah. A butcher.'

The words were accompanied by images of hypnagogic clarity. A torrent of hot blood from an open throat. A skinless, earless head, fixed in an agonised gape. Her first sight of the butcher, with the huge, fat-marbled haunch slung across his shoulder. Duncan was right. What on earth was she thinking of? What had come over her?

I had no alternative but to back off, diminished, defeated, as Duncan took centre stage. Sarah remembered the moment she had realised that he would always be with her. The funeral was over, and the best and closest of Duncan's friends and supporters had been standing beside the river, where they had loaded his few possessions on to a hazel raft and set them afloat, surrounded by candles. Sarah had watched the flickering flames sailing away into the darkness, and experienced an emptiness so profound that she couldn't see how life could continue at all. It was as though someone had scooped out her innards and hidden them aboard the little craft, and everything that animated her was floating away on the current. She had stepped to the water's edge and squatted on her heels. The breeze that was blowing from behind her was light, but it was enough, she knew, to tip her fragile balance. The waters beneath her were dark and swift. What use was an existence devoid of spirit? She could not move without Duncan. Could not take a breath or a step or a decision.

She had begun to topple forward, and no one in the gathering had noticed. But a hand, a spirit hand had risen up from the river and pushed her back on to the shore, so hard that she sat down on the cold ground with a bump. And, as she stood up again, she realised that she wasn't empty any more. Wherever Duncan had been for the past few days, he was back. Her heart was full. Her spirit was strong and keen; bolstered by the presence of his, in her and around her.

There was work to be done.

Duncan was buried in a churchyard in Dorset, where he had been born. But he had never died. He had just shucked off his body like a worn-out coat, and continued as though nothing had changed.

And nothing would change. Sarah's flighty mood evaporated. She pushed the dog away and picked up her notebook.

There was, indeed, work to be done.

Malachy lay in his damp, lumpy bed in the bungalow. He went to bed early and got up early. Usually, he dropped off to sleep the moment he lay down. But tonight he was restless. The rain had grown heavier again. It was tapping on the roof and piddling down the gutters, reminding him that he had forgotten to water the cattle in the coach-house. He could never understand how they got through so much water, and it was high on his list of priorities to put in automatic drinking troughs. But he hadn't got around to it yet. They would be thirsty tonight, but they would survive.

The rain also reminded him of his weak bladder, and the likelihood that he would have to get up again before long. It was a curse, and one that he had inherited, it seemed. It meant that if he had more than a couple of pints on any occasion he would be tormented by a night spent padding backwards and forwards to the bathroom. It was one of the reasons he rarely went out, but not the only one. The other was that he had long ago come to the end of the common ground he shared with most of the local people. He was respected for his industry, the good meat that he sold and the fact that his shop brought people from all over the outlying areas to do their business in the town. But he was not understood.

He turned over, parking himself carefully between the

springs that shoved up through the fabric of the mattress. His loneliness was driving him mad; making him old before his time. He had made a few efforts to get to know some of the women in the area, and had never been refused when he asked someone out for a date. But nothing ever got off the ground. He wanted sex, but not without love. It was his misfortune, he knew, to have experienced the real thing, and to see anything less as icing without cake. But he was seriously interested in this woman, this Sarah. He had been from the moment he first laid eyes on her. He had been interested in her even before they met.

Mairead had spoken about her in disparaging tones, about her unreliability, her lack of sense and of money and of security. He had heard about Duncan's death. Mairead had only just started the business when he died, and had gone over to attend the funeral, leaving the shop in the care of various rather haphazard friends. When she came back she was annoyed with Sarah. Duncan's demise hadn't succeeded in knocking any sense into her, it seemed. On the contrary, she appeared to be more fanatical than ever, as though she were setting out on some kind of crusade to redeem him. She had no money, no job, not even the dole. She was a liability to the family, a constant worry for her parents, and a dead loss in life.

But Malachy had read between the lines. Sarah was someone with an integrity of purpose, he knew, and he admired that, even from a distance. When Mairead told him she was coming to take over for a while he had been delighted. But whenever he had encountered her on the street behind the two shops, she had cut him dead.

Malachy knew the value of patience. He never killed a bullock until it had become entirely relaxed in the slaughterhouse crush. Some of them seemed fearless from the beginning. Others took longer to become accustomed to the smell of blood. But they all came around in the end. He believed that Sarah would, as well.

But things weren't going as he had hoped. Sarah's resistance to him seemed unbreachable. He wished that she hadn't tried so hard to be distant and cool. He wished that she had asked for the long version, not the short one. He wished that he had given it to her anyway. But now that he thought about it, he wasn't so sure that she would have listened. Not really listened. No one ever had.

The wind was coming up, and the gutters were gurgling like plug-holes. The butcher threw off his bedclothes in exasperation and went out to the bathroom one more time.

Sarah was almost asleep. For some reason, she couldn't get the butcher's name out of her mind. Malachy Glynn. It was like a galloping horse or the sound a train made speeding over the rail joints. Malachy Glynn, Malachy Glynn, Malachy Glynn. Was he there, perhaps, to bring her along some unknown part of her journey? The thought made her smile guiltily to herself and, before Duncan could start getting heavy again, she turned over in the bed and snuggled closer.

'I know,' she said. 'He's a butcher.'

John's head was aching from drink and tobacco smoke. He made several attempts to draw Liam from the throbbing, squirming rabble in the nightclub, and eventually left without him.

His car was parked on the edge of town, but the walk through the wet streets did nothing to improve his condition. The headache he could bear. What he couldn't tolerate was the fuzziness that came with it; the loss of self and purpose. As he drove home, with exaggerated care, he resolved that he would never do it again. A hero needed a clear head. He would have to outwit, as well as outmanoeuvre, his adversary.

His parents were both in bed and asleep when he got home, but they had left the television on in the sitting-room, as though they felt someone had to wait up for the lads. John turned it off and tidied up the strewn crisp-bags and mugs. Then he washed, brushed his teeth and set his alarm-clock for six hours later. He didn't have anything in particular to do the following day, but too much sleep dulled the mind.

9

Malachy got up early and went out around the land. The wind had dropped and the light rain wasn't serious. Out to the west, Malachy could see fine weather coming in behind it. He wondered if Sarah would consider walking with him after the shops were closed. Were there any ecological flash-points he could take her to see? The proposed site of the new super-dump, perhaps. Or the incinerator site in Clarecastle? Perhaps there would be an interesting case on in the district court? A farmer found with growth promoters or an effluent leak into some water-course? Or maybe, even better, they could find something unspoiled together.

He had a feeling that she wouldn't come.

The bullocks out on the land hadn't been hand-fed now for weeks. They flocked around him anyway, inquisitive as children, and escorted him among their hot, heavy bodies until he climbed over the gate and left them behind. Then they went lumbering off at a gallop along the hedgerow, and he could feel the water-logged ground juddering beneath his feet.

John dreamed that he was on television, commentating on a journey across some wild and uncharted terrain. There were others with him, but he was the mainstay; the Man.

He crossed a deep, barren valley in the middle of which was a trickling stream of blood, which led from the throat of a slaughtered bull. The others in the party hung back, unsure how to ford it.

'It's nothing,' said John to the invisible camera crew, and his heart was full of pride as he prepared to give a demonstration of his courage and skill. Dropping his knapsack, he jumped into a tiny pool where the stream widened. And went straight down.

The warm liquid was over his head. He had enough air for some time, and he wasn't unduly worried. For a while he stayed still, assuming that he would just float up again to the surface. Then he realised that he wasn't going to. His feet were stuck in the mud at the bottom. He flapped his arms like a chicken, trying to swim up, but the mud was too deep, too holding. With both hands he began to tug at one knee, and then the other, but his feet wouldn't come free. His air was running out. He began to panic, and woke in a gluey sweat, impossibly tangled in the bedclothes. His heart was hammering, and every beat caused a colossal pain in his head.

Suddenly desperate, he kicked free of the clinging sheets and made a dash for the bathroom. He barely made it in time, and afterwards he sat on the edge of the bed, his sweat slowly cooling, his head gradually clearing. Outside a car door slammed, and he heard Liam's heavy tread cross the yard. It was 7.15 a.m.

The department vet arrived on time at the slaughterhouse. Because Malachy killed his animals singly, and not in batches, he had come to an agreement with the vet which, although not entirely legal, suited both of them well. The vet came on one day of the week; examined all the animals Malachy proposed to kill over the following week, and made a note of their tag numbers. The ones he was recording

today on his official form were the ones he had seen
the previous week, and he now inspected their carcasses
and the offal that Malachy had set aside in compliance
with the current legislation. On paper, it appeared to the
department that Malachy killed several cattle on the same
day. The arrangement suited the vet, who didn't have to
call more than once a week, and it suited Malachy, whose
principles wouldn't allow him to have cattle waiting in
the pens while their comrades were being slaughtered
inside. It worked because Malachy kept healthy animals
and was scrupulous about his slaughtering procedures. The
vet trusted him absolutely.

As soon as she had opened the shop, Sarah phoned the
Clare Champion and asked to be put through to the editor.
There seemed to be some difficulty about finding him, and
she was left holding for a long time, listening to indistinct,
questioning voices in the electronic void. Eventually he
came on to the line.

'Hello?'

'Hello,' said Sarah. 'I was wondering if you were interested in buying a story.'

There was a long pause, and then the editor said, 'Are you
sure you don't want the *Sun* or the *News of the World*?'

Sarah thought about that for a minute or two. Would
they be interested? 'No. I don't think so.'

'What kind of a story is it?'

'It's about . . . well, it's about the treatment of animals in
this county. The way farmers go about things.'

'Was there something in particular?'

'Well, yes. There was, actually.'

'Something like a calf found alive on a dump?'

Sarah said nothing. She ought to have known how fast
news travelled in a small community.

'Why don't you write us a letter?' said the editor, in an

infuriatingly patronising tone. 'If it's good enough we'll print it. It always helps if you can make it funny.'

'What's funny about a calf dying on a dump?'

'You're the one with the ideas.'

The line went dead and Sarah slammed down the receiver. Maybe she would write a letter. Maybe letters were the way to start. She could send the same one round to all the papers, national as well as local. And still try the article on some of the periodicals.

She took out her notebook again, but the string of cowbells on the front door started clanging, demanding her attention in the shop. It was Daniel O'Dea, his ruddy fists already full of sweet packets.

'Did you hear the news?' he said. 'They fished Gerry Fitz out of the river this morning.'

'Gerry Fitz?'

'The vet. No one's surprised, mind you. It was clear he wasn't coping.'

'You mean it was suicide?'

Daniel shrugged. 'I wouldn't go that far,' he said.

Malachy heard the news as soon as he arrived at his shop that morning. Oliver was already behind the counter, separating meat from fat and gristle to make mince.

Malachy hung the shoulder he was carrying on a hook in the cold room and came through to the front. He hadn't known Gerry well, but what he had seen of him he had liked. The thought of his suicide terrified him. Suicide was one of Malachy's most constant and unwelcome companions.

'Who said he meant to do it?' he asked Oliver. 'Was there a note?'

Oliver shrugged.

'We shouldn't leap to conclusions. He could have had a few pints. Slipped.'

'Oh he could,' said Oliver, whose persistent good humour was sometimes wearying. 'He could indeed.'

Throughout the morning, the details of Gerry Fitz's unhappy life began to emerge. He had been overworked, everyone agreed, and wasn't up to the hours and the pressures of that kind of job. He was good with small animals, the more pet-centred people said. They always preferred to bring their cats and dogs to him than to Mr Leary. He was soft-hearted; quiet and sensitive. His wife, of course, was devastated.

Mr Leary was on his way back from the Canaries.

'He should never have left,' said Eileen, who came in for nothing, it seemed, other than a chat. 'Not without making sure that relief fellow was going to be any use. Didn't he get bitten by one of Jimmy Daley's sows on his second day at work, and she broke all those little bones in his hand. Put him out of work for weeks, it did.'

'Couldn't they find anyone else?'

'There's other vets around,' said Eileen. 'But everyone likes to deal with their own man, in the end of the day. It's a thing of trust, you see.'

'I wouldn't be a vet these days for love nor money,' said Suzie Dean. She was one of the regulars who kept the shop ticking over, and Sarah always felt slightly guilty whenever she came in, knowing how much of her money would end up in her own pocket. She was a local entrepreneur, a German who had come over and married an Englishman during the heady days of the folk revival and its extension into the uncharted territory of Ireland. Now the two of them worked together, manufacturing hand-made instruments. As far as Sarah could tell, they were doing pretty well.

'I wouldn't go that far,' said Eileen. 'It wouldn't be so bad if you were cut out for it.'

Suzie shook her head. 'How could anyone be cut out for it? All that testing. All those mountains of paperwork.

Identity cards always getting lost. We wanted to keep a cow once. Just a little Jersey cow, for milk for the house. A herd number, they said we had to have. Just for one cow!'

'It's the badgers, you see,' said Eileen. 'That's how the TB is spread.'

'Nonsense,' said Sarah. 'They disproved that years ago.'

Suzie nodded her head, but Eileen wasn't impressed. 'I don't know what "they" it is you're talking about,' she said. 'Sure, it's a well-known fact that badgers are the cause of it all. When we got tested positive Liam and PJ were out in all weathers lamping them on the land. They got dozens of them. And we're clear since.'

'Isn't that illegal?' said Sarah.

Eileen suddenly got interested in the stock, and began to wander around the shelves. 'What's this I came in for, now?' she muttered.

Suzie shrugged and paid, and while she was packing her things into the jute bags she had brought along, Eileen left the shop.

Afterwards, Sarah went back to her cigarette and her notebook. But as she picked up her pencil she realised that the story was no longer as simple as a calf on a dump. Beneath her eyes it was growing into something far bigger. An overall picture of the madness at the heart of farming was beginning to emerge. The country was inhabited by suicidal vets and maniacal badger-hunters, husbanding unwanted calves and vicious pigs. And they were all gradually being buried beneath a mountain of paperwork.

Sarah wondered if her creative gifts might stretch to drawing cartoons. She rolled another cigarette. One thing at a time.

She began to sketch an outline of her ideas. There were, she soon realised, two ways to go about the job. One was to write it from the point of view of someone like herself, who knew nothing about CAP reforms or GATT treaties or any of the bureaucracy that governed the farming community. The other was to begin with the policy, the headage schemes, the market interference on the European and global scales. The first plan, she saw, had limitations. The second would require a lot of research. Sarah wondered if there was anyone she could ask.

'I see where this chain of thought is heading,' said Duncan.

Sarah sighed. 'Vigilant today, aren't you?'

'I know what you're thinking before you do, Sal. I always have.'

Had he? Or had he instructed her on what she was thinking?

'We'll see how we go with the first idea,' said Sarah.

The shop bells rang again, and she put down the cigarette and went inside. It was Mairead, struggling with a suitcase and several carrier bags. Sarah helped her. They didn't hug.

'Are you smoking in here?' Mairead asked.

'Um,' said Sarah. 'It's just that . . . Did you hear about Gerry Fitz?'

Mairead nodded. 'I just met Suzie on the street. When's the funeral?'

'I don't know.' A cold wind blew through Sarah's awareness. She thought about the funeral, about all the days to come. Life would be going on in the little town. Without her, presumably. She had known that Mairead was coming back, but she hadn't thought beyond it at all. What was she going to do now?

In the late morning Malachy called in to a contractor friend a few miles out of town to book someone to cut and bale his hay and silage. On his way back through town, he stopped outside the wholefood shop and went in. The day was completely clear now, and he had made up his mind. If she rejected his offer, so what? He could take it. Probably.

But it was Mairead who came in from the back room in response to the bells.

'Malachy.' She sounded surprised. 'How are things?'

In the kitchen, where she was still labouring over her notes, Sarah heard.

'Grand, grand. Welcome home, Mairead. Did you have a good time?'

'Oh, you know,' said Mairead. 'Parents.'

'Parents,' said Malachy.

There was a pause in the conversation, and Sarah realised she was holding her breath.

'Anything in particular you were looking for?' said Mairead.

'Ah, no,' said Malachy. 'Just . . . Did you hear about Gerry Fitz?'

'I did. Poor Gerry. When's the funeral?'

'We'll hear, I suppose,' said Malachy.

Again there was a silence.

'Your sister manage all right while you were away?' said Malachy, at last.

Sarah reached for her cigarettes, then remembered the rules and put them down.

'As far as I can tell,' said Mairead.

'She'll be going home, then, I suppose,' said Malachy.

'Wherever home is. She'll be moving on, anyway.'

Again the pause.

'Did you want to speak to her or something?' said Mairead.

'No, no.' Malachy sounded cornered. 'You can say good-bye to her for me. I'll see you, Mairead.'

The cowbells rang dismally and he was gone.

Sarah let out her breath. Relief and despair struggled for ascendancy in her heart. But one thing, at least, was certain. It was over.

*   *   *

One of the bullocks in the coach-house had been fasting since the previous evening. Malachy let it out and, although it was a little uncertain about being on its own, its hunger led it along its habitual route to the slaughterhouse.

Malachy didn't make it wait. As soon as the crush was closed behind it, he went round to its head and fired the pre-loaded bolt-gun. The bullock didn't suffer at all, but Malachy did. It was always the same. For years he had struggled with himself, trying to bring his instinctive reactions into line with his principles. For all the right reasons he had chosen this life, and he had made a firm commitment to it. He was the first and only prelate, in a religion of his own making.

And he was constantly besieged by doubt.

When Liam finally emerged from his bed in the afternoon he bumbled heavily about the house like a bear wakening from hibernation. He nodded blearily at John, who was sitting in the kitchen, then yelled for their mother and ordered her to make him a fry. John told him to cop on and make it himself, but Eileen bustled in, fussing and fawning, taking the great lumps of rashers and sausages from the fridge. John went out into the yard and set himself the task of collecting the eggs.

When Liam had eaten he came looking for John.

'Are you going to the club tonight?'

'No.'

'Can you lend me twenty quid?'

'No. I'm broke myself after last night.' It was a lie, but one that he didn't regret at all.

Liam was silent for a few moments. Then he said, 'Will you give me a lift back to Ballinasloe, so?'

'I will,' said John. 'Gladly.'

10

Sarah cooked that evening while Mairead changed the sheets on her bed and made up another one for Sarah in the narrow little attic. The meal was a success, a pie made from mushrooms and eggs and stale bread, and they chatted about their parents and their mother's overwhelming contrition. But there was a tension in the air as well, as though there were something that was waiting to be said.

'Is everything all right?' said Sarah, at last.

'Fine,' said Mairead.

'Books in order?'

'Yes. You've done a great job. Thanks for coming. It was great to get away.'

'You're welcome. Any time.'

'Any time we can find you, you mean. Where are you planning to go now?'

Sarah shrugged. She had been brooding on the question for most of the day, but hadn't come to any clear decision. 'I had an idea about becoming a journalist,' she said. 'Maybe a kind of wandering commentator on the environment and animal abuses. Stuff like that.'

Mairead brightened. 'It's a brilliant idea,' she said. 'But you'd have to do a bit of training first, wouldn't you?'

'Training?'

'Well, you can't just head off into the blue and expect everyone to hail you as the new John Pilger.'

'I wouldn't expect them to.'

'Thing is,' said Mairead, 'Mum and Dad were talking about this, actually.'

'Were they?'

'Not exactly that. But about the possibility of setting you up in some way.'

Sarah said nothing. Her hackles were rising.

'Not to be pushing you or anything,' said Mairead. 'But if you wanted to go to college or something like that. They helped me with setting up the shop, you know, and they'd like to be able to do something for you.'

The sound of the river in the weir seemed impossibly close. Either that or there was a dangerous volume of blood reaching Sarah's brain.

'So, you have it all worked out for me, have you?'

'It's not like that, Sarah. Don't be ridiculous. But you can't go on living like this, don't you see? You deserve more out of life.'

'Deserve? Who are you to say what any of us deserves? We're all living beyond the planet's means, Mairead. You know that's true.'

'But you're not saving the world by denying yourself! Especially when . . .'

'When what?'

'It's just . . . I believe in what you're doing, Sal. I really do. But it's a waste, don't you see that? You could do far more if you were in a position to have some influence.'

'Ah. Patrician environmentalism, then. That's what you're advocating, is it? Set myself up somewhere nice and cosy with oil-fired central heating and a tidy set of recycling bins so I can continue consuming more than I need and convince myself I'm a good citizen.'

It was a bit close to the bone, she knew. Mairead hit back.

'All right, Saint Sarah,' said Mairead. 'Have it your own way. Follow your holy man to his early grave if it makes you feel better. But there's nothing particularly heroic about dying of malnourishment and pneumonia, you know.'

It was below the belt. 'Damn you to hell,' said Sarah. 'You know it didn't happen like that.'

Mairead knew she had gone too far. 'All right. Maybe that is an over-simplification. But you worry us, can't you understand that? It's as if you're on another planet!'

'It's you who think you're on another planet!' said Sarah. 'I know exactly which planet I'm on.'

She left the table and went downstairs, tripping over the hairy muddle of dogs lying at the turn in the stairs. Outside the day was still bright and clear, and she stood for a few minutes blinking in the sun before following her feet around the side of the houses to the shed where Mairead's bike was kept.

It still wasn't too late. She would be going tomorrow and she had promised herself that she wouldn't leave the area without a visit to the mountain.

John took his time coming back from Ballinasloe. He drove slowly and carefully, working on clarifying his mind and body and spirit. What he intended to do would require his utmost. He needed to be ready.

After dinner Matty asked him to help with the dogs again, and he agreed. They brought them to the Long Hill, a steeply sloping field on the boundaries of the family land, which had always been a favourite place for the boys. Halfway up the land levelled out for a while in a kind of platform, and thickets of sally willow had always grown there; the forests and dens of John's childhood games. But as they approached the gate, he saw that they were gone.

'What happened?' he asked Matty.

'To what?'

'The old scrub. What happened to it?'

Matty seemed at a loss for a moment, as though the question had struck an uncomfortable nerve.

'Ach, it was a waste of grass. I got Micky Spillane to root it out with the digger there. February, it was. Made a fair bonfire, so it did.'

'But you loved that place, Dad. You were always on about the wild places on the farm. You used play there yourself when you were a lad. You used say life wouldn't be worth living if they were gone.'

Matty's jaw was slack, and for the first time, John saw that he was getting old. Then his expression hardened again.

'You would have done the same thing if 'twas you,' he said.

'I wouldn't,' said John.

Matty didn't answer. On the other side of the gate, he handed the leashes to John and walked slowly and steadily up to the top of the hill.

John watched him go, bracing himself hard against his own sentimentality. Maybe his father was right about the sally. It was no use to anyone. But the games returned to him none the less and his mind filled with their images. There had always been some element of hunting in them. The Sheriff of Nottingham pursuing Robin Hood and his gang. Butch and Sundance on the run from the Pinkerton posse. And earlier, when they were smaller, the old hare and hounds game.

Since there had rarely been anyone smaller than he was, John had always been the hare. The game involved giving him a head start and allowing him to hide himself among the sally. Then the others would come in after him. Suddenly, physically, he remembered the terror. The smell of the earth as he crouched beneath the bushes. The clutching claws of the briars as he squirmed further in, desperate to escape the attention of his brothers and their friends. The rules were always the same. The first one of them to find him would stand off and start to howl, alerting the others. As soon as that happened, John would make a break for it, pelting through the undergrowth and heading for the steep, downward slope. He would run so hard down the field that he was practically airborne. The others would come hurtling after him, whooping and yipping. If he reached the gate before they did he was free; a winning hare. But it seemed that he never did. The others were so much taller and faster, and the fear when he heard the sound of their feet on the hill behind him would loosen his bowels and send hot, painful currents through his blood. When they caught him it was awful. One of them would bring him down with a flying tackle, and the rest would pile in, biting and pinching and punching and scratching. He had to 'die', finally, by going limp and lifeless, but he wasn't allowed to do it too quickly.

'You couldn't be dead yet! We only just caught you.'

'My neck is broke!'

'No, it isn't. He's just pretending to be dead. We all back off, and then he jumps up and starts running again.'

'No!'

'Go on! Get up!'

Once he started crying. The lesson he learned from that convinced him never to do it again.

'Let 'em off!'

His father had reached the top of the hill and the dogs, who knew the routine, began bouncing and tugging at the leashes. It was important that they all went off together, competing against each other up the hill. John slipped one leash through the four collars and unclipped the others, struggling with the frenzied hounds. When he was ready he signalled his father, who blew a shrill blast on the whistle. The dogs tore off up the hill, their lean, powerful anatomies clearly visible beneath their supple skin. They were beautiful, a triumph of nature's design.

When they reached Matty, the greyhounds transformed themselves from sleek killing machines into playful, sycophantic pups. John called them back, and they bounded and tumbled down the slope, bumping into each other and having little conversations on their way. Once more Matty called them up and then, all too quickly, it was over. John could have watched them run for ever.

It was a lot further to the foot of the mountain than Sarah had expected. As well as that, it seemed to be impossible to find a direct route. Every road she took began by heading out in the right direction, then changed its mind and swerved off towards somewhere entirely different. But when she finally left the bike leaning against a brambly ditch the sun was still high over the horizon and the mountain turned out to be a lot smaller than it had appeared from a distance.

There were no paths at all, as far as Sarah could see. The first part of the climb took her across steep meadows, pitted by the deep footholds of grazing cattle and bounded by impenetrable hedges of blackthorn and gorse. Beyond the farmland the going was even worse, with thick heather and sudden, dangerous bog-holes. Sarah had to backtrack on several occasions, and by the time she was finally approaching the summit the sun was alarmingly low on the western skyline.

She ought to have turned back while there was still light enough to see by. But the anger that had launched the expedition was still burning strongly and fuelling her to go on. Duncan was unusually silent. He wasn't sulking. He never sulked. But he had been deeply wounded by Mairead's flippant remarks, and Sarah nursed his resentment for him as she walked. Somehow she had always felt that her family understood what she was doing; why she was living the way she did. They didn't have her commitment or endurance, that much was certain. But she had never before had cause to doubt their support for her. Now she felt alone and misunderstood.

There were several false summits before the top finally came into view. When it did, Sarah's sense of desolation was compounded, not lifted. There was no cairn to greet the tired pilgrim. Only the tall spike of a radio transmitter; a robotic phallus aimed at the heavens.

John was in the pub again, because on a Saturday night there was nowhere else a young man could conceivably be without drawing attention to himself. He was in with the crowd, being macho and raucous, but he was watching himself carefully. Not only that, but he was playing a wizard game with the pints.

Whenever John put down his glass, after taking the barest sip, he would quietly exchange it for one that had a lower level of beer in it. If anyone noticed, they were unlikely to mention it, since they were always getting the better end of the deal. It worked well, and his head and his body remained clear and uncontaminated. There was an eagerness within him that he could barely contain, and he had to work hard at restraining his excitement from spilling over into the company. If he allowed that, his energy would become dissipated. Now, more than ever, he needed to remain focused and strong.

Malachy took his depression off to an early bed. It was becoming painfully clear to him that he had invested more of his dreams in Sarah than he had intended. The suddenness of their curtailment had been a shock, and had brought him up hard against his loneliness again. He knew that he was, to some extent, solitary by nature. He preferred his own company to the carefree, shallow companionship that was always available in the local pubs. But he had never intended solitude to be a permanent condition. When, as often happened, suicidal temptations assailed him, he would keep himself afloat with dreams of connubial bliss. The woman that he imagined would understand what it was that he did, and why. She would provide relationship, family, safety from his self-destructive desires. He believed that for every man there was a woman. The suspicion that he might already have met her, and lost her, was a constant threat to his fragile equilibrium. When Sarah arrived in town, he was certain that he was being offered another chance. But now, it seemed, it was being snatched away from him.

Malachy had three spirited and energetic sisters, all older than he was. Their father was largely absent from the chaotic household. He worked long hours in his slaughter-house and spent three or four evenings a week at the pub with the lads. When he was at home, he tended to keep out of the way as much as possible, and when Malachy left school at the age of sixteen to go into the family business he discovered that he hardly knew his father at all. Nor, he was shocked to discover, had he ever taken the time to think about what it was that his father actually did.

The slaughterhouse appalled him. He became anxious and nervous, prone to ghastly nightmares which woke him several times a week, sometimes shouting into the indifferent darkness, sometimes clutching at his pillows as though he were holding on for dear life. But at no stage did it occur to him to approach his parents and suggest that he might not be suited to the work. His father was a butcher. Malachy was the only son.

But he knew he wouldn't survive if he stayed there. Before the first month was out he was making plans. He saved his wages and, as soon as he had collected enough, deserted.

There was plenty of work for Irish lads in London at that time. He got the first job he applied for, on a building site in Islington. One of the other men took him under his wing and, the same night, took him to the block of squatted flats where he was living and found him his own place.

For a while Malachy was in paradise. The work was rough and tiring, but compared to the slaughterhouse it was a pleasure. The flats were full of strange and interesting people from all kinds of different backgrounds; mostly young; mostly fleeing from one form of persecution or another. He developed a strong sense of solidarity with the other residents, especially the child prostitutes and rent boys, whose wild and cheerful demeanours concealed histories of abuse that made his experiences in his father's slaughterhouse seem innocent in comparison.

All the same, he would never go back there. Of that he was certain. He rang home occasionally in the evenings, and caught up with the family news. On the rare occasions that his father answered the call he hung up, ashamed and afraid to speak to him. His mother tried to convince him that he was forgiven; there were no hard feelings; he was welcome to come home any time he chose, and there would be no pressure on him to work in the abattoir. She said that his father understood and bore him no grudge. But he couldn't believe it, somehow. He couldn't square what he was hearing with his own conscience; his own sense of shame at having failed his father at the most fundamental level. He never told them where he was living or what he was doing. He had made an outcast of himself.

Sarah started straight back down the mountainside. There was nothing to see up there; whatever magic the summit might have possessed in the past had been siphoned away by the radio mast. As she made her away across the bog, she realised the danger of her situation. The same false summits that had confused her as she was climbing now concealed the direction of her descent. She could see nothing that she recognised as a landmark, only the heather-clad hill sloping gently away on all sides. And it was getting dark very quickly indeed.

She hurried on, and, as though it sensed her growing apprehension, the mountain chose that moment to make a grab for her. Her right foot, stepping forward, landed in a bog-hole and went straight down until her whole leg, up to the groin, was beneath the cold, black mud.

She was lucky that it was only one foot. The other provided enough of an anchor for her to resist the terrifying suck of the bog. But getting out was another matter. There seemed to be something down there, clutching hold of her foot, resisting all her efforts to pull free. Eventually, by throwing herself flat on the ground and grabbing a nearby bunch of rushes, she succeeded in getting enough purchase to pull herself out. But as she sat on the damp ground to get her breath back she was shaking. The night had brought the cold with it and, although the sky was clear, Sarah had lost confidence in her senses. Next time she stepped into a hole she might not be so lucky.

There were two options open to her. The first was to camp out. It was summer, and although the night was cold she had spent enough time living out of doors to know that she could survive if she had to. The alternative was to blunder around in the darkness and hope that she would stumble upon her way home.

Sarah decided to stay, but the decision didn't hold for long. Something large and pale flew over her head as though it were checking her out, then disappeared into the night again. The wet leg infected her whole body with its discomfort. The mountain was not like the trees. It was a hostile environment. It didn't want her there. Retracing her steps, Sarah started out again, giving a wide berth to the scene of her narrow escape.

Malachy padded to the bathroom, then returned to bed. But he was still too distraught to sleep. He was thinking about Maeve; about how their relationship started and how, to his continued regret, it ended.

He had been living in the squat for more than a year when he first met her. She was passing through on her way from Dublin to Amsterdam; visiting a friend who lived in the flat across the way from him. She was two years older than he was, but it didn't matter. They hit it off immediately and in no time at all Malachy found that he had entered into the first serious relationship of his life.

A few weeks later he followed her to Holland and got another building job there. For six months they shared a flat, and together they planned a trip to India. But when the time drew near, Malachy began to get cold feet. He wasn't ready yet for a journey like that. There was unfinished business at home which was holding him back. He would have to make a visit first, and then he would follow her.

But he got stuck; seduced by the easy living in Amsterdam. He fully intended to make both of the journeys, but the first one somehow became more difficult the longer he left it. Maeve wrote long letters from India, giving new Poste Restante addresses each time. Malachy answered every one, even though Maeve seemed to be drifting away from him into a world that grew more incomprehensible to him all the time. He promised that he would come; gave dates which grew more and more distant, until it became clear that neither of them really believed that he would make it. Then, one evening, when he made a phone call home, his sister informed him that their father had died.

So, he finally got on the Dublin flight. But it was too late now to make his peace with his father.

He died at work. Those were the days when bullocks were often pumped so full of hormones that the lack of testicles was no guarantee of safety for their handlers. Malachy's father was with two other men, shifting cattle around the holding pens at the back of the buildings when one of the bullocks suddenly swung round and slammed him against the wall. His ribs and lungs were crushed by the power of the attack, and although he survived for longer than the bullock did, it wasn't by much.

Malachy never made it to India. He never heard from Maeve again, either. The addresses he had for her were already out of date, and the friend who had promised to forward her letters either forgot or couldn't be bothered. Malachy's life had moved into a new phase, now. But wherever his mind wandered, Maeve was never far from it.

Malachy's mother kept the slaughterhouse running for another year or so, but when the expansion of Dublin brought it into a highly desirable development zone, she sold the whole shebang without a second thought. She divided the proceeds equally between the children. At the age of twenty-one, Malachy was suddenly a very rich man. But his future was an empty house, and he had no idea how to go about furnishing it.

Every step was a strategic gamble. Three times Sarah arrived at the squelchy borders of bog-holes and had to backtrack and make a detour. It was a good hour later when she finally reached the edge of the unfolding slopes and got a clear view down into the valley. Lights glimmered in houses, and the headlights of a car bounced along the winding road far below. There was nothing to suggest where Sarah had left the road and the bike, but at least there were people down there. At least there was a road. She had never imagined that she would be so eager to see tarmac.

11

John gave two of the lads a lift home in his car and then drove out along the route he had been imagining all day. Once he left the main road there was no other traffic at all. All the same, he was reluctant to leave the car in the gateway of the field, and drove on past until he came to a boreen with high hedges. The track was wet and soft, and John drove as far along it as he dared before parking and turning out his lights. He left the radio on for a while, then turned it off and opened the window, listening to the sounds of the night. There might still be a few late revellers returning home from town, and he wanted to be sure that there would be nothing to disturb him and his opponent. There were magic hours ahead.

The heather and bog-lands were behind Sarah now, and the going underfoot was easier. But as she came into the farmland below, a new set of problems faced her. Time after time she came up against the impenetrable hedgerows, where the standing thorns had been interwoven with cut or fallen branches, making fences that were far more difficult to cross than barbed-wire would have been. Sometimes she succeeded in barging her way through, only to be faced with a deep, murky ditch, far too broad to jump. On other occasions she would find a way into a field, but could find no way out.

It was some kind of test, she knew, set by her karma, or the spirit guides who watched over her. Sarah didn't have a particularly clear idea of who or what it was that negotiated her fate on a daily basis, but she was quite certain that something did. There was Duncan of course, but he was just a part of some larger and less tangible power that watched over her every thought and action. But its purpose was obscure tonight. Sending her through blackthorn mazes was not one of its usual functions. Helping her out ought to have been.

After a particularly vicious passage, during which she got several nasty scratches and narrowly avoided losing an eye, Sarah stopped for a while to see if Duncan had anything to offer.

'What's going on?' she asked him. 'Why am I being put through this?'

There was no answer.

'Is there some particular lesson I'm supposed to be learning from it?'

The voice that replied was unclear; possibly Duncan's, possibly her own. 'Don't go climbing mountains at night.'

'Very profound,' she said. 'Now get me out of here, okay?'

She meditated for a moment, and tried to visualise Duncan's pointing finger. But for some reason the image wouldn't come to her, and instead her mind began to flood with strange and unsettling visions. She saw a winding column of men, carrying pieces of the radio spike, like a procession with a crucifix. She saw angry, witchy faces in the shadows around her, and smelled the butcher's shop. She opened her eyes. There was no sign, no message, except that she ought to get out of there.

She set off again, and struck lucky. The next hedge she

came to was as dense as the others, but after walking along beside it for a few minutes she came upon a gate which opened on to a narrow road with grass growing along the middle of it. Before long she was on level ground, and the brisker walking began to warm her up a bit. But when she came out, at last, on to the main road, she had no idea which direction she would have to take to find the bicycle. Nothing looked familiar at all.

Two more cars did pass along the road that evening. John waited for half an hour after the second one had gone, and then decided it was time to make a move. Leaving the keys in the ignition, he got out of the car and took two long knives from the boot. He felt their edges, then pulled on his soft leather gloves and polished the black handles with his palms. The spirit of the matador flooded into him, and he could hear the hushed respect of the crowds as he walked with a long, casual stride up the boreen and out on to the road. This was what he had been waiting for. Above him the moon shone down, so brightly that a dilute shadow moved ahead of him across the ground. Everything was perfect.

Sarah walked along the road. The mountain had been to her right as she arrived, so she kept it on her left now. It was a brooding presence, a cold old hag that scowled down at her, annoyed by her escape. Now that she was safe, or safer, Sarah felt a twinge of compassion for the mountain. Who wouldn't be bad-tempered and spiteful with a steel spike driven into the top of their head? The image expanded; the bog-holes were pustulant abscesses, spreading out from the centre of aggravation, poisoning the land below, probably the water supplies which drained down from the highlands as well. Everyone was affected by it; the whole population was drinking the toxic effluent of the mountain's pain. Perhaps she could do something about it? Start a campaign to have the transmitter removed. Or take a healer up there with her to remove the bad energy.

A couple of cars passed by, but Sarah didn't try to hitch a ride. Sooner or later she was sure to see something that she recognised, which would give her a clue to where she had left the bike. Finding her way home would present another set of problems, but she had the feeling that once she was clear of the pernicious effects of the mountain she would get back into contact with her instincts. Cycling would be a pleasure.

It was a beautiful night. If she hadn't been so tired and hungry, Sarah might have delighted in the walk.

John climbed over the gate and walked across the field. The moon was so bright that he wasn't sure whether he was seeing colours or merely imagining them. He could see the cattle, bunched together at the top end of the field, bulky shapes lying down on the ground. He remembered a plastic cow he had loved as a child. There had been several of them, but the one he liked best was the one who was lying down. She was chunky and compact, completely flat on the bottom, with no sharp legs sticking out, no bits to be snapped or bent. Except her horns. He had chewed them off one day when he was nervous in school. He could still remember the tiny plastic points between his teeth. Afterwards he regretted that he had done it. She had looked better with the horns.

He had that much of an advantage over the Spanish matadors. His bull would be hornless. Not that it would make much difference if he was brought to the ground; the power of the bull was in its neck and shoulders and it could do as much damage without horns as with them. But John would at least be spared the danger of having a horn snagging in his clothes.

His blood began to race, and he took a detour to allow

himself time to calm it. It was the same fear that had always ambushed him when he was sent to kill the cockerels, and he resented it, as though it emanated from some other man, a sniveller who resided in the dark chambers of his heart. It was there when he went to work as well, but quieter, drowned out by the bustle of the plant and the voices of the other men. It was important now that he deal with it conclusively. If he didn't, it threatened to betray him at some crucial moment during the contest that lay ahead.

For several more minutes he walked around the field, keeping to the shadows of the hedges, just in case there was someone about. He breathed deeply, counting his inhalations and exhalations, well practised in the art of listening to his own hard pulse and persuading it to quieten. On the slope above, the cattle grew restless and, as though guessing his purpose, rose to their feet and faced him.

It was a sign. John stood still, summoned his resolve, and began to move slowly towards them. As he approached, they shifted anxiously, bunching together, keeping their eyes fixed on him. He could pick out the heavy hulk of the bull even at a distance of fifty yards, and he was disappointed to notice that it didn't come forward to face him but shuffled backwards and mingled among the cows and heifers. He hoped it had some balls.

A car came along the road behind Sarah and pulled up just ahead of her. The passenger door swung open.

'It's all right,' said Sarah. 'I don't need a lift.'

'Where are you headed?'

Sarah could tell that the man was drunk even before she saw him. His speech was too careful and toneless.

'I'm just going to collect my bike and head home.'

'Where's your bike, then?'

'Just down here,' said Sarah.

'I'll bring you to it, sure,' said the man.

Warmth spilled out of the car as Sarah drew level with the open door. It was tempting.

'To be honest,' she said, 'I'm not exactly sure where I left it. I was walking on the mountain and it got dark.'

'Ah, sure, we'll find it,' said the driver. 'Hop in.'

Afterwards Sarah wished she hadn't. The man looked her up and down out of the corner of his eye as he pulled back out on to the road. ''Tis awful late to be wandering the roads.'

'It is,' said Sarah. 'But I like the dark, actually.'

'Do you?'

The question was loaded. Sarah ignored it. The headlights were handy; she could see the houses more clearly and the small roads that occasionally branched off their route. But there were still none that she recognised.

'Where are you from?' said the driver.

'Galway.'

'Ah. On holiday?'

'Not exactly.'

'Where are you staying?'

Sarah didn't want to answer that. If she told him, he might offer to drive her home.

'With my sister.'

'And who's your sister?'

Suddenly Sarah knew where she was. The road where she had parked the bike was there on her left, marked by a ruined cottage surrounded by tall, straggly spruce trees.

'Stop here,' she said. 'Just here.'

For a moment she thought he wasn't going to, and various horrific possibilities flashed through her mind. But the truth was that his reactions were slowed by drink, and a moment or two later he jammed on the brakes and came to a halt in the middle of the road.

'Thanks a million,' said Sarah, jumping out.

'Ye're welcome. Good luck, now.'

* * *

The cattle stood still until John reached a certain, critical proximity, then they bolted along the hedgerow and into the furthest corner of the field. John waved his arms and whistled, trying to attract the bull, but it kept its back turned and took no interest.

When the herd came to rest, John advanced, more slowly this time, but more confidently. His heart was turbo-charged with adrenaline again, but this time it was driven by fight, not flight; it empowered, rather than unmanned him. The cattle huffed and turned to face him, the bull submerged in their huddled midst. It was practically impossible for one person to corner a herd of cattle, and John wished he had a picador, or at least a dog. But if the bull would act like a bull he could still retrieve the day. As soon as it began to advance instead of retreat they were in business.

'Hey, Toro!' he barked.

He took off his jacket and waved it enticingly, but the only effect it had was to send the entire herd bolting away again, along the side of the field towards the gate.

John put the jacket back on. A quiet rage rose in his gullet. Maybe the bovine race didn't warrant his concern. Maybe they were as corrupt and spineless as people were, deserving the terror and indignity they were exposed to in the abattoirs and processing plants, day after day. Maybe he was wasting his time.

Sarah found the bike and set off along the road. She was ravenous, and looking forward to raiding the shop for something sweet and satisfying to go with a hot cup of tea. Her legs were tired from all the walking, but her energy was sufficient, and she settled into a steady rhythm.

Before long she spotted a turn to the right that she recognised. It was one of the advantages of cycling or walking. Everything was seen at closer range. She began to feel optimistic about finding her way home. Perhaps there had been some purpose to what had happened. Some lesson to be learned. Her heart was full of her own heroism, and the realisation struck her that she had acted alone and come through the most rigorous ordeal.

There was something vaguely heretical about the thought, and she felt a momentary guilt, as though she were betraying Duncan's memory. But the truth was that he hadn't made his presence felt. When the chips were down he had deserted and left her to her fate. And she had come through.

She recognised another turn-off, and then another. The narrow roads were beautiful and mysterious, faintly dappled by moonbeams. Her leg was drying out; she was warm and she was getting her second wind. The work of pedalling became effortless, and Sarah was suddenly aware that she was cycling through a magical landscape, guided by the ghostly radiance of the moon, towards a new and unknown dawn. Leaving the safety of Mairead's shop was no longer something to be dreaded but something to be welcomed. Her life, her future, her soul's path were in her own hands, just waiting to be explored.

John drove the bewildered cattle back up the hillside to the narrowest corner. The bull acquiesced without a backward glance, and it seemed to John that, far from protecting the members of its harem, it was consistently seeking shelter in their midst. Rage burned brightly in his breast, but he would not allow it to unsettle him. His work needed to be planned carefully and undertaken with cunning. Things weren't working out as he had expected, but he wasn't about to abandon his scheme.

He kept his distance until the cattle came to rest in the tightest corner, at the top of the hill. He stopped for a while to let them settle, then began to creep forward. A step, a pause, another step. The herd turned towards him, every eye upon him. This time the bull was in the front line.

The road that Sarah was on suddenly seemed unfamiliar. Although she had no mental map of where she ought to be, she felt that she had been on that particular narrow, winding lane for much too long. Surely there should have been a house that she recognised, or another inviting turn-off. There had been a fork about a mile back, and she wondered whether she had taken the wrong branch. She began to consider turning back.

Step by step, inch by inch, John advanced. He didn't look into the frightened eyes of the cattle, but away from them, towards the other, unoccupied corner of the field. They stayed still. He edged forward.

The bull was watching. He began to speak to it, sing to it, insult it quietly and calmly. He could see the whites of its eyes.

'Come on, you big wanker. You big, pink, lump of an eejit. What are you waiting for? Where are your balls, brother?'

Something was happening. The cattle shrank back, but the bull did not. It fixed John with an impassive stare, and watched him come on. Another step. Another.

'Hey, flabby Toro. Remember your wild ancestors, eh? Wild and free. Feel their power in your lazy blood? You want to have a go at me?'

But the bull did not. When John got to within a few paces, it wheeled around and shoved its way in among the confused cows. But it was too late. They were too tightly bunched for it to make an escape, and John didn't waste the opportunity. He sprang forward and grabbed the bull by the tail.

It lurched away from him, but the other cattle were still too slow, and it ploughed into a wall of flesh. John leaped alongside and grabbed an ear, clinging as tightly as a tick with one hand, whipping a knife from his belt with the other.

The bull shook its powerful neck, yanking John off his feet, practically dislocating his shoulder, but failing to shake itself free of his grip. Dizzying memories of the heifer's enormous feet threatened to swamp John's resolve, and the bull might have succeeded in breaking free if it hadn't come up against the solid bulk of a hawthorn tree standing like an innocent observer in the hedge. The bull stopped, its visible eye wild and white, but still it made no attempt to attack John. It came from a line selected for its placid temperament, and it had been gently handled all its life. The worst it had come to expect from human beings was the sharp sting of a needle. Experience told it that there was no point in making a fuss. It would all be over soon.

But its behaviour infuriated John. It had surrendered without a fight. It was a fat, feeble excuse for a bull. It didn't deserve his respect. He raised his arm and plunged the knife into the flesh between its shoulder blades, feeling the resistance of muscle and sinew, the skid of the blade against bone.

The bull let out a desperate bellow, dropped its great boulder of a head and swung it at John, just as he buried the knife for a second time into its flesh. He was off-balance, and the bull's poll caught him beneath the ribs with the power of a demolition ball hanging from a crane. He was thrown through the air and landed flat on his back, doubly winded by the take-off and the landing.

Despite having no breath, John rolled over and got to his feet, realising as he did so that his hand was empty; he had left the knife sticking into the bull's neck. For all those long moments as he scrambled to his feet he was a sitting duck; one lunge from the bull would have had him pinned to the ground and ready to be finished off. But still it didn't come on. As his vision cleared and he succeeded in getting a shallow breath into his lungs, John saw that the bull was moving drunkenly off along the hedgerow, its head down as though it were charging at wraiths. John felt for the second knife at his waist, relieved that it was still there and that he hadn't impaled himself upon it during the fall. As he waited for his breathing to return to normal, he watched the injured bull make a faltering return to the anxious herd. He could see the dark blood against its cream coat and knew he had made a crucial blow; damaged the muscles that allowed it to lift its heavy head. He experienced a glow of pride. He had no picador but he had done the picador's job. All that remained was for him to close in for the final coup.

But he had no further chance of getting close. The herd, panicked by the smell of blood and the strange behaviour of their bloke, refused to allow John to get anywhere near them. The field was too big and they avoided the dangerous corner again and again, breaking back each time he tried to drive them in that direction. For a while he hoped that the bull would weaken further and become separated, but it lumbered groggily along behind the others, always just that bit too fast.

Eventually John stopped. He was tired himself and, although his breathing was easy enough, he was experiencing a certain amount of pain from his bruised ribs. He had taken a bad knock. A momentary pity for the bull swept over him and he hardened himself against it, transforming it into anger at its cowardice; its total lack of bull nature.

There were other fish in the sea. This was his first attempt, and he had done well. He would learn from his mistakes, find better bulls in better circumstances. As he turned towards the gate he was fuelled by a sense of his own strength. He had not failed. No matador could be blamed for the insufficiency of the bull.

* * *

Sarah intended to stay on the small road until she came to a junction of some kind. Even if she had taken a wrong turn there would probably be a sign to put her right. But as the road went on and on she became less sure of herself. Her second wind had passed her by and there was, she discovered, no such thing as a third one. Her legs were aching and the magic that she had perceived around her seemed to have vanished back into the shadows, like fairies retreating before the dawn. She had, she realised, come to the end of her reserves.

Ahead of her the road began to rise and Sarah knew that she didn't have the energy to pedal up that hill. She stopped and looked around. She had a vague recollection of having passed through such a valley on her way, but how far it was from town or whether she was heading in the right direction along it she couldn't remember. The fluctuations in her fortunes and her spirits were suddenly of no interest to her. Duncan was an absence in her heart. She was alone and abandoned, and had no idea what to do next.

She looked at the hill ahead. Behind her was another gentle slope. Neither prospect was attractive. For a while she just stood, a forsaken warrior without a mission, and then, as though her batteries had taken on a small amount of charge, she began to push the bike on up the hill.

It was slow going; a step at a time. When she eventually reached the top the road sloped invitingly down and she got back on to the bike and freewheeled until the ground levelled off and she would have to pedal or stop. She stopped. To her right a boreen opened off the road, with high hedges on each side. Some way along it someone had parked an old car. Parked or abandoned.

Perhaps it was open. Perhaps it could be her home for what remained of the night. Sarah leaned the bike against the hedge and walked down towards it. As she approached, it occurred to her that she might have stumbled across a pair of illicit lovers, and she crept the last few steps with caution. But the car was empty and the driver's door was unlocked. As she opened it warm, musky air escaped and enveloped her. The key was in the ignition. Whoever had left the car there had done so recently, and the disappointing likelihood was that they would soon be returning.

Sarah looked around again. It seemed like a crazy place to park. The boreen looked unused; brambles and uncut branches leaned in from both sides. It was highly unlikely that there was a house at the end of it, and there were no other habitations in the area. The car and its owner were a mystery, and the longer Sarah stood there the more certain she became that they were a mystery she had no interest in solving. Disappointed, she returned to the bike and began to walk on again.

She passed the gate into a field on her way up the next incline. Beyond it, in the far reaches of the field, a herd of cattle was moving around rapidly. Sarah was aware that it was unusual; that throughout the night any cattle she had seen were completely peaceful, lying or standing in the moonlight. But she was too worn out to pay any attention to the irregularity. She knew nothing, after all, about the night-time habits of cattle.

Beyond the first rise in the road was a second one and then a third. As she stood looking at them, a badger scuttled out of the hedge and shambled ahead of her for a few yards before turning off the road again. When she came to the spot where it had gone into the hedge, Sarah saw a tiny path leading into a diminutive tunnel beneath the branches. A badger highway in the night, created for a purpose Sarah could never imagine.

'Good morning, Mr Badger,' she said, then corrected herself. 'Mrs Badger. Ms Badger, that is. Good morning, Sister Badger.'

She stayed for a minute or two but no one answered,

so she trudged on. The bike seemed impossibly heavy, and she kept checking the tyres to see if they were flat. They weren't. She was exhausted.

John returned to the car. He hadn't come down from his high, yet, and his heart was still pumping adrenaline. He was a returning hero and the roads were empty. For once he could put his foot down and burn some gas.

Sarah's body was so numb that it began to feel like another machine; a machine pushing a machine up a hill. Her mind, as though suddenly realising that there was an alternative to ceaseless nagging, became detached, and floated among the leaves in the trees above her head. Before she knew it, Sarah had come to the top, and a mile or so across the open landscape she could see the town, glimmering like a fairy fort.

It was true, what they said. The darkest hour was just before the dawn.

Behind her, Sarah heard the car starting up and the engine revving frantically as John reversed along the slippery boreen. Then the lights hit the sky above her head, and she could hear the rapid approach of the racing engine. She reacted far too slowly, her limbs set in their own strange ways after the long, rigorous ordeal of the night. The bike was barely clear of the tarmac when the car came flying over the crest of the hill and shot past, missing Sarah by inches, the bike by even less. Shaking slightly, she got back on to the saddle and wobbled her way unsteadily down the hill towards town.

12

There wasn't a cloud in the sky when Malachy went out, and the sun was already beginning to drench the tracks and the yards in hot light. The birds were delirious with excitement. Somehow the heat in their blood emboldened them, and they fluttered and foraged in full view, sometimes only feet away from Malachy. In the west of Ireland that kind of morning was rare. Malachy knew that his heart should have been lifting, but he couldn't shake off the depression of the night before. He was convinced that he had made a bags of his friendship with Sarah, and let a golden opportunity slip past. There might never be another one.

The yearlings in the coach-house pushed forward to meet him. He climbed over the gate and moved among them, running his hands over their backs and shoulders, blowing their hot breath back at them. He never ceased to be surprised at how different their characters could be, and how gentle their dispositions were. It seemed to him that they understood the circumstances perfectly; that they knew the name of his game and forgave him for it. Absolved him in advance for the crime that he was destined to commit against each one of them.

Their comical competition for his attention began to lift Malachy's spirits. The floor was ankle deep in sloppy, stinking shavings, and he decided it was time they had a change of scene. He went out and prepared a route for them, then opened the gates and followed them as they charged out into the sun and along the muddy lanes to a nearby paddock. For a minute or two more they tore around, revelling in their release. Then they fell upon the long grass as though there were no tomorrow.

The demand for Malachy's meat was growing. He delivered two whole carcasses to a popular shop in the centre of Galway every week, and he had recently had a serious enquiry from a delicatessen chain in Dublin. Malachy was stuck in every successful businessman's dilemma: expand or stay small and sane. He already found it difficult to run the place on his own. If he took on the Dublin trade he would need to buy in a lot more cattle and to do that he would need someone else around the place. But the chances of finding the right person seemed more than slim. It was crucial that anyone he took on should understand what he was doing. Really understand, not just nod and obey.

On the way back, Malachy separated two of the mature bullocks from their companions in another paddock and drove them before him. The rooks were squabbling amongst themselves in the sycamores. The ground underfoot was white with their droppings. He had seen it so many times, more times than he had seen the rooks themselves. His eyes were consistently cast down, reflecting his sunken spirit. Sarah could do so much for him, if only she would look at him; look into his heart and see that it was good.

He steered the suspicious bullocks into two empty cage boxes.

'Death row, pals. I'm sorry.'

The sun at Eileen's window woke her earlier than usual. Matty was snoring beside her in the bed, and the house was quiet. She enjoyed waking early and having the opportunity to turn over and go back to sleep, but there was an urgency about the bright morning that made her restless and eager to get ahead with the day.

She made herself a cup of tea and cleared away the previous evening's clutter of cups and toast-plates, then gathered a heap of washing to put in the machine. To her surprise, there was a load already in it; one that she hadn't remembered putting through. When she opened the door she discovered that the clothes all belonged to John. A pair of jeans, a shirt and a T-shirt, underpants, socks, and a pair of leather gloves. Eileen smiled to herself as she pulled them out. He was a godsend, that boy. If only her other men were half as considerate.

Mairead looked into the bedroom in the attic. She was relieved to see that Sarah had come home, but alarmed by her appearance. Her face was scratched and puffy, and her hair was tangled and full of small twigs and leaves. The clothes beside the bed were caked with black mud, still damp in patches.

She was also wheezing quite badly. She had suffered from asthma since she was a child and Mairead realised, with a pang of guilt, that she shouldn't have given her the dusty old bed in the attic. She considered waking her and moving her into her own bed, but she was sleeping so deeply that she decided to leave her.

The dogs came worming up the stairs to meet her. As she let them out through the back door the sun streamed in, revealing the collections of gnawed and splintered bones in the corners. Mairead gathered them and dropped them into the bin.

Malachy was having breakfast when the phone rang. It was Seanie Walsh, one of the farmers who regularly sold him young bullocks. He bred fine beasts, and had an unusually high regard for them. Malachy liked dealing with him.

'I don't suppose you'd buy my bull,' he said.

'Why would you want to sell him to me?'

Seanie swore down the line and told Malachy what he had found when he went out to check on the cattle in the morning. 'I never came across anything like it,' he said. 'The vet says there's no future for him.' Seanie paused. 'I don't know who would do a thing like that.'

Malachy didn't, either. Seanie's description of the maimed bull shocked him deeply.

'He isn't, you know, infected or anything. There'd be nothing wrong with the meat.'

'I'm sure you're right,' said Malachy. 'But it isn't the way I do things.'

'I know,' said Seanie. 'I didn't think you'd want him.'

'Have you called the guards?'

'I have. They're on their way.'

'Does anyone have a grudge against you?' said Malachy.

'Not that I know of. But listen here to me. Would you kill him for me anyway? I'll put him in the freezer if no one'll buy him. I can't just bury him, you know.'

'I know,' said Malachy. He didn't want to have any part of this, but he couldn't let Seanie down. 'Can you get him here?'

'I might,' said Seanie. 'But I'm afraid he might be dangerous if I try to handle him. Would you be able to give me a hand?'

'All right. What time shall I come?'

'Any time. The sooner the better.'

He gave directions to the field and hung up. Malachy put down the phone, waiting for the horror of the event to drag him into despair. But his mind suddenly leaped in a completely different direction, and as he reached for the phone again he was filled with eager anticipation.

Mairead answered.

'Has Sarah gone yet?' he asked.

'No. Who is this?'

'Sorry, Mairead. It's Malachy. Don't let Sarah go, all right? There's another story she might want to know about. I'll collect her there in half an hour.'

Mairead woke Sarah with a cup of tea.

'Malachy was on the phone. He says there's another story you might be interested in.'

Sarah opened her eyes with difficulty. She hadn't been in bed for long, and the sleep was so delicious. But the sound of the name stirred her interest.

'Who's Malachy?' she said.

'The butcher, you know. My neighbour.'

Sarah sat up and tried to cough. In all the time she had been living in the trees her asthma hadn't bothered her. It wasn't activated by pollen or by damp or by animals. The only thing that set it off was house dust. Rarely used beds were the worst. Her chest was tighter than it had been for years.

'I got lost on the mountain,' she said, remembering. 'Someone stuck a metal spike in the top of her head. The bastards.'

She coughed again, and wheezed. She would have to get out of that bed.

'What is it with you and Malachy?' said Mairead.

'Me and Malachy? There is no me and Malachy.'

Sarah sat up and reached for the tea. Her hands were as scratched and inflamed as her face.

'What on earth happened to you?' said Mairead. 'You look as if you've been dragged through a barbed-wire fence.'

'Worse,' said Sarah. 'You wouldn't believe it if I told you.'

By the time Malachy arrived, she had changed into fresh clothes and drunk several pints of tea. She had the theory that smoking helped her asthma, and Mairead had indulged her, even though she hated the smell in the mornings. Whether on account of the cigarettes or not, Sarah's attack had largely passed, but she was still very tired and dithery, and when she opened the door for him Malachy was horrified by her appearance. He reached out and touched her face.

'What happened?'

'I'll tell you about it some time,' said Sarah. 'What's this story?'

Malachy filled her in on all that he knew as they drove out of town and along the narrow lanes. Sarah found the information hard to absorb. She knew she ought to be outraged, but every muscle in her body was protesting like an abscessed tooth, and she hadn't much attention left over for anything else. But when they reached the crest of a long, steep hill, she suddenly woke up.

'Stop! Stop a minute!'

Malachy pulled up and Sarah eased her stiff limbs out of the van. A few yards back along the road was the badger tunnel beneath the hedge. There was no mistaking it. Sarah returned to the van.

'I was here last night,' she said. 'Or early this morning, I should say.'

'Were you?'

'Yes. I got lost. I didn't get home until dawn.'

'Did you see anything?'

'A badger. A few bats.'

'I don't think any of them did this,' said Malachy.

The garda car was parked in the gateway. Malachy pulled the van in on the other side, one wheel on the verge, the other in the road.

Seanie had parked the Land-Rover and trailer halfway up the hill, and was standing beside it with the two guards, inspecting the bull from a respectful distance. Even from the gate, Sarah and Malachy could see that it was in a pitiful state. It was standing with its legs splayed and its nose practically touching the ground. It wavered slightly on its feet, as though it were sleepy. The knife handle looked like a bloated tick buried in its broad neck.

'Maybe you'd rather wait here?' said Malachy.

'Why?'

'Well, it's not going to be a very pretty sight.'

'I think I can handle it.'

'He could get nasty when we try to move him.'

'We'll cross that bridge when we come to it.' Sarah was surprised by her own courage. Just two days ago she had been terrified by a herd of young bullocks, and now here she was walking calmly towards a full-grown bull that could, at any moment, become enraged. She realised that she had forgotten her notebook again and began to commit images to memory. 'It was like the last round in a bull-ring . . . final moments in a bull-fight. The great white beast . . . great hamster-coloured beast . . . creamy beast . . . stood with its head down, bewildered and defeated but not yet dead . . . as if waiting for the final blow . . . the killing stroke . . . the matador's final thrust.'

'Who would do something like that?' said Malachy.

'Who would do something like that?' Sarah wrote, in her imaginary notes. 'What kind of a mentality would provoke . . . would produce such a savage attack . . . a psychotic attack.'

They were halfway up the hill and Sarah looked around her. 'Amidst the wild . . . half-wild countryside of north Clare . . . gorse in the final flux of blooming . . . flux? Gorse losing its blossom . . . thick, concealing hedgerows . . . shadowy hedgerows . . . badger-filled hedgerows . . .'

She saw the entrance to the boreen further down the road.

'There was a car here last night.'

'Was there?' said Malachy.

'I saw it parked down that little path over there. It started when I was a bit further up the road. It nearly knocked me over.'

'You'd better tell the guards. What kind of a car was it?'

Sarah didn't answer. She was breaking out in a cold sweat, realising how close she had been to a knife maniac. What if he had encountered her when she was snooping around the car? Caught her with the door open? Pushed her inside?

'It seems as though your reporter . . . this correspondent may have narrowly escaped . . .'

'Sarah?'

His voice was full of concern, and her face must have been registering her horror.

'Um. Car. It was dark. I think it was a grey one.'

'Saloon? Hatchback?'

'I don't know anything about cars, Malachy. I don't approve of them.'

'Ah.'

They had drawn level with the group of observers. Above their heads a heron passed over, lethargic and gangly as a teenager. The bull hadn't moved. It seemed unaware of their presence.

'He's a quiet old creature,' said Seanie. 'Never did anyone a bit of harm.'

'Have you insurance on him?' asked Raymond Murray.

'Ach! I don't believe in that old nonsense. They'd fleece you, those boys.'

The guard gave a large sigh and turned away. 'We'll make some enquiries around the place, Seanie. It's all we can do.' He looked towards Malachy. 'Seanie says you're going to finish him off.'

'I am.'

'If you could hang on to the knife for us. It could be useful.' He handed Malachy a sterile evidence bag.

Malachy took it and put it in an inside pocket. 'Sarah here saw a car last night.'

'Last night? What were you doing out here last night?'

Sarah could see his mind ticking over. If there was someone like her hanging around in the dark then maybe there had been hundreds of them. A rave perhaps, or some dark, hippy ritual.

'I was cycling home.'

'From where?'

'From the mountain.'

'And what was at the mountain?'

'Nothing. A radio mast.'

Raymond wasn't thrilled with the answer, but he didn't pursue it. He questioned her about the car but, since her most vivid memory of it was its smell, her answers weren't much use to him.

'How did your face get scratched?'

'An encounter with a hedge.'

'On the mountain?'

'On the mountain.'

'I see. Well, I wouldn't mind hearing a bit more about this nocturnal journey of yours.'

He took her name and address and asked if she would be prepared to give a statement. She agreed, somewhat reluctantly, and Raymond and his partner moved away. 'We'll leave the loading to you, lads, if you don't mind. Watch yourself, missus.'

Sarah considered taking objection to being called missus, but decided against it. Somehow it wouldn't sound right in the general atmosphere of gloom. Besides, this was one occasion when she was quite happy to see the men do the work, and she didn't want anyone to take her up wrong.

The guards walked away down the hill and Seanie leaned into the back of the Land-Rover and took out two heavy sticks. He handed one to Malachy.

'He doesn't like sticks. If he turns on you give him a quick dig in the nose.'

Malachy took the stick.

'Maybe you should sit in the jeep?' he said to Sarah.

She chose instead to clamber up on top of the trailer, where she would get a better view of the proceedings. After the months she had spent in the trees, climbing was her strong point, but she hadn't accounted for the acute stiffness in her muscles and joints, and her ascent was anything but dignified.

'Stay quiet up there, now, missus,' said Seanie. 'Don't be banging around and scaring him, all right?'

'Fine,' said Sarah.

As the two men approached, the bull stared out at them with white-rimmed eyes.

'Did you ever lead him with a rope?' said Malachy.

'I did,' said Seanie. 'With the hook, like. And the man who had him before me. He's well used to it. But I wouldn't like to be anywhere in front of him the way he's feeling just now. Especially when he starts moving.'

Malachy nodded. He followed Seanie round behind the bull and they flanked it, one on each side. It didn't look round.

'Hup now, Tiny,' said Seanie, waving the stick.

'Tiny the bull,' said Sarah to her imaginary Dictaphone, 'is a misnomer which must qualify for the *Guinness Book of Records*. This magnificent creature . . . once magnificent animal . . . is a walking bulldozer . . . a bulldozer on legs . . . a muscle-bound tank of a creature.'

Tiny didn't move. He appeared to be planted in the mud. Seanie edged forward. 'Come on now, lad. On you go.' He gave the bull a gentle tap on the rump. Its whole body jerked, but it didn't go forward, just returned to its pathetic swaying.

Seanie tapped a bit harder. Tiny snorted, but still didn't move. 'He'll have to shift,' he said. 'We'll never move him once he's dead. Not without a flaming JCB.'

'But how to move a crippled bull?' Sarah dictated. 'Tiny was hurt. Tiny was confused. Tiny wasn't going anywhere.'

Malachy came forward and took hold of the bull's tail. He twisted it gently and pulled it upwards and forwards. 'On we go, Tiny,' he said..The bull took a single step, then froze again, paralysed by pain. 'And again, old fellow,' said Malachy.

Step by step, inch by inch, the hulking beast went towards the trailer. Sarah was enjoying herself, perched up there in the royal box. She rolled a cigarette and lit it.

'The gentleness of the creature was moving . . . was poignant. There seemed to be no aggression in him, despite the ordeal . . . the trauma he had undergone the night before . . . the previous night. Whoever did this . . . committed this outrageous deed . . . outrageous act . . . was a coward . . . was not a brave man . . . brave person.'

Could a woman have done it?

The little tableau was beneath her. Tiny had come to the edge of the trailer ramp and clearly intended to go no further.

The men were quite confident now, assured that Tiny meant them no harm. They were standing one on each side of him, pushing at him from behind. Suddenly his patience gave out. He backed up and, with an enormous effort of will, swung around towards the side where the butcher stood. Malachy dodged sideways and away. The bull's head swung against thin air, but there was little doubt about what would have happened if it had connected.

Sarah continued her commentary, even though her heart was in her mouth. 'The power of the beast . . . the sheer, brutal strength . . . even so close to its end, the bull's strength was prodigious.'

But the effort cost the bull dearly. As he brought his head around to the front again he gave a grunt of anguish and collapsed heavily on to his knees. The blood was welling out of the wounds again, adding new layers to its own dried tracks.

'Jaysus,' said Seanie. 'What the fuck are we going to do with him?'

'Get him up again,' said Malachy, quietly.

'If I ever find the bastard who did this I swear to God I'll give him cause to regret that he ever lived.'

Seanie went to the Land-Rover and took out the stick with the hook on the end. Tiny's nose was on the ground and he had some difficulty connecting with the ring, but he finally succeeded and gave a gentle pull. The bull made an effort to lift its head. Seanie pulled again, forward and upward. The bull gave another grunt and heaved itself unsteadily to its feet.

'I'm not going in there ahead of him,' said Seanie. 'Will we try again from behind?'

He unclipped the stick and moved gingerly back to Tiny's side. Malachy edged in again. The bull gave no sign of having noticed them.

'Link hands,' said Seanie, reaching around beneath the bull's tail. Malachy took a good grip and together the two men leaned into the work.

'Like raising Stonehenge . . . laying a stone in a pyramid . . . the combined strength of two strong . . . two fit men could hardly make the Behemoth budge.'

But it did. The bull's resistance had finally come to an end. It lurched forward and staggered into the trailer as though it were a longed-for sanctuary.

Seanie closed the ramp and screwed the wing-bolts tight. Sarah looked out across the countryside and saw the garda car parked in the entrance to the boreen. She hoped that she was right; that it was the place where she had seen the car. She hoped they would find tyre marks.

Malachy was grinning up at her. Was she supposed to compliment him? But as she slid down on to the wheel-arch of the trailer she realised that she was impressed. There had been no violence or aggression; no macho posturing from either of the men. They had treated the bull kindly and respectfully, even when it looked like turning nasty.

'These men were truly brave,' she observed. 'The hero of the hour wasn't the cowardly bully who assaulted the bull . . . cowardly villain . . . cowardly . . .'

Malachy had reached up to support her as she jumped down the last of the way. She didn't need his help but she could hardly refuse the offered hand. As she stepped on to the broken turf she lost her balance momentarily, and found herself leaning against him. Whether he had engineered it or not was suddenly irrelevant to her, as a dam-burst of desire flooded through her blood. She stepped rapidly away.

'We'll meet you back at my place,' said Malachy to Seanie, as the Land-Rover engine chuntered into life.

13

Sarah didn't look at the butcher on the way back. She spent the entire journey composing herself, defending with a straight bat against his solicitous questioning, bringing her mind and her emotions back to an equanimous level. She met with a fair degree of success, but what followed shocked her profoundly. When Seanie arrived at the abattoir they discovered that the bull had collapsed in the trailer. They made a few efforts to raise it, but it had clearly given up hanging on to life, and they were left with no alternative but to reverse the trailer into the slaughterhouse and stun the bull where it lay.

That moment was shocking to Sarah, but it did, at least, bring a sense of release along with it. What happened afterwards was more frightful. Malachy wrapped a heavy chain around Tiny's hocks and winched him up until he was hanging above the floor of the slaughterhouse. Then he slit the throat with a razor-sharp knife and the blood pumped out, splashing Malachy's boots and streaming away across the concrete.

'You don't have to watch this,' he said to Sarah. But it was Seanie who left; the slam of the Land-Rover door and the revving of its engine the only leave-taking he made. Somehow Sarah had to stay. It was part of the job. She had to watch the removal of the weapon, the spilling of the guts, the stripping of the skin, and all the disfiguring business that followed with the electric saw. By the time the butcher had finished, the bull was nothing but a hollowed-out shell; plump as a pig at a banquet.

Sarah's stomach was strong, but her spirit was bruised by what she saw. Desire drained from her heart like the blood from Tiny's arteries. It would take some time for her to recover from this; to forget the fact that beneath her own soft skin she was just the same as that poor bull. Meat and bone.

Afterwards Malachy went into the house to change and Sarah wandered around the outbuildings, speaking softly to the bullocks in the cage boxes, aware now of the fate that awaited them a stone's throw away. She would have liked to set them free, but she knew that life wasn't as simple as that. There was nowhere for them to go; no bullock kingdom beyond the borders of butcher-land.

She set out for the bungalow, but stopped beneath the trees to commune with them; to salve her spirit beneath their sage and benign shadows. Malachy found her there and stood with her quietly for a few minutes. He had changed into clean jeans and a fresh, white shirt that emphasised his tanned skin, but Sarah found she couldn't look at him. He had been polluted by the act. Blood clung to every pore of his being.

'I'll be going into town in a few minutes,' he said at last. 'If you can wait while we have a cup of tea I'll give you a lift.'

Sarah knew she ought to walk, but she was still too tired and too stiff. 'All right.'

The tea was hot and strong, just the way Sarah liked it. Just what she needed. They drank it in silence for a while, then Malachy said, 'I don't suppose you enjoyed that very much.'

'No. But I wanted to see it through. To have the whole story. Guts and all.'

'You got that,' said Malachy. He sighed and leaned forward, parking his elbows on the table, then went on, 'I don't like it either, Sarah. I don't know if you can believe that. I hate it, and it never gets better, no matter how many years and how many carcasses I put behind me.'

'Why do you do it, then?'

He stared hard at his mug, and twisted it this way and that. Then he looked up and tried to meet her eye. 'I have a philosophy,' he said.

'A philosophy!' Sarah might have laughed if her mind hadn't been filled with the sounds of splashing blood and breaking bones. 'That's a good one.'

'But I have,' said Malachy.

'Well, so what? Hitler had a philosophy. So did Jack the Ripper.'

'Yes, but mine is—'

'But that's what they all say,' said Sarah. 'That's what Blair and Clinton say whenever they want to bomb civilians. That's what developers and road-builders say. It's all for the common good.'

'But Sarah—'

'I don't want to hear it, Malachy. All right? I don't want to hear any waffle about the holy righteousness of slaughtering innocent creatures.'

Malachy tried another angle. 'You don't eat meat, I know that. But you drink milk, don't you? You eat cheese?'

'No one gets killed so I can have my milk and cheese.'

'But they do! That's what I'm trying to tell you.'

Sarah shook her head. 'I think I'll walk after all.'

Malachy stood up. 'I'll drive you.'

John slept through his alarm and got up much later than he had intended to. His ribs were stiff and sore, and he spent a few minutes doing gentle exercises to loosen himself up before he dressed and went into the kitchen.

The first thing he saw there was the empty washing-machine. His heart turned sideways and he looked around, close to panic, until he saw the clothes hanging on the line across the haggard. Of course. She was bound to be washing on a day like this. But the gloves worried him. He ought to have kept them out; washed them separately. No one wore gloves in the middle of July.

Something else was worrying him as well. Had he really seen a woman and a bicycle on his way home, or was he imagining it? She had appeared out of the darkness so suddenly and he had gone past her in a split-second. But the image of her frightened face was too clear to be a product of imagination.

As they drew up outside the shop, Malachy turned to Sarah.

'Are you leaving, then?' he said.

Sarah had forgotten everything except the bull. 'I don't know. I suppose I'll have to hang around and talk to the police.'

'Maybe you should stay longer? See if they find who did this?'

'Maybe,' said Sarah. But as she got out of the van she was astonished that she could ever have thought Malachy was attractive. He was repulsive to her, now.

Matty was in the machinery bay of the hay-shed, trying to work out the settings on the new rotary mower.

John went over to help. 'Isn't there a book with it?'

'Ah, there was some ol' lump of papers. I threw them in the bin.'

It was a variation on the usual haymaking crises. Matty's equipment had, until now, always been ancient. He never took time to maintain it, but somehow expected the fairies to keep it oiled and cleaned. Each year he dropped off the

old mowing bar and left it as it was, wet and grass-choked.
Each subsequent year he flew into a fury to discover that it
was rusting or seized; there were teeth broken or bent; there
was work to be done. Matty was chronically disorganised.
He spent half his life searching for towing pins or tractor
keys or spanners; things that could so easily be minded but
never were.

'It's amazing, all this new gear,' said John. 'I thought
there was supposed to be no money in cattle?'

'There's money at your end of the business,' said Matty.
'The barons are raking it in.'

'Looks like you're not doing so badly yourself,' said
John.

Matty turned and looked at his son. The uncertainty
was there again, like the time on the hill where the sally
had once been. It seemed to John as though his father
were about to say something; something of enormous
significance. But he turned away again and inspected the
mower. 'Hand me those Allen keys, there, will you?'

'I wouldn't start messing with Allen keys, Dad, if I was
you.'

'You're not me, John. Hand them over.'

John indulged him, then slipped away and eased himself
into his car. The aching ribs were a mark of his gallantry and
he suffered them with pride, like a sporting injury or a war
wound. It was a shame that he couldn't tell anyone.

The high pressure was holding and it was another
glorious day. Suddenly every tractor in the county was
out around the roads; some armed with mowers, others
with hay shakers. The heavy mob were out in force
as well: the contractors with their huge machines for
cutting and wrapping silage, crawling along the lanes
like military convoys. John drove carefully, yielding to
oncoming vehicles, often choosing to reverse rather than
get into a tight squeeze. He provided himself with an alibi

to explain why he was on a particular road at any given time. He was going to Ennis to look at a lurcher pup, or to Miltown to meet a school friend. But although a lot of people waved and nodded to him, no one had time to stop and chat. The fine weather was too precious to waste.

Indeed. But bulls were scarce, and John had to be careful about his methods of searching. It would look odd to be found leaning against a farmer's gate. The news of his previous night's work would spread rapidly. He had to be careful.

It was Sunday, but whenever Mairead was at home the shop was unofficially open, and the occasional person popped in for a bag of muesli or a chat. Mairead listened to Sarah's story with astonishment, then sent her off to get some rest, in her own bed this time. She felt magnanimous; unusually fond of her errant sister.

Sarah snuggled down under the duvet. Despite the warmth of the day she was cold, as though her thermostat had been damaged. She longed for the anaesthetic of sleep; believed absolutely that the only cure for mental stress was to hand everything over to the unconscious mind for as long as was necessary to process and heal the psychic wounds. But she found that she couldn't sleep. Too much had happened too quickly. Her mind was overloaded. She couldn't think of a single emotion that she had not experienced in the last few hours.

She sent out a distress call to Duncan, but there was no response. To her horror, Sarah found that she couldn't even remember his face; not really; not with the usual clarity. Somehow she had offended him; severed the spiritual partnership that had sustained her since his death. The sense of loss was acute. Her heart felt like a battlefield, where nothing stirred except dark, carrion birds.

There was only one other thing that she could use to

bolster her flagging spirit, and she reached for her tobacco. Mairead would kill her, but it might be a blessed relief.

She smoked the cigarette down to the last, soggy half-inch and buried the tarry remains among the roots of Mairead's pot-bound spider plant. Then sleep hit her like a freight train, and carried her along on its speeding cow-catcher into the gory realms of her disturbed id.

John saw several bulls on his travels, but none of them was in a suitable situation. One of them was on its own in a vast field surrounded by barbed-wire. The others were all too close to some habitation or other. He didn't find what he was looking for until the early afternoon. He was a long way from home by then but it didn't matter at all. The further the better. The bull was similar to the last one: a bulky Limousin with haunches like boulders. It looked younger than the last one, though, and John hoped it would offer more sport.

The only problem was the group of buildings that stood in the corner of the field. It was possible that there was a house beside them. John started the car again and crawled past. He was in luck. There had been a cottage there once, but only the shell of it remained. He drove on. The next inhabited house was half a mile away, over the brow of a hill. Perfect. John turned round at the next junction and cruised back, looking for a suitable place to park the car. The buildings themselves seemed to be the most promising. He would have to open a gate and drive in among them, and a quick getaway would be impossible if he should need it. But it was probably worth it. The car would be completely concealed from the road and the chances of his being disturbed were remote.

He straightened up in the driver's seat, felt the exquisite pain in his ribs, and turned the car around. But he wasn't looking forward to going home. There was something wrong there. His parents were involved in a lie; they were keeping something from him. John knew the current price of cattle. Farmers were going to the wall because of it. So where had the new car come from? And all that flash machinery?

14

Mairead had some difficulty waking Sarah when the police arrived. She called her name gently a few times, then shook her arm, and finally pulled the bedclothes off her, the way she had sometimes done when they were children. Sarah sat up in wide-eyed confusion and stared around her.

'The guards are here,' said Mairead.

'Guards?' There had been some sort of military activity in her dream. Was she being bombed or was she the bomb?

'They said you'd agreed to give them a statement.'

Everything came back. 'Jesus H Christ. I must have been off my head to agree to it.'

'What else could you do?'

'Run,' said Sarah.

Mairead went ahead to put the kettle on, and Sarah finally succeeded in dragging herself out of bed, feeling like a grub turned up by the spade, and cruelly exposed to the sun. One of the scratches on her face was quite deep, and was beginning to feel as if it might be infected. It burned with a fierce ache and made her whole cheek glow vividly beneath her deeply shadowed eyes. As she crossed the landing outside the bathroom she caught a glimpse of herself in the mirror. Her mind was still swarming with dream images and the face she saw looking out at her fitted better with them than with any former self she could recognise. Perhaps she had been bombed?

The guards were waiting in the sitting-room. They stood up as she came in, and introduced themselves politely.

'Garda Sergeant O'Shea and Garda Detective Murray.'

But they were both regarding her closely out of frosty little eyes, and she felt the familiar criminal guilt that is always lurking around in those who despise authority.

Mairead came in with the tea, but only Sarah accepted the offer. It was a bad sign. It meant that the guards were on serious business. One of them produced a witness statement sheet and a pen.

'Stay with us, Mairead, if you don't mind,' said Sarah. She had been raked over the coals by the police plenty of times in the past, and knew her rights.

'I'll just close the shop, then.' Sarah recognised her sister's delight in any kind of drama and vaguely wished that she could deprive her of the pleasure. But the alternative, of being alone with these two goons, was infinitely worse. As they waited for Mairead to come back, they continued to examine her as though she were a specimen of some kind, but whenever she tried to catch either of them in the act they quickly averted their eyes. Shifty characters.

Mairead came in and closed the door behind her. Sarah sipped her tea.

'We'll just go through your evidence, if that's all right with you,' said the sergeant. 'Then we'll take the statement down. What's your name?'

'Sarah O'Malley.'

She spelled it out for them, and the detective wrote it down.

'Address?'

She gave them the address of the shop.

'Is that your permanent address? Are you resident here now?'

'No,' said Sarah. 'I was expecting to move on today, until all this happened.'

'I see. So what's your home address?'

'I don't have one.'

'Between residences, are you?'

'You might say that.'

'Can you give me your last address, then?'

Sarah gave them her last address in London. Mairead looked uncomfortable.

'And when did you leave that residence?'

'About two and a half years ago.'

'I see. And where have you been living since then?'

'Various places,' said Sarah. 'Nowhere in particular.'

The guards exchanged glances. 'Can you be more specific?'

'I stayed with some friends. Then in a tree-house.'

The detective cleared his throat, disguising a cynical smirk.

'What is your occupation, Sarah?'

She hated it when they did that: got all chummy and used her name. Patronising bastards.

'I don't have one, currently.'

'You're unemployed.'

'That's not a label I accept,' said Sarah, her blood rising despite herself in rebellion against established assumptions. 'I'm not in a job, if that helps.'

'So you're on the dole?'

'No.'

'How are you supporting yourself, then?'

She ought to have been prepared for all this. She had been through it often enough, after all. It was always the same, trying to plough new ground and sow new seed in infertile minds. It sapped her energy.

'I don't need much,' she said. 'I survive without money.'

There was a long silence as the two officers surveyed her.

'A few nixers, is it?' said the sergeant, at last.

'I don't know what a nixer is.'

'Unofficial jobs here and there. A few quid into your hand.'

'I've been helping out my sister if that's what you mean. She has been supporting me while I did that. But she doesn't pay me a wage.'

'I don't pay myself one, either,' said Mairead.

The detective glared at her, and she apologised. 'I won't say anything else,' she said.

Sergeant O'Shea sighed pointedly. 'All right, Sarah,' he said. 'You don't have any fixed abode and you're unemployed and not on the dole. Can you show us some form of identification?'

'No,' said Sarah.

'Passport? Driving licence?'

'No.' Sarah did, in fact, have an old, English driving licence in her bag upstairs. The name on it was Judith Chambers, and there was no photograph.

'Cheque book? Bank card?'

'I don't believe in banks.'

'A letter, perhaps? With your name on it?'

'I don't keep letters.'

'She is who she says she is,' said Mairead. 'I can vouch for that.'

O'Shea nodded with a dramatic display of tolerance. 'We appreciate that, Mairead,' he said. 'But it's just a matter of our records.'

'Sorry,' said Mairead.

He turned back to Sarah. 'So, you have no address, no job and no ID.'

'No.'

'When did you arrive in Kilbracken?'

'About ten days ago.' She glanced at Mairead for confirmation and she nodded. 'I took over the shop while Mairead went to visit our parents.'

'All right. So let's move on to last night, shall we?'

'Fine.'

'You told Garda Murray earlier that you saw a vehicle parked in a boreen near the place where the bull was attacked?'

'I did.'

'What time was this?'

'I don't know, exactly. It was shortly before dawn.'

'Can you tell us what you were doing there at that hour of the night?'

Sarah poured herself a second cup of tea and wrapped her hands around it.

'I went to climb the mountain.'

'Which mountain?'

Sarah pointed vaguely. 'The one over there. The nearest one.'

'That's quite a distance from here. About seven or eight miles.'

'That'd be it. I cycled there. It was further than I thought.'

'And what time did you set out?'

'In the evening after dinner. I suppose it was around seven o'clock or so.'

'Very late to be setting out on an adventure like that, wouldn't you say?'

Sarah glanced at Mairead, who gazed into the empty fireplace. 'I know that now,' she said.

She filled them in on the disastrous events that had overtaken her, keeping quiet about her feelings towards the injured mountain, sticking to the facts as she remembered them.

'Did you meet anyone along the way?' O'Shea asked.

Sarah shook her head. 'Oh, wait a minute. I did. A man gave me a lift.'

'Where to?'

'Just a few yards along the road. When I was looking for my bike.'

'What time was this?'

'I have no watch. No idea at all. But I'd say it was after closing time.'

'Did he give you his name?'

'No.'

'What kind of car was he driving?'

'A red one, I think. Or orange. It smelled of beer.'

The detective was still taking notes. Sarah ploughed on with the story, recounting her retrieval of the bicycle and her long journey home. O'Shea questioned her closely about the car in the boreen, but she could remember no more than she had told the others earlier in the day. When she came to the end the two officers exchanged quiet glances.

'How did you come by the injury to your face?' said the sergeant.

'Climbing through the hedges on the mountain.' She showed them her scratched hands as well.

O'Shea shook his head. ''Tis a very strange story altogether.'

'It is,' Sarah confirmed.

'A strange coincidence that you should have chanced to pass just as a crime was being committed.'

Sarah decided not to expound upon her theory of coincidence. 'It is,' she said again.

'And how did you come to accompany Malachy Glynn to the scene this morning?'

Sarah flushed. 'I . . . He . . . Well, you see, I was covering another story he was involved with.'

'Covering?'

'I was thinking about becoming a journalist.' It felt as lame as it sounded.

'I see.'

'There was a calf found on the dump the other morning.'

'We're aware of that.'

'I wanted to write about it. Then Malachy told me about the bull, and I went along.'

'Malachy told you, or you told him?'

Sarah's hackles rose.

'He told me,' she said. 'How could I have known about it otherwise? What are you implying?'

Suddenly she saw herself through their eyes: a misfit with no credentials and all the signs of having been through a recent, violent ordeal.

'You don't suspect me of having anything to do with it?' she said. 'I'm a peace activist. A vegetarian. I campaign for animal rights.'

'We're not suggesting anything,' said Sergeant O'Shea. 'But you might stay around for a few days if you have no other pressing engagement. In case we should have any more questions.'

'Is that a request or an order?'

'Just a request, that's all.'

15

Malachy was in a profound depression. The contractors had arrived and their heavy machinery was out on the land, ploughing deep tyre-tracks in the low-lying fields, probably breaking the old drains. He wished he hadn't appointed them; wished he had sold the grass for grazing and bought in hay and silage. But it was too late now. The damage was done.

He couldn't get Sarah out of his mind. He was still certain that she would understand him if only he could get her to listen. The need to be heard had reached a critical point in his heart. He had no idea how he had survived in isolation for so long. Maybe he had been wrong to talk of philosophies. Maybe he should have just launched straight into it and made her listen. Instead she had made him feel even worse: a murderer seeking a sympathetic hearing. Hitler, she had said. Jack the Ripper. Was that how she saw him?

His head ached, and the sound of the huge machines in the distance was like the drone of a hundred bees inside his skull. He walked quietly through the buildings, whispering to the cattle, topping up their water barrels. They were all that was keeping him sane.

After the guards left, it took some time for Sarah's blood to cool. She paced the kitchen, subjecting Mairead to

an outraged monologue about authoritarianism and the
vanishing rights of the individual. But as her bluster
began to wear out, she became besieged by doubt. The
detective had read out everything that he had written,
but he had subtly changed her words from time to time
and she wondered how it would all read if it came
to court.

It couldn't. It couldn't possibly. But she had to admit that
she was afraid. On the farm and in the tree camp Sarah
was a hero; a warrior amongst warriors, at home and at
ease. But here, in the settled community of rural Ireland,
she was a fish out of water. And she had the uncomfortable
feeling that if she didn't get back to her element soon, she
might find herself in serious trouble.

Sunday was a day off for the dogs, and when Matty had
mowed the three meadows he spent the rest of the afternoon with his feet up in front of the television. When he
came back from his drive, John joined him there. Cork
were playing Tipperary in the Munster final, and Matty
was shouting for Cork, not because he had any particular
allegiance, but because Tipp had put Clare out in the semis.
Eileen put on a big roast of beef and as she joined the men
with a cup of tea, she brought the smell of it in on her
clothes.

'You staying for dinner?' she asked John.

'I'm staying for more than dinner, Mam. I'm staying for
me holidays.'

'You on holiday? You never told me that.'

'I did, so. On the phone.'

'I never heard you.'

'Sure that's great,' said Matty. 'There's the world of work
to be done around the place.'

'I've just remembered,' said John. 'I'm going to Barbados.'

Eileen laughed, her delight at her son bursting out, too

big for the cramped sitting-room. 'You're a great lad to be spending your break with your old people.'

'I am that,' said John. 'One in a million, me.'

Malachy ate his Sunday dinner in the Weir. It was a custom with him, and he always believed that it was one he enjoyed. But as he surveyed the heaped plate of stodgy bacon and cabbage he wondered if it had ever been true. What was it that Maeve had said about the Irish and their food? It was in one of the first letters she had sent from India. How could a rural people with acres of land to cultivate be satisfied with the same old mush, day after day? Meat, potatoes, one or two of the same four vegetables; everything boiled to breaking point. And it was true, that people are what they eat. The Irish were a dull and stodgy race. Nothing like the adroit vegetarians of India.

There had been so many letters. She wrote to him, she said, instead of keeping a journal. She hoped he would hold on to the letters. They were the only record she had of her experiences. Malachy promised. He kept his promise, too. The letters were still in his possession, carefully sealed in plastic bags in the loft of the bungalow. He would never part with them. It was a long time since he had last taken them out, but he could remember them clearly. Written in watery blue ink on crisp, micro-thin sheets of airmail paper. Quite often there were enclosures: newspaper clippings, bizarre advertisements, snippets of strange scripts, the occasional photograph. She wrote about Hindu gods and customs, village life, the people, the politics, the heat. One letter came from a yoga ashram, where she was taking a basic teaching course. Another was written outside a slaughterhouse in Hyderabad, where she was keeping a vigil with a group of Gandhian activists she had met on the road. They didn't object, she said, to the Muslims butchering their own cattle. They were protesting because the small Hindu farmers in the area were becoming mechanised. They no longer needed bullocks to plough their fields and transport their goods. The Hindus themselves were selling their sacred cattle to the slaughterhouses, and it went against the most basic tenets of their religion.

It was around the same time that she had sent him the *Bhagavad Gita*. He read it over and over again; it had been constantly at hand when he was speculating over how to spend his share of the developers' money and what to do with his life. It had, in a certain sense, become his bible.

During those days he could never get his father off his conscience. He had been wrong to run away and cut himself off. Even when he was told that his father held no resentments, he stayed away; refused to speak to him. The rejection had been total and unwarranted, and the guilt it provoked colonised every aspect of Malachy's thinking. In the end, there was only one way he could assuage it and make amends to his father. But it had to be on his own terms. It had to be a solution that would be acceptable to both of them: the living and the dead. And, though he couldn't have articulated it, it had to appease his anima; the living memory in his heart of the woman for whom he still yearned.

He put down his knife and fork, his meal half eaten. A waitress whipped away his plate. 'Apple pie or cheesecake?'

'Just a cup of coffee, please, Moira.'

It had seemed to be the perfect solution; it had satisfied him and quieted the ceaseless nagging of his remorse. But for some time now the cracks had been appearing in his life, and no matter how hard he tried to mend them, they continued to widen. Increasingly he was faced by great crevasses; alluring voids that promised peace. It would be so easy to give in. Just step forward into the dark.

16

Sarah woke briefly when Mairead came in to get her nightdress, then woke again a few hours later. It was still dark but a blackbird was singing tentatively from a tree on the other side of the street behind the house. Sarah turned over and tried to go back to sleep, but she had gone to bed too early, and she was wide awake.

She turned on to her back and looked up at the ceiling.

'Duncan?'

The blackbird answered and, beyond it, the river.

'Duncan?'

Sarah was alone. But why? Why at a time when she needed guidance more than ever before had she been abandoned?

'Are you sulking? Are you jealous or something?'

She ought to be able to get some sort of an answer, even if it was manufactured by her own mind. But nothing came.

The bird sang again, each clear, fluty phrase concluded by a raucous squeak, as though the singer were ridiculing his own skill. In the tree-houses the birds had been so close, their songs so clear and vibrant. Sarah had learned to identify them all, and spent countless mornings watching the activity in the air around her. The memories made her homesick.

Should she go? If she got on to the road now, hitched a lift with some early traveller, she could be in Dublin before the police woke up, and heading out along the road to Wicklow before anyone realised she was gone.

'Should I? Duncan?'

She wasn't used to making decisions on her own. But it seemed to her as she lay there that everything was telling her to get up and go. The fact that she had woken so early was a sign in itself, and the blackbird's song was surely a summons. Sarah lay still for another few moments, waiting to be sure. Immediately her mind began to fill with the gruesome and threatening events she had witnessed. There was no doubt about it. It was time to go.

If anything, she was even stiffer than she had been the day before. She did a few gentle stretches to try and ease the pain, suppressing the moans and groans that tried to emerge. Then she began to gather her stuff. She had brought everything she owned with her, and still it didn't amount to much. A few clothes. A paperback she had been reading. A couple of crystals representing her sun and moon signs. A torch with dead batteries. Her best jeans, one leg stiff and brown with peat, were up in the attic room where she had taken them off the previous night. She decided to abandon them, rather than risk waking Mairead. But she did leave a note on the kitchen table.

'Made a snap decision to move on. Many thanks for everything. Will phone. S.'

And then she was closing the door behind her, stepping out into the breaking dawn, embarking again.

It felt wonderful. The stiffness in her limbs was forgotten as she walked away down the street. There was no doubt at all in her mind that she was doing the right thing. Her path was quite clear again, even without Duncan's ratification of it.

There was no one about. Behind every closed door and drawn curtain people were deep in dreams, taking refuge from Monday morning. Sarah congratulated herself. That was something she would never have to do, no matter how long she lived or where she ended up. She would follow Duncan to the grave before she submitted to the enslavement of materialism and a nine-to-five job.

Before long she had left the town behind her and was walking briskly along the main road towards Ennis. More birds were awake now, and the light, though still blue, was becoming brighter by the minute. It was a glorious time to be up and about. It was a glorious time to be alive.

'Please share this with me, Dunc,' she said. 'No questions. No demands.'

But he was gone. Celestial business, perhaps. A campaign meeting in the heavens. Working out a new agenda for mankind. Or planning another experiment on a new planet, which would never get into the kind of mess this one had.

She laughed. Her body was awkward and uncomfortable, but her heart was as light as air. The sun had risen on to the horizon and washed the last of the night-stains out of the sky. A milk van zipped past, heading towards town with the morning deliveries. Soon the creamery lorry would be around, heading in the opposite direction. It was another of the insanities of civilisation, that the farming communities sold their milk to the big dairy conglomerates and then bought it back from them at several times the price. No more churns and dippers. No more jugs with the cream settling on the top. Everyone drank homogenised piss out of cardboard or plastic.

The thought reminded her of her journalistic mission. That stuff about the milk could be part of it as well.

'What about a book, Duncan?' she said.

While she was waiting for an answer, a car appeared on the road ahead, coming towards her at high speed. It was a grey car, and there was something familiar about it. Sarah stopped and waited as it sped up to her and passed her by. When he saw her, the driver lifted a gloved hand, as though to shield his face from her eyes. But it was already too late. She had seen him. And she had seen the blood that was smeared all over his face and his arms. As the car sped past she saw more blood: a cluster of smudges around the handle of the driver's door.

For a few moments Sarah stood still, paralysed with shock. It was certainly the car that she had seen the night before. Whoever he was, he had done it again. She swore under her breath.

John was swearing as well. He was thumping the steering wheel with both fists and dragging every profanity he had ever heard from his memory. What the fuck was the stupid bitch doing out on the road at that hour? She was the same one he had seen on the bicycle, he was sure of it. What was she? Some kind of vampire or something? She looked a bit like one, with her skinny face and her dark eyes.

Every fucking thing had gone wrong that night. The bull was no better than the last one. It was worse. He had lost his cool, and remembering what he had done frightened him a little. He preferred to think about other things. Maybe he should go back and finish the woman off? Just a little swerve as he passed her on the road. No one would see. No one would know.

He was coming into town and he needed to keep his eyes open. The milk truck was ahead of him, parked outside the supermarket. The driver's door was opening. John swerved up a side street and made a circuit of the town, past the cattle mart and the hurling pitch. A drunk was sleeping it off on the side of the road, but John gave him a wide berth and he didn't wake.

He didn't think of the woman again until he was well out of town and on the way home. Too late, now, to go back and sort her out. She had seen the car, but she hadn't seen him. He was sure of that. Besides, she looked as though she were on her way somewhere. With luck, he would never set eyes on her again.

Sarah wanted to move, but she was glued to the spot. She had seen him now; she knew what he looked like. But what could she do about it? The thought of going to the police appalled her. Should she just sneak away? Pretend it had never happened? With a chill she realised that there was nothing to suggest it was another bull he had just attacked. What if he had killed a person?

Was that worse? Was a person's life necessarily worth more than an animal's? Some of her friends didn't think so. Before she could decide, Sarah's musings were overtaken by a new thought. What if he came back to silence her? Could he have recognised her? It was a small place, after all, and the shop had made her into a fairly public figure during the time she had spent there. What if he was biding his time now, planning to return at night and get rid of her?

She swore again. For the first time in days, Duncan's voice came into her mind.

'Run,' he said. 'Get as far away from this mess as you can.'

But, unaccountably, Sarah found herself retracing her steps, heading back towards the cold comfort of the town. Something was happening there. The coincidences were too extraordinary to understand. For some unknown reason she had been singled out by fate to play a part in the sinister drama, and turning her back on it all was not an option.

Garda Raymond Murray, patrolling in the squad car, didn't see John driving through town in the blood-smeared Ford. He didn't see Sarah, either, but she assumed that he had when she saw the car pass along the end of the narrow street. The stray bitch growled menacingly from her concealment in the butcher's doorway. Inside Mairead's house, the dogs barked in reply. The whole town suddenly seemed to be crawling with enemies.

17

Sarah screwed up the note she had left for Mairead and made a pot of tea. She had the awful sensation of being stuck in one of those nightmares where there is a corpse lying in some other part of the house and the powers of authority are about to move in and discover it. She knew that she'd had nothing to do with the killing, but she was implicated anyway and was suffused with guilt. There was also, as in dreams, nowhere to turn.

She switched on the radio, but it was too early for news. For the moment, at least, there was nothing she could do except sit and wait.

Eileen woke early again and lay listening to the strangely harmonious sounds of birdsong blending with Matty's snores. Gradually, she became aware that there was another noise as well, a household noise that made her feel uneasy because it was an unusual one to be happening at that hour. It was the washing-machine.

She got up and padded along to the bathroom in her dressing-gown. There was a steamy warmth in there as she stepped in, as though someone had just taken a bath. The tub was wet and warm. Eileen looked at her watch. It could only be John; there was no one else in the house. Why on earth would he be up so early?

She tiptoed along the corridor to his room and peeped inside. He seemed to be asleep, but his hair was wet. Her heart went out to him. Her best boy. A lot of lads didn't bother to take baths at all. What did it matter to her if he chose to take them at strange hours?

In the kitchen the washing-machine was churning away. For a few weeks now it had been making an unpleasant, grinding noise whenever the drum turned. She meant to get the man in to look at it, but had put it on the long finger. She had lived for so long without any money at all that she couldn't get used to her changed circumstances. She could buy a new machine today if she felt like it. But she wouldn't. The lump of capital in the bank still felt like blood money. Matty didn't seem to mind spending it, but she preferred to pretend it wasn't there. As long as the washing-machine kept working it would have to do.

She put on the kettle. There was something a bit odd about the bubbles churning around inside the glass door. They seemed to be pink. Eileen hoped John hadn't used the wrong detergent. Windolene or something.

She smiled to herself. Men. You had to excuse them their little weaknesses.

Despite her uneasy stomach, Sarah ate a large bowl of muesli and milk. She thought about what the butcher had said. 'You drink milk, don't you? You eat cheese.' Only because she needed protein. She had tried being a vegan once, along with Duncan. There was a lot of cruelty in the dairy farming business, she admitted that. But Sarah hadn't been efficient enough to be a vegan. She had cut out milk products without replacing them with other proteins and the diet had brought her close to death's door. It had, she suspected, taken Duncan right through it.

After he died, a trusted friend had pointed out to her that even Gandhi was persuaded by illness to break the vow he had taken against milk. He had limited himself to drinking goat's milk, but there was, as far as Sarah had been able to ascertain, no quantifiable moral difference between the treatment of both animals. For a while she had used goat's milk when she could get it fresh, but she didn't particularly like it, and over a period of time she had let the issue drop. But perhaps, now, it was time to examine it again.

Sarah turned up the radio when the morning news programme started. There was nothing about a knife murder, but there was something else of interest. Throughout the country, farmers were picketing the meat-processing plants. They were getting fifteen pence a pound less than farmers in the North for their beef cattle, and thirty pence less than their counterparts in some European states. They were claiming that the prices were artificially low; set in advance at meetings of the plant owners, who were reaping vast profits at the farmers' expense.

Sarah listened intently. A week ago she would have had no interest, but now she was becoming more and more fascinated by the whole absurd business. She found that she had little sympathy for the farmers. Anyone who reared cattle for slaughter deserved what was coming to them. On the other hand, the picture that the picketers were painting of the beef barons was even more obscene. These were pariahs; profiting from blood without getting their hands dirty. The living, breathing beasts who formed the foundation of the grisly pyramid were nothing more than commodities; weighed by the kilo and converted into Mercedes cars and grand country estates.

More research for her book. It was beginning to firm up, take shape in her mind, divide itself into chapters. How many acres was necessary for a hard-working smallholder to become self-sufficient? And how did that compare with the acreage that commercial farmers considered necessary

before a living be made? That would be a good
starting point.

She allowed the thoughts to run on in her mind. A chapter on human food, another on animal food, one on dairy, one on beef, one on new alternatives like angora goats and ostriches and deer. Something about sheep, perhaps. She knew nothing about sheep.

But like the spectre at the feast, the man at the wheel of the car invaded her thoughts. The book sank like a stone into Sarah's subconscious, usurped by more immediate concerns. Above her head, she could hear Mairead moving around. She put the kettle on again.

Eileen forgot about the clothes in the washing-machine until John got up in the early afternoon. He looked pale and thin, and she set about making a fry for him, even though she would shortly be putting on the dinner.

There was tea in the pot and she poured him a cup.

'Thanks, Mam,' he said. But he didn't drink it. Instead he unloaded the washing-machine and took the clothes outside to hang on the line.

Eileen watched him. The same thing as yesterday. Everything he had been wearing the day before had gone into the machine. A whole set of clothes. It was wonderful, of course, that he should take it upon himself, but all the same there was something a bit unusual about that. She hoped he wasn't getting one of those weird obsessions about cleanliness. A cousin of Matty's had got that, once; had spent her life washing her hands and cleaning everything in sight. It had seemed funny at first but she had ended up in the mental hospital. She didn't want to see John go that way.

'Very tidy, these days, aren't you?' she said, when he came back in.

'Ah, no,' he said, reaching for the mug of tea. 'Some

eejit spilled beer on me in the pub last night. Everything stank of it.'

Eileen smiled with relief and turned the rashers in the pan.

'Have you heard the news?'

John froze. 'What news?'

'The farmers are picketing the meat factories. Over the low prices. Your place is closed.'

John turned on the radio but there was only music.

'Picked a good time for my holliers didn't I?' he said. 'Any other news?'

Eileen shrugged. 'Nothing worth remembering, anyway.'

18

It was late afternoon before the news of the dead bull found its way to the shop. It was delivered by a local teenager, calling in for sesame sticks on her way home from her shift in the supermarket.

'Did you hear about Tom Deverix's bull?'

'No,' said Mairead.

Sarah, who was checking an order in the back room, came into the shop, her face pale.

The girl wasn't pale at all. She was clearly delighted to have found someone who hadn't yet heard. 'Found dead in the cattle crush,' she said. 'Hacked to bits, it was. There's a sick fecker out there somewhere.'

'Where?' said Sarah. 'Where was it found?'

'Way over Miltown direction,' said the girl. 'I never heard of the place myself. But it's sure to be the same person, isn't it? Who had a go at Seanie's bull the other night.'

'Sounds like it,' said Mairead.

The girl went out. Mairead turned to Sarah, but she was already out in the hall, putting on her coat.

Matty arrived in for dinner just as Eileen had decided to start without him. He was slightly unsteady on his feet. John found it difficult to look at him. How could such a creature have fathered him?

John had been like cat on a hot tin roof all afternoon. He had heard his mother creep into his bedroom that morning and had pretended to be asleep. But it was several more hours before he had fallen into a kind of uneasy half-consciousness, full of the desperate deed he had committed earlier in the morning. Waking or sleeping it horrified him. Waking or sleeping he played and replayed what had happened. The bull had stayed lying down even when the cows had got up and moved away, and he had been tempted to fling himself upon it then and there. But he had held back; allowed it a sporting chance, thrown his arms around and persuaded it to lumber to its feet.

It had been lame, God damn it. Not very lame, but limping; shuffling along behind the herd like an overgrown calf. He ought to have left it. In one of the dreams he did leave it, and walked on to a golden mountainside where an icy stream threw silver knives like trout on to its banks. But in the other dreams, as in reality, he went after it. Chased the whole fecking herd round and round the field. Trapped them in a corner once, ran right up the bull's arse, but still it wouldn't play ball. So he had separated it off from the others and driven it into the cattle crush.

It had been too easy. He ought to have left it.

Because what happened afterwards was a disaster. His memory and his dreams hurt and bled like a knife wound in his head. He had lost control. Something had got into him. An overwhelming rage, a black train hurtling through his mind, driving him on. He didn't even remember half of it. He just remembered looking up and seeing that the daylight was beginning, and then looking down, at what he had done. There was blood everywhere. He was drenched in it.

Matty sat heavily into his usual chair and Eileen started banging around with pots at the stove. Matty's plate came out first. It had always been that way, as long as John could

remember. The family was a patriarchy, not a meritocracy.
No wonder his brothers had both ended up in such a mess.
A wave of anger rose up in him, touching on the raw place
in his mind. It was easy to make it go away.

'There you are, John. Wrap yourself around that.'

Had she always said that, or was it just recently that she
had begun it?

'Thanks, Mam.'

He was still full of rashers and sausages, but there would
be emotional recriminations if he didn't eat it all. He picked
up his knife and fork.

'Did you hear about Tom Deverix's bull?' said Matty.

John knew he ought to have been prepared for it, but he
wasn't. He dropped his knife, grabbed for it too quickly and
knocked it on to the floor.

He bent down to pick it up. 'What about it?'

'That sicko was on the prowl again, whoever the fuck
he is.'

'What do you mean?' said Eileen.

'Got the oul' bull into the crush and cut him to shreds.'

'Oh, no.'

John's hands wouldn't function properly. He put down
the knife and mashed up his potatoes with his fork.

'He was quiet as a lamb, the creature,' said Matty. 'Deverix
had him since he was a calf. Made an oul' pet of him.'

'Who would do something like that?' said John. He was
pleased with the way his voice came out. Maybe it wasn't
too late for him. If he went to the priest. If he swore that
he'd never do it again.

'Well whoever it was they'd want their head seeing to,'
said his mother. 'I don't know what the country's coming to.
That kind of thing never used happen in the old days.'

'No,' said Matty. 'It didn't.'

John decided to divert them. 'There was no picketing
meat plants, either.'

'There was no need,' said Eileen.

'How come you're not there, Dad?'

Matty looked down into his plate. 'I was never much of a political animal,' he said.

'I thought something like this might get your blood up, though,' said John. 'Bit of crack, like.'

Matty and Eileen exchanged glances. John was aware of that secret again, lurking just beyond his vision.

'Where did the new tractor come from, Dad? Where did you get all that money?'

Matty didn't answer, and John knew better than to push him. But the mystery created a pressure in his head; an anger about being excluded. For the rest of the meal there was no sound other than the clack and scrape of cutlery on plates.

Sarah had intended to cycle to Miltown, until Mairead told her how far it was. Instead she walked through town and out on to the main road, then stuck out her thumb and hitched.

There were lines and lines of cars; tourists mainly, heading for Spanish Point and the sea. None of them stopped for her.

It didn't matter. There was plenty of daylight left. Plenty of time. She walked on, her back to the traffic, her thumb describing a regular arc through the empty air. Sooner or later someone would give her a lift.

She didn't see the white van until it pulled up in front of her. Malachy was so surprised and delighted that he jumped out of the driver's side and came around to meet her in the road.

Sarah grinned despite herself. It seemed that she and Malachy were destined to see this through together.

John went out as soon as dinner was over. He filled up with

petrol at the garage on the edge of town. Every time he got in or out of the car he inspected it carefully, making sure again and again that he had really got rid of all the blood on the door, and that he hadn't left gory stains on the seat covers or the floor.

After he had paid he counted what was left of his money. If he used up what he had in the tank, he would need another tenner's worth of petrol to get him back to Athlone. That left him with fifteen quid for the rest of the week. He would have to be careful; eke it out. If it hadn't been for Liam, he would have had plenty.

He was just like that bull, was Liam. Big and clumsy and stupid; all balls and no brains. No pride. No ambition. He was heading the same way as their father, except that he was worse. At least Matty had his dogs. Some kind of reason to come home from the pub.

The lads at work were the same. Work and beer and women, day after day. John couldn't understand how it could be enough for them. There was something missing in all their lives, some element that was necessary to be wholly human, but he didn't know what it was. He had thought he would find it by tackling the bulls. But he hadn't. At least, not yet.

He didn't want to go home, and it was too early to go into a pub, so he cruised the roads again. He wasn't really looking for another bull, but he found his eyes scanning each herd of cattle that he passed. Whatever the nature of the hunger that existed in his soul, it was still not satisfied.

Inside the white van, Sarah told Malachy her story. Gradually the smile left his features, replaced by intense concern.

'Did you get the car reg?'

'I didn't think of it,' said Sarah. 'I was too shocked by all the blood. There was blood on the car as well. Around the door handle.'

'But you saw his face?'

Sarah nodded. Her skills of observation were notoriously bad, and she knew she would have trouble if she was asked for a description. But when she started talking she was surprised by how much she had taken in.

'He was quite young. Late teens or early twenties. Not tall. Dark hair.'

'Would you recognise him again if you saw him?'

'I think so.'

Malachy was silent for a moment. He was, of course, alarmed by the new turn of events. But there was something else that was on his mind, and it had to be asked.

'Why didn't you tell me?'

Sarah didn't answer.

Her silence told him more than he wanted to know. It took him a while, but eventually he mastered his disappointment and went on, 'Have you been to the guards?'

Sarah found herself telling him everything; more than she had even told herself. About how threatened she had felt by the interrogation; how accused.

'I don't live like other people, you see. I'm not part of the system. They can't understand that. They want to put everybody into a neat little category, but I don't fit. I'm not even a square peg in a round hole. I don't have a hole at all.'

Malachy ignored the sexual inference that tried to nudge its way into his thoughts. He was struggling with other, more powerful emotions. Everything Sarah said about herself was true. It was what made her so interesting. It was why he admired her. Why he loved her.

He fought back an impulse to reach out and take her hand. 'I'll stick up for you,' he said. There was a catch in his voice. 'I won't let the bastards grind you down.'

She looked up into his eyes, surprised and slightly alarmed by the intensity she saw there.

'We'll crack this thing, Sarah. We'll get to the bottom of it and you'll have your story. Your exclusive.'

'It's not just about that,' she said.

'I know. I couldn't sleep last night, thinking about that poor bull.'

He lost her, and he knew it. The softness left her features.

'Come off it, Malachy. You kill every day. Don't give me that . . .' Bullshit wasn't the right word. She couldn't think of a better one.

'But it's not like that, Sarah. I keep trying to explain it to you. What I do. Why I do it. You won't listen.'

'Are we back to your philosophy again?' Sarah turned decisively towards the window. They were coming into Miltown.

As John pulled up in the yard, his father was coming out of the shed with five dogs, two of them muzzled. They were all bouncing with delight, winding their leads around his legs; a chaos of bridled energy.

John checked the seat covers for the twentieth time, then closed the car and met Matty in the yard. He said nothing, but took two of the leashes and walked with his father towards the gate.

For the first two or three hundred yards the dogs sniffed and pulled and added to the trail of turd piles in the grassy centre of the lane. Then they began to relax, and John did, too.

The day was one of the calmest and warmest that he could remember. The hedgerows were thick with blossom and alive with thrushes and finches. Beyond them, the rush-blighted fields stretched away to the horizon, as green as they would ever be.

'You know why it is that I'm not on the pickets, don't you?' said Matty.

'No. How could I know?'

Matty walked on for a few more yards before he replied. 'I sold the farm.'

John stopped in his tracks. 'You what?'

'That's where the money came from. The machinery and all. I sold the farm to Slattery's.'

It was the local meat-processing plant; one of the main competitors of the company that John worked for.

'I don't get it,' he said. 'I don't understand. If you sold the farm, what are you doing here? What are any of us doing here?'

'That's the deal, see,' said Matty. 'They buy the farm and the stock. I keep the house and I get to stay on and work for them. They pay me a wage.'

John walked on, trying to absorb the information. It was the most absurd thing he had ever heard. People only did that kind of thing in the third world, or in American films about the depression.

'It's all very well to stick your nose in the air,' said Matty. 'I'd like to see what you would have done in my place.'

There were answers John might have given, but he didn't. There was no point. 'I wasn't sticking my nose in the air. I'm walking the dogs.'

His father came alongside him again. 'You won't tell Liam or PJ, sure you won't?'

'I won't.'

'They're not like you. They wouldn't understand. Especially PJ.'

Especially PJ. He had assumed he would inherit the lot. Now there was nothing. A small, damp house marooned in the middle of someone else's land.

'It isn't right, Dad. It isn't right that you had to sell it.'

'No. You can be sure it isn't right. And you might tell that to your boss the next time you see him.'

'I will if I see him.' But John had never seen him; not the man at the top. He didn't even know what he looked like.

19

Malachy and Sarah stopped in Miltown and asked directions to Tom Deverix's farm. He wasn't at home, but his wife told them where they would find him.

The field to which she directed them appeared to be empty at first sight. Like everywhere else in that part of the world it was wet and muddy, even after the two days of fine weather. Sarah wondered if the land around there ever dried out. As they went through the open gate they saw the renderer's lorry parked in the corner near a hay-shed, its winch arm standing idle. They walked over to where the driver and Tom Deverix were standing together, leaning over the bars of the cattle crush. They stepped back together as Sarah and Malachy approached.

'Evening,' said Tom.

Malachy introduced himself and Sarah. 'We saw the other bull, the one over towards Kilbracken,' he said. 'We were interested to see this one.'

'Ye're welcome to see him,' said Tom. 'What's left of him, that is.'

When Sarah saw the carcass her lunch came back. Malachy was solicitous, but kept his distance and watched with the other men as she heaved into the nearest hedge.

'Sarah's a journalist,' he said, as she returned to them, pale and slightly unsteady on her feet.

'You'll be writing all about it, so?' said Tom.

'Yes.'

''Tis an awful thing.'

'It is.'

It was. This bull had not just been killed. It had been driven into the cattle crush and, when it was hemmed in by steel bars on all four sides, it had been hacked to pieces. The eyes were gone, and the ears and the tail and the testicles. Great gouges of flesh hung from its back and its sides, and there was hardly an inch of the bull's coat that wasn't pierced or gaping.

'What kind of a lunatic would do that?' said Tom.

'I never saw anything like it,' said the lorry driver. 'I do be picking up all kinds of animals. I picked up a horse once that had been hit by a train. 'Twas nothing as bad as this.'

'It'd make you fear for your life,' said Tom, looking around him as though his neck hairs were rising. 'Where would you be with a fella like that hanging around the place?'

'What time did it happen?' asked Sarah.

'I have no idea. I was making silage all morning. It was after that I found him.' He paused for a moment and then went on. 'First thing I did was to move all the cows into another field. They were all just standing there and looking at him. It didn't seem right.'

No one had anything to say, and Sarah realised that yet again she had forgotten her notebook. But this time the running commentary didn't come. This was too serious. Too scary.

Behind them a car pulled into the field and stopped rather suddenly as its front wheels sank into the mud. Garda Murray and Sergeant O'Shea stepped out and began to walk gingerly across the sparse grass. Sarah realised that she had made yet another mistake. She reached for her tobacco and rolled a cigarette.

Garda Murray, who had clearly been there earlier, introduced the sergeant to Tom. He nodded curtly and walked over to look at the carcass.

'You're hardly going to put that one in any freezer,' he said to Malachy.

'No,' said Malachy. 'We were just . . .'

'I wanted to see it,' said Sarah. 'For my piece.'

'Your piece,' said O'Shea. 'And have you got a press card?'

'No. Not yet.'

'Then I'd ask you to leave the scene, if you don't mind.' He looked pointedly at Garda Murray. 'This area should have been sealed off as soon as the crime was discovered. You may be interfering with vital police evidence.'

'Ah, sure, they were interfering with nothing,' said Tom.

'They didn't touch a thing,' said the lorry driver.

O'Shea looked closely at everyone's shoes.

'We'll be off now, anyway,' said Malachy. 'Won't we, Sarah?'

As they drove home a few flossy clouds were inching their way across the sky, driven before some slow breeze that was absent down below. Malachy drove carefully, aware of the width of the van on the narrow roads.

Sarah looked into the back for the first time. Both sides of the roof had been reinforced to take two steel rails, from which a few empty meat hooks swayed gently with the motion of the van. The floor was scratched but spotlessly clean, and empty apart from two or three coils of rope and a steel toolbox. There was no smell of blood.

'Have you read the *Bhagavad Gita*?' said Malachy.

'The *Bhagavad Gita*?'

'Yes. Have you read it?'

Sarah always implied that she had, if ever it was referred to in conversation. But the truth was that she hadn't. She

found religious texts of all descriptions extremely difficult, and preferred to read modern interpretations wherever
possible.

'Have you?' she asked.

Malachy nodded. 'An old girlfriend sent it to me from
India. Have you been to India?'

'I don't have money. And I don't hold with that eastern
mysticism stuff.'

'You have your own brand of mysticism, I suppose,' said
Malachy.

'I prefer no mysticism, in general.'

It wasn't entirely true. Half of the tree people were
adherents of Druidism, some more sanely than others.
The tarot cards were regularly brought out to help the
Great Spirits of Nature guide their mortal helpers, and
Sarah found that it was hard to resist finding some kind
of significance in a reading spread out beneath the trees,
seen only by candle- and firelight.

'The *Bhagavad Gita* is one of the main reasons I do
what I do.'

'But Hindus are vegetarians, Malachy. You can't quote a
Hindu text to justify being a butcher.'

'Ah, but that's where you're wrong,' he said. 'Hindus are
pacifists, too, on the whole, but Arjuna was a warrior. He
didn't want to fight, you see. He didn't want to kill his
friends and his uncles and cousins, but Krishna told him
that he had to. He was of a warrior caste, and he had to be
true to his birth, even though it didn't seem right to him.'

'How profound,' said Sarah. 'That's the long version, is
it? Back to your dad being a butcher again?'

'Yes. No. There's more to it than that. The meat that
I sell—'

Sarah interrupted him. 'Oliver told me. You finish it
yourself, organically. People come from all over the county,
bla bla bla.'

Malachy pulled into a gateway to allow an oncoming car to pass. 'You're missing the point, Sarah.'

'What point am I missing?'

'Will you come with me? Look around my place? See what I do?'

'I've already been to your place, remember? I've already seen what you do.'

'You haven't, though. Not really. You've seen the worst, not the best.'

Sarah shook her head. 'I'd better get some notes taken down about this case,' she said. 'Some other time, perhaps.'

'Is that a promise?'

'No.'

Malachy didn't speak again until they were on the out-skirts of town.

'Why don't we take a stroll around the streets tonight? Take a look inside the pubs. See if you recognise the man or the car.'

The prospect of encountering the maniac filled Sarah with dread. But she could see the sense in what Malachy was saying. If she wasn't going to tell the police, it was incumbent upon her to take some other kind of action. And she would far rather do it with a bodyguard, whatever his persuasion.

Malachy pulled up between the two shopfronts. 'What do you say?'

'All right,' said Sarah. 'Let's do it.'

20

Malachy called for Sarah shortly before nine. He had taken
about twenty minutes to decide what to wear, and in the
end had decided on an old, soft shirt and a pair of faded
black jeans. Sarah was in the same jumper and combats
she was wearing earlier, but it didn't matter to Malachy.
That was the way she was; careless of appearances, free
of fashion ordinances, completely and utterly herself. If
she had dressed up, he realised, he would have been
disappointed.

Sarah had invited Mairead along, as a sort of unofficial
chaperone. She had said that she might join them later. First
she had to go and pay her respects to the unfortunate Mrs
Fitz, and she didn't know how long she would be away.

They spent the first twenty minutes walking around the
town, checking out all the parked cars. Sarah found that
she was pleased to be walking with Malachy. He cut a fine
figure beside her and she felt safe, despite the nature of
their search. Malachy felt good about it, too. He resisted
the temptation to take Sarah's hand, but he noticed that
they gravitated towards each other as they walked; their
shoulders kept bumping and they had to make adjust-
ments.

It was almost as though some force unknown to either

of them was guiding their steps, insisting that they come together, whatever they thought of the idea.

The car was nowhere to be seen. There was a grey one that looked a bit like it, but the passenger seat was covered by a grimy blanket and was occupied by a sad, weary collie, who looked like a permanent fixture. There was no rear seat, and the back was strewn with empty fertiliser bags and pieces of string and chocolate wrappers. Even if the collie had been left at home and Sarah had failed to notice the mess in the back, that car wouldn't have the smell she remembered. Besides, it wasn't a young man's car.

'He may not be in town at all,' said Malachy. 'It is Monday, after all.'

'We may as well have a look, anyway,' said Sarah. 'Now that we're out.'

'We'll have to have a drink, then,' said Malachy. 'It would look a bit weird if we just poked our heads in and then went out again.'

'We might just be looking for someone,' said Sarah.

'We are,' said Malachy. 'Do you want us to advertise it?'

As they walked on, Malachy dismissed three of the pubs out of hand. They were old men's pubs, he said, and no one under forty would be seen dead in any of them. Two others were unlikely and one was always closed on Monday. That left three to explore.

'We'll have one drink in each of them,' he said. 'To start with, anyway.'

They had a pint in Reagan's and a pint in Fahey's. As they were heading across the street to Burke's, Mairead caught up with them.

On Fridays and Saturdays, Burke's had an electric band playing and was usually bursting at the seams with young people. But on a Monday the clientèle were quite different. Apart from a pair of tourists sitting on their own up at the far end of the long room, there seemed to be no one under fifty in the pub. Seanie Walsh was in there, leaning against the bar with two other farmers, Micky Mac and Danny Mahony. Another group of men, none of whom Malachy knew, were propping up the nearer end of the bar. The postman and his wife were sitting against the long wall of the pub, where wooden partitions about three feet deep made each table semi-private. There was no one else to be seen.

Sarah took a seat at a table beside the window, overlooking the front door. Mairead sat opposite, facing into the smoky room. Malachy went up to the bar and leaned beside Seanie.

From where he was sitting, behind one of the partitions with a newspaper, John saw him. He liked Malachy, and on another occasion he would have greeted him and had a superficial chat. But that evening he wanted to stay quiet. He was still trying to gather his thoughts and assess what had happened to him the night before. The newspaper was open, and he had read several articles, but none of them had registered. The only reason he was in the pub was that he couldn't bear to be at home, and there was nowhere else to go. Malachy was entirely wrong about Burke's. On a Monday night it was the last place in the world that the young people of the town would gather. That was why John had chosen it. He wanted to keep his head down, and as much of his money as possible in his pocket. The pint that sat in front of him would have to last the whole evening, however warm and bitter it became.

'You well, Malachy?' said Seanie.

'Grand, sure,' said Malachy. 'And yourself?'

'Good, good. How's my bull?'

'Getting better every day.'

Seanie laughed.

Behind them, too close for comfort, John squirmed in his seat and turned the page of the newspaper. Beside the unlit fire, the tourists were adamantly enjoying the atmosphere, even though there wasn't any.

Malachy gave his order and watched the barmaid begin the long, slow process of pulling the pints of stout.

'Will you buy a few weanlings off me?' said Seanie. 'I'll have to get hold of a new bull before all my heifers go barren.'

'I have a fair bit of stock just now,' said Malachy. 'Let me have a think about it.'

He liked to buy bullocks from Seanie. They tended to settle well into his system. They had never been abused.

'You'd want to watch him closely,' said Danny. 'If you buy another bull.'

'I will that,' said Seanie. 'I'd move the lot of them up beside the house and keep a grip on my shotgun. Slimy bastard that did it. He wouldn't get another chance.'

John read the same paragraph over and over again. Ireland lost yesterday to Germany. Ireland lost yesterday to Germany in the final minutes of . . . Ireland . . . But his mind was too finely tuned to the conversation at the bar. It was creepy, hearing himself talked about like that, but it was exciting as well. There was a daring in holding his ground and listening. Like an outlaw; a hooded man, spying on his enemies.

Ireland . . . He turned the page.

'He won't be bothering me, anyway,' said Danny. 'I don't know why anyone keeps a bull these days. 'Tis far easier to get the AI man.'

Micky laughed. 'Jaysus, you'd never catch me going in for that caper. Ferrying them hither and yon, standing around waiting for your man.'

''Tis fairly straightforward these days,' said Danny. 'And you get the best bulls.'

'You wouldn't know what you're getting inside in them glass jars,' said Seanie. 'It's pure madness.'

'Have you still got a bull, Micky?' asked Malachy.

'I have, begod,' said Micky. 'The same old shorthorn lad.'

'Isn't he getting a bit old for the job?' said Seanie.

'He isn't,' said Micky. 'I had a hundred per cent last year. Good strong calves, every one. And I'll tell you something else as well. There's no need for me to bring that fellow up to the house. I pity the lad tries to tangle with him.'

John was staring at an advertisement for a hair clinic, but he wasn't seeing it at all.

'You want to watch yourself, Micky,' said Danny. 'Colm Maloney's young lad was killed by a bull there last year.'

'Two years ago, it was,' said Seanie. 'But he's right. What if someone wandered in on him?'

'Ah, I wouldn't have him near the road,' said Micky. 'He's down on the inch and a big sign on the gate. No one ever goes down there.'

'All the same,' said Malachy, 'you'd want to watch yourself as well.'

'I do,' said Micky. 'He isn't a bit afraid of people but he's pure terrified of the oul' dog. I couldn't keep him else.'

When Malachy came back with the drinks Sarah leaned forward.

'I'm not sure I can manage another pint,' she said. 'Maybe we should just leave these and go home?'

Malachy looked at his watch. 'What's the rush?'

'I've only just got here,' said Mairead. Her upper lip was white with cream from her Irish coffee. 'Cheers, Malachy.'

They drank in silence for a while. Sarah was feeling distinctly unsettled, and she wasn't sure why. She was disappointed that the search had been unsuccessful, but there was more to it than that. She had found the conversation at the bar nauseating, but Malachy, despite his earlier protestations, had been a part of it. She was among enemies.

For the first time in days she was actually aware of Duncan's presence at her shoulder, egging her on.

'Do you know what I'd do to them?' she said.

'To who?' said Mairead.

'To your man, the bull-murderer. And the rest of them as well. This evil lot.' She swept her arm around, indicating the loose gathering at the bar.

Mairead laid a restraining hand on her sleeve, but it was already too late.

'I'd have them standing knee-deep in mud for half the year and sleeping in their own shit for the other half. I'd castrate ninety per cent of the males and coop up the rest in an artificial insemination station.'

The men at the bar had turned to listen.

'Shh, Sarah,' said Mairead. 'You've made your point.'

But she hadn't. Not yet. 'I'd bring some luscious young floosie in and tease them till their eyes were popping out of their heads, then make them shoot off into a plastic bag and then . . .' She thumped the table so that all the glasses jumped. Every eye in the place was upon her. 'And then I'd tie up their wives while men in white suits stuck syringes up them. And exactly nine months later I'd winch their babies out with calving-jacks.'

The farmers were sniggering. The barmaid was blushing. One of the tourists was staring, wide-eyed. The other was busy with a pocket dictionary.

'Okay, okay?' said Mairead. 'That's enough.'

But my mother hadn't finished. 'I'd whip their children away from them at two or three days old and stick them all together in a pen and feed them on liquid soya derivatives out of buckets. And when they were big enough . . .'

Sarah stopped, appalled by her own direction.

'You'd hand them over to me,' said Malachy.

There was a brief hush in the bar, then someone said, 'I won't be voting for you, so.'

Everyone laughed except for Mairead, who was struggling into her coat. Sarah dropped her eyes to her pint, astonished by her own outburst. But my father leaned in close to her.

'Fair dues to you, Sarah. That's great talk, that is.'

Sarah looked up, straight into his eyes, then turned quickly away, light-headed with desire. Malachy leaned back in his chair.

'Goodnight, all,' said Mairead, from the door.

'Goodnight, Mairead,' said Malachy. But his attention was still on Sarah. She stood up, intending to tag meekly along behind her sister, but as soon as she did so she knew her bladder wouldn't last the walk home.

Her face was hot with the focused attention of the entire room. Even the tourists stared at her until she made it to the door of the Ladies and gratefully closed it behind her. There was only one cubicle, with no lock and no seat. Peeing in the woods was a great deal more comfortable, and more private. She wished with all her heart that she had never left there.

As she washed her hands she looked into the mirror. Her face was lean and bony; still scratched and swollen from the blackthorn battles. Her hair was all over the place. She tended to keep it short and neat, so that she didn't need to brush it, but now it had grown; it was straggling all over the place and she still didn't brush it. How could Malachy be interested in her? How could any man?

With a cold flush of humiliation, she realised that he wasn't. He was playing some weird kind of power game with her, that was all. Playing her along. He was probably laughing at her even now, along with the rest of the local farming community.

She dried her hands on a grimy towel and stood for a moment inside the door, trying to muster some calm. She wouldn't sit down again, but go straight past and grab her jacket on the way. A curt nod. But whatever degree of composure she had attained was blown away the minute she stepped out of the door. Because there, right in front of her, was the man she had seen in the car.

John saw her at the same moment, and their eyes met. He looked away immediately, returning to the worthless rag in his hands. But it was already too late. He knew she had recognised him.

He looked at the newsprint, but all that entered his mind was, 'Fuck, fuck, fuck, fuck, fuck.' How the hell had that happened? A moment ago he was listening to her along with everyone else in the room; joining in the sniggering, feeling on top of the world. And now he was plumbing the depths. He kept his head down. She was passing him, and he could feel her gaze boring into his skull. Fuck, fuck, fuck.

It was only in John's imagination that Sarah's eyes were upon him. She didn't look at him at all as she passed, but gave him as wide a berth as she could. Malachy saw her coming. Her face was the colour of the head on his pint.

'Are you okay?'

She sat down on the stool beside him.

'No,' she whispered. 'He's there. Our man.'

'What?'

'Behind the partition. Reading a newspaper.'

'Are you sure?'

Sarah thought about it. Maybe she wasn't sure. Maybe she was just overwound, and imagining it. But he had registered shock as well. There was no doubt about that.

'I'm almost sure,' she said at last. 'What are we going to do?'

Malachy reached for her drink and set it in front of her. 'Let's not rush anything, anyway. Let's try and keep a clear head.'

*　　　*　　　*

John stayed motionless, bewildered as a badger in the beam of a sheep lamp. He was longing to look around the edge of the partition, to see where the woman was and who she was with. But every instinct told him to keep out of her line of sight.

His mind was racing. What could she do? Get the guards? They had no evidence. But there were still two knives in the boot of the car; they would be pretty damning if they were found. And there were sure to be traces of blood on the seat covers, if some forensic joker was called in.

Fuck, fuck, fuck. Was it all over, then? Should he just pick up and head for Athlone? Sell the car? Park it in some out-of-the-way place and burn it out?

Everything had gone pear-shaped. Suddenly he wasn't the hunter any more, but the hunted. How did a man react to that? Was there any alternative to flight?

He steadied his mind and began to think hard. He was clutching the newspaper so tightly that it was making little ripping sounds. He took a deep breath and relaxed. It wasn't over until it was over. He still had options.

And one of them was to stand his ground and fight. If he bolted now, he would be worse off than ever. Not only had he failed to accomplish what he had set out to do, he had shamed himself by his actions on the previous two nights. Returning to work would be a torture worse than ever. He would be better off to drive to the Cliffs of Moher and throw himself over.

For a few moments the thought possessed him. There was something attractive about the idea of looking out into the darkness, the roar of the waves far below, the waiting embrace of empty space and limitless peace. But that was a coward's way out. There was, he realised, still another possibility. If he acted fast, he could do it, and worry about the consequences later. If he had to go out, he would go out in a blaze of glory. As nonchalantly as he could, he peered around the edge of the partition. The woman was gone. How long would it take for her to find the guards and bring them back there?

He left the paper where it was and walked out of the pub.

21

Sarah and Malachy were opposite the pub in the van when John came out. He looked up and down the street, then walked away from them, head down, hunched over himself.

Sarah said nothing, but nodded towards him.

'That's John Kilroy,' said Malachy. 'He's a nice lad. It can't have been him.'

Sarah was already beginning to doubt herself. 'I was certain when I saw him,' she said. 'Where does he live?'

'His parents have a farm a couple of miles outside town. But I thought he'd left home. I thought . . .'

Malachy stopped.

'You thought what?'

'I think he works in a meat factory in Athlone,' said Malachy. 'Let's see where he goes, shall we?'

He waited until John went out of sight around a bend in the street, then started the van and drove slowly after him.

'We're hardly invisible in this flaming thing,' said Sarah.

'I'll try and keep a distance.'

As they rounded the bend, John came into view again and Malachy pulled in to the side. A couple of cars passed, their headlamps on even though it wasn't yet entirely dark. Sarah looked up. The last of the light was a vivid pink on the western horizon. Night was coming on fast.

The street was long and straight, and they were able to keep John in sight for some time before he crossed over and turned to the left, on to the road that led towards his home townland. Malachy drove forward again, and drew in at the corner. There were only a few houses on the street. Beyond them, the open countryside began. Parked on the verge, beneath an overhanging sycamore, was a grey car.

'That's it,' said Sarah. 'That's the car.'

'Are you sure?'

'Just wait. See if he gets into it.'

John hadn't looked back once in all the time they'd been watching him. When he reached the car he stopped and turned round, feeling in his pocket for the keys.

Sarah shrank down in the seat, but John gave no sign of having seen them.

'I can't believe it's him,' said Malachy. 'He always seemed so nice.'

'It would be easy, wouldn't it, if criminals all looked like criminals,' said Sarah, caustically. 'Oy, you. You're obviously a nasty piece of work. You're under arrest.'

Malachy laughed.

'They do it, actually,' Sarah went on. 'If you're black, or if you live in a tree or a new age convoy.'

The car's lights came on and it started out. Malachy switched on his own lights and followed, keeping as far behind as he could without losing sight of it. After a quarter of a mile the car indicated politely and turned left.

'He's not going home, anyway,' said Malachy.

The grey car skirted the town, then joined the main road again. It turned right, towards Ennis. About a mile outside the town was a narrow bridge where the river crossed under the road. On the other side of it the car indicated again and turned on to a smaller road.

Malachy slowed and, just as he was about to turn, switched off his lights.

Sarah made a grab for the dashboard as they were plunged into darkness. 'What are you doing?'

'I want to see what he's up to,' said Malachy. 'I don't want him to know there's someone behind him.'

As her eyes adjusted, Sarah realised there was light enough to see by. Just about. And she saw the wisdom of it. If John looked into his rear-view mirror he would think the road was empty.

The river was beside them for half a mile or so, and then the road swung away from it, to the left. John's car followed it for another few hundred yards, and then turned off, back towards the river.

'I don't believe it,' said Malachy.

'What?'

'I think he was listening to us in the pub. I think he's heading for Micky Mac's inch.'

'Inch?' said Sarah.

'It's a piece of land beside the river. It's where Micky Mac keeps that bull he was talking about.'

'Oh, God,' said Sarah.

The van hit the verge and Malachy straightened it out. Sarah clung on to her seat.

'Why are you still following him, then?' she said. 'If what he says about the bull is true, he's going to get what's coming to him, isn't he?'

'Maybe,' said Malachy. But he didn't stop.

John turned on to the cinder track that led towards the river and Micky Mac's land. A few yards down was a gateway, and he pulled into it and parked. Around him the light was fading, and it would be some time before the moon came up. He would have to act fast. His gloves were at home. He had washed them by hand this time and they were still drying out under his pillow. He would have to manage without them and ditch the knives afterwards.

Malachy pulled up on the verge, turned off the engine and rolled down the window. For another moment or two they could hear the sound of John's car and see the lights shining through the hedgerows. Then all was silent and dark.

'I don't believe we're doing this,' Sarah whispered. 'What are you hoping to achieve?'

'He needs help, Sarah. Not prison.'

'And how do you propose to help him?'

'Stop him first, anyway.'

But he didn't get out of the van. They heard John's car door close and, a few moments later, the boot.

'What are you waiting for?' Sarah whispered.

'I want to catch him in the act. Give him a chance to incriminate himself.'

Sarah's nerves were on red alert, and the night seemed full of death and disaster. She made a cigarette but she licked the wrong side of the paper and it fell apart as soon as she lit it. She rolled another one.

'You should pack that in,' said Malachy.

'When it's the worst of my worries, I will.'

Malachy laughed. He poked around in the compartment under the dash until he located a screwdriver. Then he reached up, unscrewed the cover of the inside light and took out the bulb.

He winked in the dimness, put a finger to his lips, and said, 'Come on.'

John walked down the long, winding boreen. He was well acquainted with Micky's inch. Better acquainted with it than Micky himself, perhaps. For one thing, he knew that it was not at all the quiet, out-of-the-way spot that Micky thought it was. Since he was a small boy he had been coming there to fish with his brothers and their friends. Beside the long, narrow strip of meadow, the river had gouged deep, dark pools, where big trout, and occasionally salmon, could be caught.

They had never eaten the fish themselves. Eileen's cuisine didn't stretch that far and the only fish that John or his brothers had ever tasted came covered in orange crumb. But they offered their catch from door to door in town, and never failed to sell whatever they had. For a few weeks every summer, there was decent pocket money in it.

Maybe the local lads didn't come here any more. Maybe they were all inside messing with their computers and Nintendos. It might be his epitaph. The last of the fishermen.

Something, perhaps the familiarity of the place, had sedated him. With a rush that made him unsteady on his feet for an instant, the magnitude of what was happening raced back. He was actually doing it; doing the last Butch and Sundance run, staring down into the waves from the cliffs, facing eternal darkness.

Or eternal life. He might win. He might succeed at last in what he had set out to do.

The bars of the ancient gate were bent. Rust pushed through the flaking paintwork. It had always been like that, and although it was already too dark to see the colour, John was sure it hadn't been painted since he last saw it, several years ago. Crumbly scabs broke beneath his hands as he climbed over. He wiped the dust on his jeans and walked on into the field.

The river was quiet here, without obstacles to grumble over. In winter-time it rose up and flooded the level fields, laying down a layer of rich silt which made the summer grazing some of the best in the area. On the other side of the long field the land rose sharply and was covered in thick undergrowth. If the cattle got hungry or bored they ventured up the slope and browsed among the sally and brambles, and their muddy tracks made little bushy islands of the scrub. John had taken one of Matty's lurchers up there once, and she had put up a hare. But she hadn't caught it. It had vanished, as hares tend to do, unless they are trapped and let loose on the coursing field. Or unless they are human hares.

The cattle were about halfway along the strip of land, standing in a loose group, already looking his way. John felt for the knives at his belt, and pulled out the longer of the two. Its edge was true. John tucked it back under his palm, holding it like a dagger, as though he needed to conceal it from the bull before it would consent to the fight.

The old, familiar terror rose into his throat. He turned away from the cattle and walked along the foot of the hill, breathing deeply, trying to calm his thundering blood. The run-off from the slope made the ground wetter there, and his feet sank into the sloppy mud, reminding him of the dream where he couldn't reach the air.

He was a coward. That was the truth. He had driven thousands of cattle to their deaths, but had never faced something that had any chance of fighting back. It was now or never. Before the police came looking for him. Before he made his escape to Athlone. Before he walked back into that stinking slaughter hall, echoing with the bawling of terrified beasts. He faced the herd again and walked on.

The bull watched him come. It watched people coming and going along the riverbank on most days. As long as they didn't bother it, it didn't bother them. That was a beast law, as relevant in the meadows of Ireland as on the plains of Africa. There were, however, a whole set of sub-regulations about manners, and this human was disobeying them all. He was approaching head-on, with his eyes to the front. He was coming at a steady pace, and with clear purpose. This was not a passer-by, to be watched and ignored. This was a threat.

John crossed an invisible line and the cattle swung around

and moved away. But the bull did not. John was dismayed before he remembered that he ought to be pleased. He hesitated, thought of taking another turn around the block, and decided against it. He walked on.

He could no longer feel the ground beneath his feet or the cooling air around his face. He had lost awareness of his heartbeat, and it no longer bothered him. All his concentration was focused on the bull ahead of him. The worthy adversary. The match that he had met at last.

Still the bull stood its ground. It wasn't going to run. John stopped, uncertain. The bull stared straight at him. Behind it, the cows had regrouped and were standing in a ragged semicircle, watching. Like a bloody audience. A bull-fight where cattle were the spectators. John looked around. It had to be another dream. This couldn't really be happening.

Without warning, the bull charged. It didn't make the head-down, snorting kind of charge that John had always associated with bulls. It just began to trot towards him, purposefully and fearlessly.

Instinctively, John did what his father would have done; what almost any farmer in the county would have done. He raised his hand as though it had a stick in it, and shouted at the top of his voice.

'Ga'an! Get out of it!'

The bull stopped. John stood his ground. This bull was putting it up to him. Now was the time to find out whether he really meant it. Whether he had as much bottle as he thought he had. The bull was a bit too close already. How would he play it? He had no jacket to wave; nothing except his arms. The matadors always had capes, to fool the bull while they nipped out of its way. How come he hadn't worked out any of this before?

The bull, meanwhile, had taken a look around and discovered that there were no dogs. It turned its white-eyed stare back to John. There was no comparison between this bull and the ones he had been dealing with on the other nights. This one was half the size but twice as lean and agile. In a gesture of impatience, it stamped a front foot.

He could have slipped away at that moment. The bull would have allowed it. But the moment passed and the chance was gone. The bull trotted forward for two steps, and before John had a chance to shout at it again, it lowered its head and thundered with terrifying speed straight at him.

Any ideas John might have had of mounting a counter-attack had no chance of being put to the test. There was no space for anything other than instinct in that rich, riverside meadow, and John abandoned himself to its commands. He was moving before he knew it, running with a speed he hadn't known he possessed, running without awareness of breath or legs or ground.

The bull could have caught him if it had chosen to. Its aggressive reputation was entirely justified, but it wasn't in its nature to attack something that was so clearly on the run. It stayed at John's heels, however, until he was well away from its herd. Then it came to rest and stood watching him go. Behind it, the cows and heifers trotted up to watch the sport.

John didn't stop running. The panic of the hare was upon him, his childhood nightmare pursuing him yet again down the hunting hill, his brothers on his tail. Those days had taught him a few painful lessons. Looking back lost him time. Looking back could cause him to miss his step. Worse than either of those things, looking back could let him know exactly how close the pursuers were, and bring fresh agonies of terror to weaken his racing limbs. Beneath the over-arching hedges, he could make out the paler gap where the old gate stood, and he made for it with the last of the adrenaline fuelling his blood. He wasn't even listening for the bull any more. When he was safely outside the field he could stop and think about where it was, and what to do next.

The rusting gate was barely visible in the darkness, even when he was almost upon it. But without a break in speed he launched himself at it, dropping the knife in order to grab it, throwing himself in a spectacular vault high over the top bar.

But something was wrong. As he flew through the air he could see someone emerging from the shadows and moving to intercept his flight. Before his feet had even reached the ground, John found himself captured; completely restrained by the encircling grip of Malachy Glynn's strong arms.

22 ∫

John screamed as if his entrails were being torn out. It was a terrible, unnerving sound which froze Sarah to the spot and almost made Malachy let him go. It was like the sound of a terrified and injured beast, and both of them wondered whether he was hurt, or mad, or both. It seemed to go on for ages, and then, suddenly, he stopped screaming and started to swear. He had no idea who was holding him. All he could see was Sarah. He assumed she had led the guards to him.

'You bitch! You slag! You fucking whore!'

He started to struggle as well, and Malachy was having trouble keeping his grip. John got a foot on to the ground and almost pushed them both over backwards. His arms were locked at his sides, but Sarah could see that his hands were moving with some sort of purpose, and it was only then that she spotted the knife in his belt.

She darted forward, avoiding his flailing legs, grabbed the handle of the knife and pulled it free. As though it were a dangerous insect that she had been obliged to remove, she didn't hold on to it at all, but flung it away from her into the darkness. Malachy yelled, and for a moment she thought she had hit him with it, but it was John who had hurt him, kicking him viciously in the shins with his heels.

Malachy swung him around like a father swings a child, and when his feet were clear of the ground he dropped him face-down on the muddy ground and yanked his arm up behind him in an elbow lock.

'Get some rope, Sarah!' he said. 'Quick!'

'Where?'

'The gate.'

On her bike-rides around the Clare roads, Sarah had passed a hundred gates which had bristly heaps of baler twine draped over them, or piled beside them on the verge. But Micky didn't keep the cattle on the inch in the winter, and never fed them hay there. The only piece of cord in sight was the one that secured the gate to its post, and it was bulging with a hundred knots. Sarah began to struggle with them.

'Get off me, you hairy bollocks!' John was shouting. Sarah broke a nail. She didn't know what Malachy was playing at. The violence frightened her.

'Hush, John,' said Malachy, a catch in his voice betraying his own anxiety. 'It's me, Malachy. Malachy Glynn.'

'I don't give a flying fuck who you are. Fucking get off me or I'll break your fucking neck!'

The bull slid up through the gloom and stood a few feet away, watching. Behind it, their feet squelching in the mud, the cows began to gather.

'Come on, Sarah!' said Malachy. 'What are you doing?'

Sarah broke another nail, and wished that she hadn't been so hasty in discarding John's knife. But the cord finally came free, still knotted in a dozen places. She handed it to Malachy and he wrenched John's other arm behind his back and tied his wrists together.

'What are you doing, you crazy bastard?' John screamed. 'You don't have any right to be tying me up!'

'You don't have any right to be killing bulls,' said Malachy.

'Who said I was killing bulls? I was fishing.'

'Fishing my arse. Get up now, John.'

John got to his feet and launched himself at Malachy,

swinging at his face with his head. Malachy dodged out of the way and slipped around behind him, grabbing a handful of hair at the back of his head.

'Be good, John. I won't hurt you if you behave yourself.'

'Where are you taking me?'

'I'm going to bring you home to stay with me for a while. That's not too bad, is it?'

Sarah fell in beside Malachy and gave him a searching look. He smiled, back in control of himself. 'Can you drive?' he asked.

It wasn't the time to expound on her theories of the car and the profligate wastage of Mother Earth's royal black blood. 'I used to,' she said. 'But I haven't done it for years.'

'You'll manage. It's not something you can forget.'

Malachy's words kept ringing in Sarah's ears as she tried to back John's car up the boreen in the dark. It had no reversing lights, and she drove into the ditch several times before she discovered the trick of opening her door and leaning out. Every muscle in her neck and back was stiff with tension, and she was physically shaking by the time she made it as far as the tarmacked road. She wanted to get out and tell Malachy she couldn't do it, but he drove off before she had time, and she had no option but to follow as well as she could.

They took back roads all the way to the old estate. Sarah fixed her eyes on the tail lights of the van and tried to keep all other thoughts out of her mind. But they crept in on her anyway. What the hell did Malachy think he was doing? What was he going to do with John? What if someone stopped them and heard John yelling and kicking in the back of the van? By the time they pulled into the cobbled yard she was rigid with fear, and almost drove into the gatepost. She stopped the car where it was and got out.

Malachy was already out of the van and about to open the side door.

'What are you going to do?' she asked him. 'Why did you bring him here?'

'Trust me, Sarah,' he said.

'Why?'

Her response disappointed him. He dragged John, still kicking and screaming, out of the van, and half pushed, half carried him across the yard towards the coach-house. At the door he freed a hand to switch on a light, then shoved John inside. Sarah followed, hesitantly. Malachy stopped beside one of the cage boxes. A bullock's nose appeared at the bars, blinking at the sudden light.

'Open the door, there,' said Malachy.

Sarah hesitated, then slid the heavy door across. The bullock moved aside politely, still blinking. Malachy bundled John inside, pushed him down into the shavings in the corner, and dodged back out again. He had barely closed the door when John flung himself against it with such ferocity that the whole building shook.

'Let me go, you pair of perverts,' he yelled. 'Untie my fucking hands!'

He launched himself against the bars again with bone-bruising force. The bullock had retreated to the furthest corner of the box and was gazing out at the extraordinary proceedings with acute anxiety.

'Jesus, Malachy,' said Sarah. 'He's going to kill himself.'

'I'll let you have your hands again when you cool off a bit.'

'I don't want to fucking cool off,' John screamed. 'I want to fucking get out!'

Malachy went into the narrow tack room and rummaged around in a box until he found a padlock with a key. He slipped it through the hasp on the door and clicked it shut.

'I'll be back in a while,' he said to John. 'Don't worry. No one's going to hurt you.'

'You already have fucking hurt me!' said John. 'I'll have the guards on you.'

'I'd say you'd have an interesting story for the guards, all right,' said Malachy.

He walked away and Sarah followed. At the open end of the building, where the yearlings had been penned, he began to move bales of hay around.

'I don't know which of you is madder,' said Sarah. 'What are you trying to do?'

John was still shouting at them from the cage box, and they spoke in the pauses between his outbursts.

'Do you want to turn him over to the police?' said Malachy. 'Do you think that they would have the appropriate response to what he's done?'

'No, I don't. But what can you do? I mean, he's obviously deranged, you can see that.'

'Maybe I have a treatment for him.'

'You can't do that!' said Sarah. 'You can't just take the law into your own hands.'

'Isn't that what you do?' said Malachy. 'Setting up camps in the trees? Sabotaging hunts? Harassing people who do animal experiments?'

Sarah found herself hoist on her own petard. 'That's different.'

'How is it different?'

'It just is. We don't hurt anyone.' Her words were lost beneath another of John's profane outpourings.

'Give me a hand, would you?' said Malachy.

Together they moved enough of the bales to make room for John's car, then Malachy drove it in. The exhaust fumes in the enclosed space made Sarah dizzy, and she walked out into the yard. Malachy stayed inside, moving the bales back to hide the car. After a while, Sarah went back to join him.

'Someone's going to notice he's missing,' she said. 'Someone's going to come looking for him.'

'Not down here, they won't,' said Malachy. 'No one ever comes down here.'

'Not even Oliver? Not even the postman?'

'Not even Oliver. Not even the postman.'

'You must lead a pretty lonely existence, then,' said Sarah. She meant it sarcastically, but to Malachy's hungry heart it sounded like concern.

'I do, Sarah,' he said. 'You wouldn't believe how lonely.'

Malachy had assumed that Sarah would understand and be an accomplice in his plans. But she wouldn't come into the house with him, not even for a cup of tea, and began to walk out along the drive.

'I'll give you a lift,' he said.

'I don't want a lift. I don't want anything to do with what's going on here.'

But he went back for the van anyway, and when he drew up beside her she got in.

When he heard the van pull away, John realised there was no more sense in shouting. His rage subsided, and for a few minutes he shamed himself by blubbing like a baby. Malachy had left the lights on for him and he was grateful for that. Once he stopped shouting, the bullock lost its anxiety and seemed bemused by him; not in the slightest bit aggressive. But he would have hated being locked up in the dark with it.

When he had finished crying, John felt empty and numb. He remembered the flight through the field and knew that was when everything had gone wrong. He ought to have stood his ground, even if it meant losing. Once again the warm darkness beckoned. An honourable death would have been better than this humiliation.

He made a cautious tour of the box, avoiding the corner that the bullock had claimed as its own, hoping to find some way of freeing his hands. But there were no sharp edges, not even a protruding nail in the woodwork. The manger had a rounded concrete lip, darkened by the rubbed-in grease of countless dewlaps. The water was in a blue plastic half-barrel, but the sawn edge had been filed smooth. He turned his back to the bullock.

'Chew through that, mate, will you?' he said.

The bullock, as though happy to oblige, took a step towards him. John swung round.

'Keep away from me, you filthy bastard,' he said.

The silence in the van was excruciating. They were already nearing the town by the time Malachy succeeded in breaking it.

'If only you'd listen to me, Sarah.'

Sarah said nothing.

'I know what you think of me, but you're wrong. You've never given me the chance to explain myself.'

'Your *Bhagavad Gita* trip, is it?'

Malachy stopped the van. 'You know something?' he said. 'You think you're so superior to everyone because you have an ethical standpoint of some kind. But you're not, you know. You're as narrow-minded as everyone else. How can you expect to change anything if you won't allow dialogue? If you won't hear someone else's point of view?'

They were still some distance from the shop, but Sarah opened the door and got out.

'Thanks for the lift,' she said.

Malachy revved the engine and made a U-turn in the road.

Mairead was still awake, sitting in the kitchen reading a recipe book. She didn't look up, and Sarah was reminded of her mother, punishing her misdemeanours with passive aggression. It was a while before she remembered the cause of Mairead's displeasure. The drink in Burke's pub seemed like something from a different era.

'I'm sorry if I embarrassed you.'

Mairead looked up, but the state of Sarah's shoes and jeans made her forget her well-rehearsed grievance.

'What on earth have you been up to?'

Sarah hadn't noticed the mud. 'Oh. Just . . . We went for a walk beside the river.'

She wanted to tell Mairead everything; share the burden that was weighing on her so heavily. But it wasn't only her sister's censorious mood that held her back. Mairead would almost certainly feel compelled to tell the police. She was like their parents; a good, moral citizen of the empire. And although Sarah wasn't at all sure of her own position, she didn't want to shop Malachy. Not yet, anyway. Not before she had given it some more thought.

'You're old enough to know what you're doing,' said Mairead. 'I suppose.'

The last words were heavily weighted.

'I'm going to bed,' said Sarah.

John was leaning against the manger.

Malachy fed a pair of grey blankets through the bars. 'Made friends, yet?' he asked.

'He a pet, is he?' said John.

'Sort of.'

Malachy never gave names to the bullocks he bought. But this one had a clear, circular patch of white around each eye, and although he had never spoken the name out loud, Malachy couldn't help thinking of it as 'Goggles'.

'You're seriously sick, you know,' said John. 'This is false imprisonment. You'll be the one who ends up behind bars.'

'Possibly,' said Malachy. 'Do you want me to untie your hands?'

John didn't answer.

Malachy shrugged. 'It's all the same to me.'

'All right,' said John.

'If you come up here and turn round I'll cut the rope.'

The bullock was lying down in the middle of the floor, chewing the cud. John moved along the walls and turned his back to Malachy, who put both arms through the bars and began to saw at the blue nylon cord. He was using an ancient hoof knife that had been hanging against the wall of the building since the day he bought it. It wasn't as sharp as it looked, and the process took some time.

As soon as his hands came free, John whipped around and made a grab for Malachy's arm. But the rope had restricted his blood supply for too long, and his hands were numb and useless. He managed to grab a sleeve, but couldn't keep hold when Malachy pulled away.

'Careful, now,' said Malachy.

John flew into a rage again. 'You can't fucking keep me here! My dad'll come looking for me. He'll make bloody mincemeat of you.'

'He can try,' said Malachy. 'Are you hungry? Can I bring you something to eat?'

'Fuck off,' said John. 'You can shove your fucking . . .'

Malachy turned on his heel and walked out of the building. As he left, he switched off the light.

John yelled until his voice gave out. He booted the wooden partitions with all his strength, but they had been built to withstand far more powerful kicks than his. The bullock stood up and cowered in the corner, a pied shadow in the darkness.

When he came to the last of his strength, John grabbed the bars in both fists and hung from them, his head down. This wasn't the darkness he had been longing for. This was not the restful, warrior's darkness that had beckoned to him. This was the long, slow, breathing darkness of the damned. He flung a last series of frustrated kicks at the wall, and the building echoed mockingly and returned to its pregnant quiet.

John turned. In the furthest corner of the box, the bullock turned as well, and although he couldn't see its eyes in the dark, he had a feeling that it could see him. In the box to the right of him he could hear the inquisitive blowing of another beast, its nose pressed against the bars. The one on the other side was empty.

As his rage subsided, John realised that he was hungry, and thirsty as well. But he was glad he hadn't taken food from Malachy. It would have given the mad fucker too much satisfaction. What did he think he was playing at, anyway? Was he just keeping him there until he got the guards? Or was it something worse?

He had always thought of Malachy as a decent sort of bloke. Everyone thought so, although they also thought he was a bit cracked, the way he kept his bullocks like pets. Kept them like pets and then slaughtered them. A cold sweat broke out under John's arms and trickled down under his shirt. He wouldn't be as mad as that, would he? Some sort of cattle worshipper, out for revenge.

He yelled hoarsely, one last time. But he knew where Malachy's buildings were. Apart from the bungalow, there wasn't another house within a mile.

The bullock began to edge out of the corner. John waved his arms and swore at it. He saw its thin tail lift and heard the liquid slop of its shit hitting the ground. Smelled the fresh, hot stink of it. Swore again. Like an echo, the bullock in the next box relieved itself as well. He would kill Malachy for this. The man was raving if he thought he could get away with it.

The sweat had made him cold. He pulled the blankets free of the bars and wrapped them around him. There were heaps of shavings on the floor, and although a lot of it was soiled, the bits in the corners were probably still fresh. He felt around in the darkness beside where he stood. The manger was the best bet, but as he began to edge towards it the bullock huffed and shrank away. Even though it had done nothing but keep its distance, John was afraid of it. He had no cattle prod now, and no knife. Micky Mac's bull had put the wind up him, and he was much too aware of the brute strength and the hulking weight of his cell mate. He stood for a long time, waiting for some better idea to occur to him. Finally he edged along the wall, swept the remains of the hay in the manger into a pile and climbed in on top of it.

He didn't lie flat, but leaned against the partition wall, watching the beast in the opposite corner. It watched him back for a while and then, with a huge sigh, it folded its knees and dropped heavily on to the floor.

John relaxed into the hay. A deep tiredness swam into his head, but the moment he closed his eyes he was beset with powerful images, more real than the darkness around him. His feet flying across the inch. The bull on his heels, breathing fire, which engulfed him, became the flames of some hell presided over by a bull-headed god. Teeth snapped at him, great maws opened to receive him. A pair of black horns reached for his entrails.

He opened his eyes again and stared into the dark. Below him, the bullock belched and began to chew the cud.

'Shut the fuck up!' he shouted.

The bullock shut up, but in the loft above his head something was scuttling around. A rat. He turned and pulled the blankets tight around his head. But now there were more images, worse ones. Rats swimming in blood. His own entrails, leaking out of his body like the guy in a war film he had seen. The bullock resumed its chewing, and this time John didn't object. Instead he listened, and gradually his revulsion subsided. His mind swam into the sound, took refuge there. There was a brief silence, another glubby belch, more chewing. Somehow, the contentment of the huge, placid creature transmitted itself through the sounds, and John was infected by it, and soothed. As he dropped towards a restless sleep, the bullock's grinding teeth were his anchor to the world; his lullaby.

23 ∫

In the bungalow, Malachy was finding it even harder to sleep. He was amazed that Sarah hadn't understood; hadn't even tried to. He found that he was angry with her; fed up of chasing her approval. What he had said to her was true: she was intolerant and full of hubris. To her he was some sort of scum; a Harijan; someone to be despised and reviled. A man with blood on his hands.

He turned on to his back and stared into the darkness. John was quiet at last. He hoped that he hadn't brained himself against the bars or hanged himself with the blankets. He hoped Goggles was all right as well. John could hardly damage him with his bare hands, could he?

Sarah lay in the same darkness, the same sleepless place. She appeared to have got herself tangled up with not just one madman, but two of them.

'Duncan?'

It was time to get out, and no mistakes, this time. But what should she do? Just turn her back and abandon the whole, dreadful situation? Or should she inform?

'Duncan?'

Instead of his face, Malachy's appeared in her mind.

'Go away.'

He wouldn't. She had come so close to liking him, despite

197 •

herself. But she was glad now that she hadn't listened to him; glad that she hadn't allowed him to seduce her, either physically or mentally.

Through the thin, wooden ceiling, she heard Mairead turn over in the attic bed. It made her feel guilty, to be usurping her sister's comfort. It was another good reason to get up and go. Early in the morning. A second attempt.

The thought made her aware that she had been awake for nearly twenty-four hours. She must be exhausted, but she didn't feel it. Her mind was jizzed up, full of activity. She hadn't a snowball's chance in hell of getting to sleep.

She closed her eyes and listened to the night. The wind was rising, feeling around the house for loose things to rock and rattle. It was one of the nice things about real houses; the security they gave against the weather. No matter how well a tree-house was constructed, the wind would always find a way in and come creeping around in the night, weaselling into her sleeping bag and giving her earaches.

She remembered Micky Mac's bull standing in the dark field, watching her struggling with the gate. She found herself wondering what would happen if all those bulls that were born every day weren't castrated and killed. The thoughts made her uncomfortable. She didn't want to follow them any further. Who knew where they would lead?

'Duncan?'

He came roaring out of the darkness, a wild, grimacing head on a bull's body. Sarah jerked upright, shocked stiff by the vision, and clutched at the bedclothes.

'Oh, no! Not like that, Duncan!'

'How then, Sal?'

He became a putrefying corpse, risen from the grave, the flesh falling away from his face, revealing white bones. A bull's skull burned on a funeral pyre. Malachy stoked the flames.

'You want me, Sal?'

'I'm going mad. It's something about this town. Everyone in it is stark, staring bonkers!'

Duncan lay among the worms, which poked from his flesh and wriggled. He was grinning out at her.

'No! Go back to the grave. Stay there!'

'You sure? You want to be on your own?'

'Yes. I want to be on my own.'

And he was gone.

Sarah shrank back on to the mattress and pulled the bedclothes up around her face. They smelled of Mairead's fruity perfume. They were comforting. She was aware of sitting tightly on the lid of something, but whether it was Duncan's stinking sepulchre or her own raving imagination she didn't know. They were the same thing, perhaps. She began to hum urgently to herself, as she had done as a child when frightening thoughts threatened her safety. All she had to do was get through the night. And in the morning everything would be all right.

Malachy got up, pulled his clothes on over his pyjamas and stepped into his wellingtons. The night was brisk with the rising wind, and the trees were answering it. He felt in his pocket for the key-ring with the little light, and tested it against the palm of his hand.

He wasn't sure what he was going to do. Perhaps he would just talk to John and see what he was thinking. They could come to an agreement: John's freedom in return for a promise to stop what he was doing. He had been rumbled, after all. If there were any more bull deaths, Malachy would put the cops on to him. Maybe that was enough?

He crept into the coach-house and stood at the bars of Goggles's box. He could see the shape of the bullock on the floor, but there was no sign of John. He stepped back and turned on the torch, suddenly aware that John could be anywhere in the darkness around him. The tiny beam made things worse, not better, casting black shadows that crouched and pounced. But as far as he could tell, John wasn't at large in the passageway.

He stepped up to the bars again and shone the light inside. Nothing. Then he saw the blanket-wrapped shape in the manger. There was no head, nothing recognisably human, but when he succeeded in steadying the tiny beam, Malachy could see the rise and fall of even breathing.

Micky Mac was restless that night as well. He had been confident enough in the pub, but he was worried about his bull all the same. He got up early, let the mangy collie into the ancient hatchback and drove down to the inch.

The first thing he noticed was that the rope had been removed from the gate. The dog drew his attention to something else. Inside the gate, trampled and muddied, was a large kitchen knife.

He put the dog back into the car and went through into the field, careful to avoid the knife. The cattle were lying peacefully beside the river, their backs to the wind. As he approached they stood up. The bull stepped forward to face him, stretching its back. Micky didn't need to go any closer to know that it was unharmed. But someone had made an attempt on it there last night, there was no doubt of that.

As he went back to the car, Micky was smiling. He hadn't just been bragging in the pub. It would take some tough lad to get the better of his bull.

Malachy got an hour or two of fidgety sleep and was pleased to open his eyes and find that daylight had arrived. Some dream he had been having had suggested to him that it never would.

His nerves were jittery as he walked towards the cage

boxes. The cattle inside heard him coming and called for breakfast, but he hesitated at the double door. What was he going to do about John? He had a feeling that he had come to a decision about that earlier in the night, but he wasn't quite clear in his mind. He remembered that he was to get a promise from the lad, and let him go. It somehow seemed too easy.

John was standing at the bars, looking out. The bullock stood beside the manger, expectantly.

'Morning, John.'

'Have you come to your senses, yet, Malachy? Are you going to let me out of here before it's too late?'

Malachy burst a bale of hay and began feeding the bullocks in the cages on the other side of the passage. 'I was hoping you would be the one to have come to your senses. Are you ready to talk about it, yet?'

'Talk about what?'

'About why you killed Tom Deverix's bull, and tried to kill Seanie's.'

'I have no idea what you're talking about,' said John.

'You didn't hear, then?'

'Of course I heard. Everybody heard. But I didn't do it.'

'What were you doing out last night, then? In Micky Mac's field?'

'I told you. I was fishing.'

'Fishing without a rod. Tickling trout, were you?'

'I did have a rod, actually. I let it fall into the river when that mad bastard of a bull made a go for me.'

'Good try, John. You'll have to do better than that.'

Malachy went into the empty box beside John and squeezed a few wedges of hay through the bars. They fell into the manger, and Goggles began to munch happily. The bullock on the other side gazed at him wistfully, but Malachy had finished with the bale and when he returned to the side of the box he was carrying a water hose.

The hungry bullock bawled mournfully.

'Shut your stupid face, you,' John said to it.

Malachy fed the hose through the bars and into the water barrel. Goggles came over and drank as it filled.

Malachy stood clear of John's reach. 'Come clean, John. Tell me about it. Wouldn't it be better to get it off your chest?'

'Get what off my chest?'

'You know what I'm talking about. All I want is for you to admit to it. We can make a deal.'

'We have nothing to make a deal about, Malachy. I have nothing to get off my chest, you understand? I didn't go near any stupid bull. I'm killing them every day of the week, for God's sake. You think I want to do it on my holidays as well?'

'How do you feel about killing them every day?'

John put on a poncy voice. 'How do you feel about killing, Mr Kilroy? Would you like to have a study session with Mr Glynn? A heart-to-heart? A mutual analysis? An exchange of innermost feelings?' His voice changed abruptly. 'You can fuck off with your feelings, you sad bastard. You're the one who needs psychoanalysis. Does it make you feel powerful to have me locked up like this? Does it?'

The change in John's tone alarmed the bullock, who moved away from him and returned to the manger. The barrel began to overflow. Malachy pulled out the hose and slid it into one of the boxes across the way. The unfed bullock moaned again. John flew against the bars, alarming both the beasts, sending them lunging in opposite directions.

'You're making a nuisance of yourself,' said Malachy. 'They're not doing you any harm. Stop hassling them.'

'Everybody knows you're weird, Malachy. The way you treat these bullocks as if they were racehorses. Maybe that's what you'd prefer to be doing, eh? Down here in your fancy stable block. The local squire, riding out every morning, all the common folk doffing their hats.'

'We're getting away from the subject,' said Malachy. 'If you seriously want to get out of here, you'd better start doing some thinking.'

John kicked the partition savagely. Every beast in the place jumped, and Malachy jerked the hose so the water slopped on to the floor.

'What do you want? A confession? All right. I did it. Now let me out of here!'

'I want to know why, John. If I knew why then maybe we could talk about it and—'

'I didn't fucking do it!' John screamed. 'You don't have any right to keep me here!'

Malachy moved the hose on again. The bullock in the next box roared like a foghorn.

'Why don't you feed the fucker? Shut him up?'

'He's fasting,' said Malachy.

'You're killing him today?'

Malachy nodded.

'And what about my charming cell-mate here? When's his turn?'

'Depends. Soon. Maybe tomorrow.'

'And is there any particular reason you chose him to room with me?'

'Don't be ridiculous, John.'

'There's only one person here who's being ridiculous, and it isn't me.'

Malachy walked away along the passage. 'Do you like rashers and sausages? Fried eggs?'

John jumped for the bars and climbed up them, wedging his fingers into the small space between the top rail and the ceiling. 'You're going to pay for this, you wanker! You'll never get away with it!'

*   *   *

Sarah's getaway plan came to nothing. She didn't sleep until the dawn was greying the window, and the mental alarm she had set failed to go off. The first she knew of the day was when Mairead knocked on her door and came in.

'Sleep well?' she asked.

Sarah groaned. 'What time is it?'

'Can you do me a favour?'

'What kind of favour?'

'Can you watch the shop for a few hours? It's Gerry Fitz's funeral.'

Sarah managed to focus on the clock. 'I meant to leave today,' she said.

'Well, you didn't say anything. I thought you'd changed your mind. Or that Malachy had changed it for you.'

For a moment, Sarah couldn't think straight. Then everything came flooding back, all at once. 'No. It's just . . .'

She tried to disentangle reality from dream. It wasn't easy.

'You could go tomorrow instead. It's late, now, anyway. What's the rush?'

Sarah slumped back down on to the bed. 'What time are you going?'

Malachy phoned Seanie Walsh before he started on the breakfast.

'I might be interested in those weanlings of yours, after all,' he said. 'If the price was right.'

'It would be,' said Seanie. 'Isn't it always?'

'In the end, maybe,' said Malachy. 'Never in the beginning.'

'Well, you'd have to look at them first, sure.'

'I don't need to, Seanie. I know your beasts and how they're reared. What are you asking?'

They haggled for ten minutes, and finally struck a deal.

'It'd suit me to collect them later this morning, if it suited you.'

Seanie was surprised. He usually delivered the stock himself to Malachy's yards. But he was willing to lend his trailer and get the weanlings loaded, as long as Malachy had the cash.

Daniel O'Dea brought the latest news to Sarah in the shop.

'Someone tried to have a go at Micky Mac's bull last night.'

Sarah tried to feign astonishment. 'Not another one?'

Daniel shook his head. 'Never got near him. They found his knife beside the gate, though. Getting serious, so it is.'

Some slight unease nagged at the back of Sarah's mind. Daniel put his sweets on the counter and handed her a grubby fifty-pound note. 'I hear you made a bit of an election speech over in Burke's last night?'

'Oh, that,' said Sarah, hunting for change. 'I suppose I'll never live it down.'

'You will,' said Daniel. He left, hurrying to catch the funeral mass. Sarah tried to remember what it was that had been worrying her, but all she could think of was John, imprisoned in the slaughterer's yard.

Malachy wrapped the breakfast in tin foil so that it would fit through the bars. John reached out to take it, but grabbed Malachy's wrist instead and yanked his arm into the box until his shoulder rammed up against the bars. Malachy yelled with pain, and Goggles crammed himself fearfully into the far corner.

John twisted the arm. 'Let me out, you fucker.'

'How can I, when you've got my arm?'

'We'll work that one out.' He twisted again and the

foil-wrapped packet fell among the shavings. 'Are you going to let me go?'

Malachy got his other arm through, grabbed hold of a handful of John's hair and wrenched his head back. John twisted harder on the arm. Malachy swore and spoke through clenched teeth. 'There's no need for any of this, you stupid little sod. Why can't you understand? We don't have to be enemies.'

'Then let me out, and we can talk about it.'

'Talk first.'

'Fuck off!' John dug his nails into Malachy's wrist. Malachy yanked his head hard against the bars. It didn't make him let go, but his hold relaxed enough for Malachy to heave his shoulders away and pull John's hands up to the edge of the partition wall. Then he released John's hair and pushed him in the face until he let go of his arm.

'That was a stupid thing to do,' he said. 'I would have thought you had more brains.'

'What gave you that idea?' said John.

Malachy laughed, and John couldn't keep the twitches of a grin from creeping into the corners of his mouth.

'Listen, John,' said Malachy. 'I understand how you feel.'

'You do in your arse,' said John.

'Then tell me. Tell me what made you do it?'

'Do what?' said John.

Malachy dropped a bottle of spring water through the bars and walked away. The hot foil packet hit him on the back of the neck and fell with a soft plop on to the flags.

Sarah watched the hearse pass along the main street in front of the shop, followed by a long cortège of cars. She had closed the door and turned off the lights, as Mairead had asked, and she was about to open up again when she realised that she couldn't stand any more waiting around.

Instead of opening the door she locked it, and hung up the BACK IN FIVE MINUTES sign.

Eileen was vaguely relieved to discover that there were none of John's clothes in the washing-machine that morning. She didn't notice that his car wasn't in the yard. She just assumed that he had come in late again and was still asleep in bed. But when Matty came in for a cup of coffee he said, 'Has John gone back to Athlone?'

'I don't think so. Why?'

'His car's gone.'

'He'd hardly be gone back. They're saying on the news there's no work for them in the plants, on account of the pickets. No cattle coming in. Maybe he's already out driving around?'

'Maybe,' said Matty. 'You wouldn't know with that one.'

There was no sign of Malachy at the house, and Sarah cycled on down through the trees to the buildings. The van wasn't there, but she could see that the bales around John's car hadn't been moved. Her heart sank. She had hoped it would all be over.

The fasting bullock heard her footsteps in the yard and bellowed to her.

'Hello? Who's there?'

It was John's voice, calling from inside the building. Sarah didn't answer.

'Help! I'm a fucking prisoner! Someone help me!'

Sarah held her breath. She had a sudden memory of putting her foot into a wasp's nest in the woods one day. When she saw what she had done, she had felt exactly as she did now.

John began to kick the partition. His voice was rising towards hysteria. 'Get me out of here! Help!'

24

'Hello?'

'In here! Get me out!'

Sarah peered into the building and waited for her eyes to acclimatise to the gloom.

'Here! Down here!'

She walked along the passage between the boxes, every nerve on edge.

'It's yourself, missus,' said John. 'Have you come to let me out?'

'Where's Malachy?' said Sarah.

'How the fuck should I know? He has me starved here. He's out of his mind, missus. You have to help me get out.'

The hungry bullock roared again, and John flew at the bars, sending it leaping clumsily away.

'Look at me!' he said. 'Are you involved in this? I'm up to my knees in shit here. Is this what you wanted?'

It wasn't what Sarah wanted. It never had been. But she was afraid as well. She kept her distance from the bars.

'It is, isn't it?' John went on. 'I heard you last night, what you were saying. About what you'd like to do to me. You're behind all this, aren't you?'

'Don't be ridiculous. I didn't mean any of that. I was just spouting off.'

'Then what am I doing here?'

Sarah didn't answer. John kicked the boards again, savagely. 'Tell me!'

'I don't know what you're doing here. It was—'

'Malachy's idea, was it? I heard him as well. About handing over the kids to him when you were finished with them.' He turned and paced to the opposite partition wall, then kicked that as well.

'You got yourself into this, you know,' said Sarah. 'Why did you kill those bulls?'

John gave a dramatic sigh. 'Oh, God,' he said. 'Not you as well. I didn't kill anything or anyone, missus. All I know is I went fishing last night and got chased across a field, and look at me now!'

'You did kill them, John. I saw you twice, remember? I saw you in your car both nights.'

'But there's an explanation for that. I go fishing every night.'

Sarah shook her head. 'There's no point in lying to me. I was there, remember? I saw you.'

John fell silent and prodded the bottom of the partition with his toe. Goggles was appreciating the softening mood, and wandered over to stand beside him and look at Sarah through the bars. John edged around him and came to the door.

'I can't keep calling you missus,' he said.

'No, you can't. Especially since I'm not.'

She saw John make a mental adjustment and wished she hadn't said it. There was a certain type of man who assumed that any woman who wasn't married was lonely and feeble-minded, and subject to their charms. It was an attitude that drove her demented.

'Well?' said John. 'You have my name.'

For some reason Sarah didn't want John to know her real name. 'It's Anne.'

'Nice name,' said John.

'Don't bother with flattery. It won't help you.'

'Fine, fine,' said John. 'But all I was going to say is that you're a smart woman. I know you're not part of this mad scheme.'

The cage boxes were nothing like the cells she and her fellow campaigners had occupied in Oxfordshire, but Sarah knew the frustration and claustrophobia John must be feeling.

'I mean,' he went on, 'I'm not your responsibility, am I? I'm not Malachy's responsibility. What you're doing here is criminal, you know?'

He was right, of course. Not only was it criminal, but confining someone and trying to elicit a confession was playing by exactly the same dirty rules that the police did. Where was the sense in it?

'I'll make a deal with you, Anne,' said John. 'If you let me out now, I swear I'll never tell anyone what happened here. Just give me my car keys and I'll be back in Athlone before dinner-time. You never have to see me again.'

Sarah glanced at the padlock. Even if she agreed to let him out she couldn't. She didn't have the key. But John had detected her ambivalence.

'If you don't let me out there's going to be trouble. Sooner or later it's going to come to light, that two people kept me locked up here. Falsely imprisoned me.'

Goggles was edging over towards John as he spoke, eager to be a part of what was going on, even if he didn't know what it was. But John waved his arms and said, 'Whoosha! Get out of it!' and the bullock moved away again, back to the manger.

'Do you have the key?' asked John.

Sarah was aware that she was being wooed.

'It doesn't matter if you haven't. It's easy enough to break an old padlock. A bolt-cutter will do it, or a crowbar, or a decent hacksaw. There's bound to be tools around somewhere.'

Sarah glanced around, and John knew he had won her over. 'Good girl, Anne,' he said.

'I'm not a good girl,' said Sarah, caustically. 'I'm a full-grown woman with a mind of my own. If you have any desire to get out of here you had better not try and patronise me again, understand?'

John put up his hands in a gesture of submission. 'Point taken,' he said. 'Message received and understood.'

Sarah walked along the aisle and into the tack room. The sides were boarded to the ceiling and John couldn't see her, but he could hear her rummaging around and moving pieces of heavy metal.

'There's a kind of a—' She stopped, hearing a noise outside.

John heard it as well. 'Anne!' he called, urgently. 'Forget it. He's back.'

The van pulled into the yard and Sarah threw the tools back into the box and came out.

'Come back later!' John said. 'Wait till he goes out again.'

Sarah passed him by and went towards the doors.

'Please, Anne!' he hissed.

She didn't turn back.

Malachy saw the bicycle as he turned into the yard, and his heart pitched with joy. He jumped out of the van and met Sarah coming out of the coach-house. He wanted to hug her, but her face showed that she wouldn't be receptive.

'You came back,' said Malachy. 'Thanks, Sarah.'

'I didn't exactly come back.' Sarah nodded towards the cage boxes. 'What are you going to do with him?'

Malachy closed the gate of the yard and dropped the ramp

of the trailer. 'I don't know. It isn't exactly working out as I had planned.'

The weanlings called anxiously, but they didn't come out. The boldest of them poked a nose around the back of the trailer and pulled it back in again.

'What if we're wrong, Sarah? What if he was just fishing?'

Abruptly, all the images that Sarah had seen earlier in the week came spilling back. The car parked in the boreen. The dying bull. The car again, hurtling along the main road, John's face inside it smeared with blood. The gory mess in the cattle crush. A minute ago she had been about to release him back into the world. Had he really succeeded in seducing her so easily?

'No. I saw him, remember? I saw the car. It was definitely him.'

Malachy thought she sounded shocked.

'Are you all right?'

'Yes. I'm just a bit confused, that's all. I'm not sure I know what's right and what's wrong. I think you've bitten off more than you can chew.'

Malachy looked abject. 'You can say that again. But what's going to happen if we let him out? He practically pulled my arm out of its socket this morning. He's a hard character, Sarah. I'm not sure that he would necessarily stop at killing bulls.'

Sarah stared at him as the meaning behind his words sank home. The fact that the same thought had occurred to her, the morning she saw John driving back from his night's work, made it even worse. Her spine tingled, and she turned to face the coach-house, half expecting to see John framed in the doorway, wielding an axe.

'Maybe we ought to forget about it,' said Malachy. 'Turn him over to the guards.'

'What's the penalty for killing a bull?'

'I don't know. Not that much, I'd imagine. It's probably covered in some ancient law that was written in the 1700s. But they'd realise he was sick in the head, wouldn't they? They'd help him?'

Sarah shrugged. 'You have more confidence in them than I do. And what's the penalty for falsely imprisoning someone?'

The weanlings came bolting down the trailer ramp as though they were making a daring getaway, then stood in the yard, looking bewildered.

'I don't know,' said Malachy.

Eileen looked into John's room. He made his own bed every morning, but she had the feeling that he hadn't been in it the night before. His clothes were still there, folded on the other bed beside his bag. She felt inside the bed and lifted the pillow. There was a pair of gloves underneath it, slightly damp, and they had left a nasty pinky-brown stain all over her sheets. She took them out and hung them over the back of the chair. It wasn't like John to do something as messy as that.

Perhaps she was expecting too much of him. Nobody was perfect, after all.

Sarah pushed the bike along the rutted track and Malachy walked with her. The leaves on the old trees were dancing with the wind, and Sarah stopped to look at them.

'You live in a beautiful place,' she said.

'I do,' said Malachy. 'But it's too much for one.' He glanced at her. 'The work, I mean.'

She nodded.

'Not just the work,' he said.

Sarah didn't look at him, but she couldn't escape the feelings that were besieging them both. It was an awful shame he had to be a butcher.

*   *   *

The wind was against her face on the cycle home and she was tired and red-faced by the time she got back to the shop. Mairead hadn't returned, yet. There was no knowing how long she'd be gone.

Business was slack. To pass the time, Sarah began to leaf through a heap of newspapers that Mairead had put aside for recycling. She was amazed by what she found. Almost every issue had an article about one aspect of the cattle industry or another. The French refused to buy British beef because of BSE, and the British then discovered that the French were feeding their cattle on processed sewage. The Americans were getting heavy with Europe, threatening a trade war if the Europeans refused to allow imports of their hormone-treated meat. And a new report found intensive cattle farming to be the number one cause of global warming. Sarah fetched a pair of scissors and began to collect clippings. The whole business was going from mad to worse. If it hadn't been so macabre, she would have laughed.

25

When John didn't arrive home for dinner, Eileen began to get anxious. She got on the phone to the mother of one of his friends asking if she'd seen him. Matty heard her.

'For the love of God, leave the boy alone, will you?' he said.

'But it isn't like him to stay out and not come back for his dinner.'

'He's grown up, Eileen. He can do what he wants. With any luck he'll be sowing a few wild oats and getting on with his life. It isn't right, him to be sitting at home all the time. It isn't natural.'

She deferred to him, and made no more enquiries. But her mind was no easier.

John pissed into the shavings in the corner of the box, beside the door. When he had finished the bullock went over and sniffed at it, then lifted its head and curled its top lip, analysing the scent. It turned and looked at John, and he laughed.

'What do you think, lad? Am I the Man?'

The bullock walked cautiously over to where he was sitting in the manger.

'Get away,' said John. But he didn't wave his arms or shout, and the bullock came to rest nearby, in an easy kind of truce.

*   *   *

The newspapers were absorbing, but it was difficult for Sarah to keep her mind away from the problem of John's imprisonment. From time to time her eyes lost their focus, or the scissors came to a halt mid-clip. John's bloodthirsty behaviour was like a storm, trying to tug her mind from its anchors. All that she believed was being challenged.

She had a deep-seated distrust of the institutions of the state, and couldn't countenance turning anyone over to the police. Besides, she had been there herself. She was, in a sense, an accomplice.

She mulled it over. She could say she was under the impression that she was participating in a citizens' arrest. She could say that she didn't realise what the butcher's intentions were. But what would happen then? There would be more of their foxy questioning; more of their derision. There would be a court case. She would have to turn up for that, to give evidence. She would have to give addresses wherever she went, become entangled in the machinery of policing, enmeshed in the dangerous web of state security. She couldn't stand that.

The trouble was, she didn't trust Malachy either. He was, in his own way, infected by the same madness that set John on the rampage. But when she tried to imagine a sane, humane solution, she came up against a brick wall.

The circling thoughts were frustrating and exhausting. Above all, Sarah wanted to disassociate herself from the whole business. But, although many would have disagreed with her interpretation of the words, Sarah had never been one to shirk her moral responsibility. That was why she did what she did. Whether she liked it or not, she felt obliged to stay and see the sordid business through to the end.

Just once, somewhat half-heartedly, she called on Duncan for help. He was there somewhere, she knew it. But all that came into her mind was the candle-lit raft, floating further and further away from her on the dark, oily river.

John was entirely confident that the hippy woman would return at the first opportunity and break him out. Despite this, he was still suffering from a mild apprehension, and he was light-headed and buzzy with hunger. It made his mind race and he found that he was quite enjoying the sensation.

After several failed attempts, he succeeded in getting astride the bullock. It was frightened and perplexed, and went bumbling around the box for a few minutes, banging against the walls. But there was no wild rodeo stuff at all, and the worst John had to worry about was keeping his legs from getting crushed against the walls.

Before long, the bullock got used to the idea and calmed down, and by the time the neighbour's roaring alerted John to the fact that someone was coming, it was so relaxed that it was snuffling hopefully around in the manger among the hayseeds. John slipped down and approached the bars. He hoped that it would be the woman, but it wasn't. It didn't matter. She would come.

Malachy went into the empty box.

'Have you come with our pardon, my good man?' said John.

Malachy opened the flask that he was carrying and began to pour milky coffee into the plastic lid. 'Everything all right?'

'Oh, splendid,' said John. 'Ferdinand and I are having a right royal time of it, aren't we, Ferdie?'

'Coffee?'

'Rather.' It was a voice that he and some of the other lads had developed, to liven up the atmosphere in the slaughter hall. 'Never knew the accommodation on Death Row was so desirable.'

Malachy handed the cup through the bars. John made a mock lunge for his arm, and Malachy jumped away, spilling the hot coffee all over his hand. He swore. John laughed.

'Your nerves are getting to you, old chap. Maybe you need a tonic?'

As Malachy shook the scalded hand, John said, 'Where's modom?'

Malachy glared silently.

'Are you two shagging each other?' John put a hand on the bullock's withers. ''Cos we're not. Not yet.'

'Do you want this fecking coffee or not?' said Malachy.

John reached up for the cup. 'Ah, service isn't what it used to be, is it, Ferdinand? How long has that chap next door been waiting for his steak and kidney pie, eh?'

'I brought you some sandwiches,' said Malachy. He handed through a package, a bunch of bananas, and two Mars Bars.

'Good show. We like Mars Bars, don't we, Ferdinand?'

The bullock chose that moment to walk up to the bars, and John laughed. 'See? Ever since Ferdinand lost his tentacles he's been partial to a bit of chocolate, haven't you, dear? They say it's a cure for all sorts of ills. I don't suppose it'll help him with that one, though. Never heard of them regenerating, have you?'

Malachy poured himself a mug of coffee. 'Have you been thinking about what I was saying earlier?'

'Of course!' said John. 'We've been mulling it over all day, haven't we, dear? Not a lot else to do in here, is there?'

'And have you come to any conclusions?'

'Let me see now. What was the question again?'

The bullock was sniffing at the bananas. John watched it out of the corner of his eye.

'You seem to be enjoying yourself, anyway,' said Malachy.

'Oh, yeah.' John's tone changed instantly. 'I'm dancing a fucking jig in here. Up to my arse in shite. Who wouldn't?'

'I want to let you out,' said Malachy. 'But you have to co-operate.'

'Yeah, I figured that out,' said John. 'You want me to make a full confession and blub all over the place like the hard cases in the movies, don't you? Bare my soul, see the reason for my sins, repent them all in a massive, cathartic demonstration of the triumphs of modern psychobabble.'

'Come on, John,' said Malachy.

The bullock was licking the bananas. John watched it, surprised by his own reaction. He wanted them, but he didn't want to take them away.

'Oh, it's all right. We can do it, can't we, Ferdinand? We've been rehearsing all afternoon. He wants to be let off the hook, too, you see. We came to a decision. We want to cave in before we get to the next stage in the coercion process. Like that poor chap next door.'

'Just talk straight, all right? Maybe we can come to an agreement.'

'I'll talk straight,' said John. 'Will you listen straight?'

'I will,' said Malachy.

'I . . . didn't . . . kill . . . any . . . bulls. Get it?'

Malachy shook his head. Goggles was chewing on the bananas, making a gluey mess. The bullock in the next box was watching. It moaned despairingly. John restrained a laugh.

'Listen, John,' said Malachy. 'I think you need help.'

'I need help all right,' said John. 'Preferably a JCB with a front loader and a chain.'

'I know you killed those bulls. You know I know. You must have been in an awful state to want to do something like that.'

'I must have been in some awful state, all right. Especially since I can't remember any of it.'

He unwrapped a bar and took a bite. Goggles had finished

the bananas and was looking for more. John offered him the bar. He took it eagerly, wrapper and all.

'Look at him!' said John. 'He's just swallowed the whole thing as if it was a Malteser!'

Malachy felt uncomfortably like a parent, trying to talk sense to an intransigent teenager. It disturbed him that John was so calm, so much in possession of himself. It seemed that there was nothing more to be achieved.

'Have a think about it,' he said. 'We can talk again later.'

He picked up the flask. 'Do you want the last bit of coffee?'

John held out the cup and Malachy poured out the dregs of the flask. This time John did throw it in his face. It was barely hot by then, and although it stung Malachy's eyes, it didn't do any damage. He walked out. John flung the other Mars Bar after him.

'Let me out of here, you sick fucker!'

The pitch of his voice reminded the weanlings in the yard that they were still missing their mothers, and they joined him in a plaintive lament.

26

Mairead came home, fairly well jarred, in the late afternoon.

'You're famous,' she said. 'Everybody's talking about what you said in the pub last night. Mairead O'Malley's mad sister.'

'Oh, God,' said Sarah. 'Will they be getting up a lynch mob?'

Mairead began to sweep Sarah's cuttings off the counter. 'Not at all. Most people think it's funny.'

'Most?' said Sarah.

One of Mairead's homeopath customers came in, and Sarah gathered up her papers. She ought, she knew, to have gone back down to Malachy's yard, but she didn't. She just couldn't face it.

'Mairead O'Malley's mad sister.' The words rumbled around her head like a mantra. Some obscene fate seemed to have drawn her into this havoc and she could see no way out of it. If, or when, John returned to society with his story, no amount of persuasion was going to get her off the hook. She had incriminated herself all along the line.

Malachy slid open the door of the next box and went in. The bullock moved around restlessly, expecting food. Malachy had none. He got behind the bullock and guided it towards the open door. As soon as it saw the way was clear it trotted along the passageway and out into the yard.

'A last-minute reprieve?' said John.

Malachy said nothing, but followed the bullock out.

'Perhaps not. Goodbye, Bertie. It was nice knowing you!'

Goggles called to his neighbour, and the faintest twinge of something like sorrow caught John off guard. The poor old hungry sod. He had no idea what was about to hit him.

Malachy was on edge during the whole process; afraid that someone might wander in and discover John. The weanlings were his watchdogs. If anyone were to come as far as the bungalow, the odd shout that John might give would be masked by their cries. But no one called. Not even Sarah.

Malachy began to fear that she wasn't coming back. He had assumed that she would; that she felt as much a part of what was happening here as he did. But, as the afternoon dragged on, he realised that nothing had been said. She might be anywhere. On the road to Dublin. On the ferry. On her way back to the Glen of the Downs to join her idealistic friends.

When the work in the slaughterhouse was finished, Malachy went home and dropped into an armchair beside the cold, empty range. The phone rang twice, and each time he was certain that it must be Sarah. But the first time it was Oliver, who was running short on popular cuts, and the second time it was the deli in Galway, who had been expecting their delivery that morning. Malachy made promises to them both, then returned to his melancholy thoughts. His spirits were sinking dangerously. If he didn't move soon he risked getting stuck.

It had happened before. On several occasions he had been ambushed by a depression so severe that he had been unable to get out of bed. Each time he had succeeded in dragging himself out of it, driven by the needs of the beasts in his care. He lived in dread that the next time he would fail.

John was huddled in the manger when Malachy went in to feed the cattle. He glared out silently, his eyes burning in the last of the natural light.

'You're a sicko, Malachy. You'll never get away with this.'

Malachy sighed. He didn't feel in much of a position to argue. 'You're probably right, John.'

'You know I am. Everybody else knows it, too. You should forget about this, you know. It's a mad whim you took. You can open that door now and it would all be over.'

Malachy pushed hay through into the manger.

'Wouldn't you prefer that?' John went on. 'To be rid of me? Aren't you afraid that my dad'll come looking for me? Or that someone will just wander into the yard one day and find me here?'

Malachy was afraid of both those things.

'I won't tell anyone you did this. I'm not particularly fond of the cops, you know. I don't want them sniffing around my business.'

Malachy finished with the hay and turned on the hose.

'I won't say anything to anyone,' John went on. 'People like you in town, even though they think you're a bit weird. I wouldn't do anything to upset that. I wouldn't even be around all that much.'

Malachy said nothing, but John could see that he was wavering. His shoulders were hunched as he stood over the hose and watched Goggles drink.

'She wants you to let me out, you know,' he said. 'Your one. Doesn't she?'

The bullock's capacity for liquid seemed infinite. The hose couldn't fill the barrel fast enough.

'I wouldn't touch her, you know.'

The suggestion, and the image that came with it, filled Malachy's mind with fury.

'You were thinking of it then, were you?'

'No, no,' said John. 'Of course not. Of course I wasn't.'

'Then why did you say it?'

'I thought you might be worried, that's all. Since you think I killed those bulls.'

'You did kill those bulls, you little shit-head. And you're not getting out of here till you come clean.'

Goggles returned to the hay and Malachy moved across the aisle. 'Don't ever mention her again in that way, you understand? Don't even think about her.'

His tone frightened John. Not for the first time, it occurred to him that he might be in real danger.

'I won't, Malachy,' he said. 'No, she's nice. I mean, I could see that you would respect her.'

'Shut up about her now, you hear? Just shut up.'

John shut up. Malachy finished watering and went out into the yard. The weanlings stared at him as he scattered hay around on the cobbles for them. He ought to have put them behind the gates in the coach-house, but he didn't have the energy to do it now. They could stay where they were until the morning.

The bungalow was a sorry place to return to, especially now that it had known the presence of Sarah. Malachy hated being in it. He knew he ought to find something for John to eat, and for himself as well. But the best he could manage was a handful of Mars Bars.

Sarah took a long, hot bath. She washed her hair and spent twenty minutes with Mairead's hairbrush, working at the tangles. Every time her thoughts returned to John, she felt a stabbing sensation in her diaphragm, as though someone were sticking pins into her effigy somewhere. She had no idea where to turn.

If you believed, as she did, that the police were the executive arm of a repressive authority, then you had to come up with some alternative way of dealing with errant souls. Somehow, Sarah had always assumed that she would know what to do if the situation arose. But now that it had, she didn't.

At the tree camp, there had been a spate of thefts. A meeting had been called, at which the perpetrator had been asked, anonymously, to return the stolen articles and thereby return the community to peace and security. It hadn't produced results, and after a while a woman was found in possession of some of the stolen things. She had been asked to leave.

That had been easy. Her behaviour was an extension of the world outside the tree settlement. Her malevolence had merely been removed from their midst and returned to where it rightfully belonged: among the avaricious consumers out there. But this case was entirely different. There was no other world to which John could safely be banished.

There was no doubt in Sarah's mind that his behaviour was the result of the corrupt society that had spawned him. If the tree was diseased, how could the fruit be otherwise? But how you healed the rot once it had set in so deeply she had no idea at all.

When she was dry and dressed she phoned Theresa to ask for some advice. But Theresa was having problems of her own. Mike, it seemed, had met someone else.

'Maybe it's not too serious?' said Sarah.

But, according to Theresa, it was. They had gone to the Sai Baba ashram in India to get married. She was coming to terms with trying to run the farm on her own.

Sarah commiserated, angling for a way to get round to her own concerns, but Theresa's emotions had too much momentum. She asked Sarah if she would consider coming back to help out.

'I might,' she said. 'It's just that I have other things on my mind just now.'

Theresa didn't ask what they were. For the moment, at least, Sarah was left to struggle away on her own.

John lay in the manger. The bullock had eaten all the available hay, and was snuffling around John's blankets, trying to get at the bits he was lying on. John gave it a Mars Bar. It drooled chocolatey slobber all over his foot. He wiped it off with a handful of hay, which the bullock then happily ate.

Later, as John lay waiting for sleep, the bullock began to chew the cud.

'Not fair,' said John. 'You get to eat your bars twice.'

Sarah dreamed that she was in a broad, wooded valley. She was walking along a path between the trees, so narrow and winding that she couldn't see more than a few feet ahead. She came upon a small, ghostly figure, dressed in a grey cowl and cloak, crawling on hands and knees along the path ahead of her. She knew that it was Duncan's ghost.

Malachy stepped out of the shadows and stood in front of the ghost. Sarah was terrified that he was going to kill it, and she tried to call out, but her voice was trapped in a cave up on the hillside and couldn't get out. The butcher picked up the ghost. It was as small and light as a balloon. It kept trying to float away, but Malachy held it to his breast and beckoned Sarah to come closer. She crept forward, terrified of what she might see. But when the ghost turned its head to look at her, it was a newborn baby with a smile as beautiful and as radiant as the sun.

She woke with that sense of expansion and excitement that big dreams bring, and sat up in bed. A pinky-grey dawn was looking in through the window. Sarah wrote down the dream in Mairead's bedside dream book, since she didn't have one of her own. Afterwards she worried that Mairead would mind, or, worse, that she would find the dream and apply some profound Jungian interpretation to it. Or some profound Jungian interpretation that differed from her own.

She sat up in bed and reached for her rollies. Mairead would kill her for smoking in her bed. She decided to get up instead, and went downstairs in Mairead's dressing-gown.

That blackbird was singing again on the other side of the alley. Malachy was in Sarah's thoughts, and she reached for the newspaper in an effort to push him out.

The book began to bubble again in her consciousness. She thought back to the beginning of this bizarre episode of her life: the calf on the dump, the mountain with the spike, the car in the boreen, the bulls, dying and dead. But wherever her thoughts led her, Malachy walked into them. Every recent memory was inhabited by him. She went over to the window and looked out, but he was still there. The dawn, the singing bird, the distant roaring of the weir: it all seemed to be an extension of the numinous dream. Duncan's poor ghost, her ailing animus, was being transformed into something new and beautiful. And Malachy, the butcher, was the catalyst.

John woke to the sound of Malachy moving around in the open end of the coach-house. He looked at his watch. Five thirty. The guy was definitely mad. He turned back over in the manger and tried to sleep again, but he had spoiled the illusion of comfort by waking.

The gates scraped on the flagged floor as Malachy penned the weanlings in. John sat up, and at the same moment the bullock got to its feet, as though the two of them were joined

by some sort of instinct. Together they went over to the door
and looked through the bars. Malachy had tied up the gates
and was throwing hay over them.

John called along the passageway. 'Er, excuse me. Room
service?'

Malachy approached between the cage boxes. 'Morning,
John. Sleep well?'

'Excellent. Have you got my morning paper? Have you
polished my shoes?'

Malachy handed him in a packet of breakfast and, while
John was eating it, he took round the hay and water.
Goggles muscled up against the bars, waiting for his share.
But Malachy left him out.

'Oh, oh,' said John. 'Your turn for the third degree. What
are you in for? I never asked.'

He made a show of listening at the bullock's mouth, then
nodded. 'Sounds like a trumped-up charge to me. I didn't
do it, either, you know. But there's no judge or jury in
this place.'

Malachy turned off the water and began sweeping the
passageway between the boxes.

'Any word in town?' said John.

'About what?'

'About me. Are they sending out the search parties
yet?'

'Not a peep out of anyone,' said Malachy. 'They're all glad
to be rid of you, I'd say.'

'I don't know what a man has to do to get some attention
around here.'

Malachy put down the broom and took a muck fork
and a barrow to the box that the bullock had vacated the
previous day.

'Is that what you were after? Attention?'

John ignored him. 'Will we be getting a new neighbour,
then?'

'Some time,' said Malachy. 'I have a couple to bring in.'

'That'll be fun, won't it, Ferdinand? Someone else to talk to. That last chap was . . . well, to be quite honest he was a bit of a bore. I mean, we're all innocent, aren't we? But methinks he did protest too much. Did he die prettily? Did he kill out to your satisfaction? Will he make a good bit of steak, Malachy?'

Malachy didn't answer, but continued to heap the wet shavings into the barrow. He was sweating, using the work as an escape, a purge for his contaminated spirits.

'You never answered my question yesterday,' said John.

'What question was that?'

'About yourself and your woman. Are you an item?'

Malachy stopped working and leaned on the fork, looking down at his feet.

'Is it a taboo subject or something?' said John.

Malachy sat on the edge of the manger and wiped his forehead with his sleeve.

'Why don't you tell me first, John? Have you got a girlfriend?'

John hesitated. He didn't have a problem with women. He knew that. It wasn't that he didn't have the same luck as the other lads did. It was just that he didn't try as hard. And he didn't try as hard because he couldn't really see the point.

He had scored in the Athlone nightclubs a few times, without too much difficulty. But the result on every occasion had been somehow unsatisfactory. All the drunken fumblings had embarrassed him. He had done what was required of him, but he hadn't made any connection with any of the women. They might as well have been in different rooms for all the real contact there was between them. After each occasion, he hadn't even been sure that he would recognise the woman again if he saw her in the street. It all seemed senseless.

But you didn't talk about that kind of thing with the lads. You just went for it and you were lucky or you weren't.

'I get my end away, if that's what you mean,' he said.

Malachy thought about that for a minute. 'And is that enough for you?' he said.

John gave a well-practised, smutty grin. 'I don't like to miss the All-Ireland finals,' he said.

Malachy shook his head, then gestured towards the bullock. 'We're like him, you and me. We're redundant males.'

'I'm not redundant,' said John. 'Though I might be soon if you don't let me out of here.'

'I didn't mean that. There's thousands of people out there going to work every day and they're still redundant. We don't have a real purpose as far as the species is concerned, you know? Like these guys. They're surplus. They're not needed by the herd because the AI man or the fancy pure-bred bull does it all.'

'Well I'm not one of these guys,' said John. 'If you put it like that, I'm one of the bulls.'

'Are you?' said Malachy. 'Are you sure?'

'Damn right, I am.'

'I don't think people are like that, though. Or maybe not all people. I'm not. I need something more. Don't you ever feel like that? Wouldn't you like to be settled with someone? Have kids? Be part of some bigger picture, not just out for yourself?'

John shrugged. 'Why would I want to get myself hitched up like that? Why buy a cow when you can get the milk for nothing?'

'Maybe you're right,' said Malachy. 'But I know it's not milk I'm after.'

'Ah,' said John. 'You're the man who wants to own the cow.'

Malachy laughed despite himself. 'But it has to be the right one,' he said. 'Not just any old cow, you know?'

John said nothing for a while, but something was dawning inside him, and before he had even thought about it, it came out.

'Maybe it's not about finding the right woman, Malachy. Maybe it's about being the right man.'

The words sent a holy shiver through Malachy's soul. 'Yes,' he said. 'That's it. That's it. And that's why you did it, isn't it?'

His own truth besieged John, and he took refuge. 'Did what?'

'No, no, John. Don't run away from this. There was some kind of integrity in what you did, or an attempt at it, anyway. To be more than a slaughterman. To meet the beast on its own terms.'

'Don't be ridiculous.' But John's voice was thin. It betrayed him.

'But the bulls wouldn't play, would they? They weren't man enough.'

'You're cracked, Malachy. Leave it alone, will you?'

'I understand, though. Don't you see? It makes sense to me.'

But Malachy's understanding was more terrifying to John than his ignorance. 'You understand nothing! You're a sad, fucked-up wanker! If you want truth, I'll give you truth. You're not getting your leg over, and this shit, keeping me locked up like this, turns you on, doesn't it? You get off on it, don't you?'

'Don't, John. Don't keep denying it.'

'Is she impressed, eh? Your hippy friend? Does she think you're a stud?'

'That's enough.'

'It's not half enough.' John threw himself at the bars and Malachy shrank back instinctively.

'Let me out. For Christ's sake, let me out. I can't stand being in here any more. It's making me ill!'

Malachy jumped down and walked out of the building, leaving the muck-barrow and the fork behind him.

27

There was supposed to be someone on duty in the garda barracks between ten and one every morning, but when Eileen arrived there at eleven the place was deserted. She did some shopping in the supermarket, then wandered in to the wholefood shop to pass the time.

Mairead had gone to chase up a man who had promised to paint her shopfront, and Sarah was at the counter.

'I was looking for the guards,' said Eileen. 'There's never anyone in there. They're short-staffed these days, I suppose. Like everybody else.'

'Out looking for bull-killers, I hope,' said Sarah.

'I hope so too,' said Eileen. 'Whoever done that should be behind bars if you ask me.'

'They should, indeed. What did you want with the guards?'

'My son John has gone missing.'

Sarah locked the muscles in her face.

'Matty says he's old enough to look after himself and I shouldn't be poking my nose into his business, but it isn't like him, you see. He's left all his clothes in his room. He wouldn't have gone back to Athlone without telling me.'

'You never know with young people these days,' said Sarah. 'They can be very thoughtless.'

'I suppose they can. But I thought there was no harm in

asking the guards. I mean, what if he had an accident or something?'

'You would have heard, surely?'

'You never know, though, do you?'

She wandered around the shop and picked up a packet of pumpkin seeds. 'What do you do with these?'

'Just eat them. Or fry them. Or grind them up in a nut loaf. Anything you like, really.'

'I might try a few in a fruit cake,' said Eileen.

She went back to the station at twelve o'clock, and found Garda Murray sitting in the car outside, eating a doughnut. She knocked on the passenger side window.

Raymond opened the door for her. 'Hop in there, Eileen,' he said. 'Bad day, isn't it?'

'Very bad,' said Eileen. 'I think we had all the summer we're going to get last week.'

'Looks like it,' said Raymond. He took another bite of his doughnut and spoke between chews. 'What can I do for you, anyway?'

'Oh, you'll probably think I'm pure stupid. But it's my son John, you see. He's gone missing.'

'Missing?'

'Yes. He went out to the pub on Monday night and he never came home at all.'

'He's the youngest one, isn't he?'

'He is. Just twenty years last March.'

'Ah, now, Eileen. He's a big lad. He's probably met up with some other young fellows and they've gone after a bit of craic somewhere.'

'I suppose,' said Eileen.

'He'll turn up, you'll see.'

'I suppose,' she said again. 'But it isn't like him. He's a good young lad. Very considerate. I'm sure he would have phoned or something.'

Raymond swallowed the last of his doughnut. 'The way it is, we can't file a Missing Persons report on someone of that age. Unless there was some way he wasn't in full possession of his faculties.'

'Oh, he was,' said Eileen. 'He is. He has a good job in Athlone and a new car and all. That's why I was thinking, he might have had an accident or something.'

'What kind of a car does he have?'

'A kind of silvery grey one.'

'Do you know what make it is?'

'What's this he told me? It sounded like a washing powder. Daz something.'

'Mazda?' said Raymond.

'That's it. A Mazda. A grey Mazda.'

'I tell you what, Eileen. I'll make a few enquiries for you, see if there's been any accidents involving a grey Mazda. How's that?'

'Oh, that's great, Raymond. That would help to put my mind at rest. To be honest, he has the heart put crossways in me, disappearing like that.'

'Don't you be worrying. He's probably having a great time somewhere. What does he work at?'

'In Greaney Meats,' said Eileen. 'They kill twelve hundred cattle there every day.'

Malachy took John a sandwich and another Mars Bar. Goggles went ape, trying to get at it, but John wasn't sharing, this time. He wasn't sharing with Malachy, either. He felt that he had somehow been walked into a trap the last time they spoke, and he wasn't about to do it again.

'Are you feeling any better?'

John didn't answer.

Malachy took up the fork and returned to the work. He took a full barrow to the muck heap before he spoke again.

'I was thinking about what you said, about being the right man.'

'Were you, Malachy. Thinking. How very stressful for you.'

'Maybe you're right. Maybe it's us men who have got it wrong.'

'You're a philosopher, I see. A philosopher butcher. How quaint.'

'Oh, come on, John. I don't understand why you're being like this. We were getting somewhere earlier. We were beginning to understand each other.'

'Don't fool yourself, Malachy. You have about as much chance of understanding me as he does.'

He walked over to the bullock and rubbed its ears. Then he took hold of one in each hand, gripped them tight, and slammed his forehead down between the bullock's eyes. It was debatable which one of them suffered more, but the bullock swung away in terror and crammed itself into the corner by the door.

Malachy dropped the fork with a clang on to the flagged floor. 'You little shit!' he said. 'There was no cause for that!'

He came around to the door and spoke gently to the bullock, but John moved in and kicked it hard in the stomach, sending it spinning round into the other corner.

'Let me out, Malachy!'

'No way.'

'Shall we see if I can kill it? With my bare hands? What kind of a man would that make me, eh?'

He kicked the bullock again, following it around the box.

'I'm going for the guards,' said Malachy.

John stopped.

'I've had enough. I thought there was another way. A better way. But it isn't working, is it? That's not what you want.'

John said nothing, but he put a conciliatory hand on the bullock's rump.

'I thought there was some kind of logic to your insanity, but maybe there isn't. Maybe you're just the vicious little bastard you appear to be. Is that it, John? Is that the truth?'

The bullock seemed ready to believe that it had all been some kind of terrible mistake. It looked enquiringly at John, and took a hesitant step towards him.

'How can you accuse me of being sick?' said John. 'How can you treat them like this and then take them out and kill them?'

Malachy found it hard to change direction. The question hit him where he was vulnerable.

'It hurts, all right? It hurts every time.'

'Then why? What's the point?'

Malachy closed his eyes and dragged a hand across his face. 'Because it ought to hurt. It's right that it should hurt.'

John rubbed the bullock's forehead, where he had struck it. It let out a bellow, of confusion, or relief, or hunger, or perhaps all three. Malachy felt ill. This couldn't go on. He had to do something that would bring it to a resolution, one way or another.

'I'll be back,' he said. 'Let's talk about it later.'

Raymond Murray had a nagging suspicion about John Kilroy and the grey Mazda. There were plenty of grey cars, but the fact that the lad worked in a slaughterhouse had raised his suspicions. It might be worth checking out.

He made the calls that he had promised Eileen, then went home to pick up his wellingtons and drove on down to Micky Mac's inch. He parked the car at the end of the boreen and walked down it. The tyre-marks from two evenings ago had been practically obliterated by the heavy rain. It had already been established that they were made by the same kind of tyres as the ones in the boreen near Seanie Walsh's land, but Raymond was hoping to find something that might have been missed. He searched behind the high hedges in the nearby fields and was both disappointed and relieved to find that the car was not hidden, as he had suspected. The fact went a long way towards disproving his theory, but he decided to continue anyway.

The gate at the end of the track was open, hanging sadly from the electric fence wire which acted as its hinges. Micky had been proud of his bull's success in warding off the attacker, but he wasn't taking any more chances. As soon as the guards had finished their investigations that morning he had moved the herd, dragging out two nieces and a nephew to help him drive them the long, slow two and a half miles to his home meadows. Raymond was relieved about that as well. He had grown up on a farm and had a great respect for cross bulls.

The level of the river hadn't risen appreciably, despite the rain. It would take several days of heavy downfall in the hills before the water would cover the inch, and it was almost unknown for that kind of rain to occur during the summer months. But the ground was gathering the run-off from the hill, and his wellingtons squelched at every step. He combed the undergrowth at the foot of the slope and walked along the hedge at the other end of the long field. Then he made his way back along the bank of the river, peering down into the peaty water.

There was no body. The bull had scared off the intruder, not killed him. But as he walked back up the muddy track, Raymond was still thinking about John Kilroy and the grey Mazda.

Mairead was concerned about Sarah. She didn't like to ask her, but she appeared to have forgotten that she was planning to leave. She was pale as well, and distracted. Her characteristic energy and focus had evaporated.

Even her appetite had gone. Mairead had made vegetarian bangers and mash for lunch; a variation on a childhood favourite, but Sarah was picking at it lethargically.

'Are you all right?' Mairead asked. 'Is there something on your mind?'

'No, no. I'm fine.'

The phone rang. Mairead went out to answer it and returned a moment later.

'For you,' she said. 'I'm amazed at you, Sal. I really am.'

Sarah picked up the phone. 'Hello?'

'Sarah.'

'Malachy. How are you?'

'I thought you'd gone. Why didn't you come down?'

'I meant to.' She reached out and closed the kitchen door, then turned her back to it. 'What's happening?'

'Not a lot.'

'He's still there, then?'

'He's still here, and it doesn't look as though he's going to crack. What are we going to do?'

Sarah had been thinking about little else all day. She kept her voice low, so that Mairead wouldn't overhear. 'You'll have to let him go. I can't see what other option there is.'

There was a long silence. So long that Sarah eventually felt compelled to break it. 'Malachy?'

She heard him take a long inhalation. The sound, so close to her ear, sent tingles through her belly.

'I don't know what we're dealing with, any more,' he said. 'I keep thinking I'm getting somewhere with him and then I realise I'm not.'

He told her about the way John had treated the bullock. 'I was half afraid to leave him alone with it, but I listened at the door, and you know what?'

'What?'

'He was talking to it. Muttering away.'

Sarah failed to see the significance. 'So what?'

'That was the point, really. One of the points.'

'Was it?'

'Yes. So he might get more of an insight. Feel some affinity.'

'But you're fond of it too. It isn't going to stop you from killing it, though, is it?'

'You still don't understand, do you?' said Malachy. 'Why I work the way I do?'

Sarah sighed heavily. 'Oh, Malachy.' The way she said it made him suddenly shaky with desire, and for a few moments he barely heard what she was saying.

'All that stuff is neither here nor there. We're in this mess together and we just have to try and find a way out of it.'

Malachy re-engaged his mind with an effort. 'You don't know what it means to me to hear you say that.'

'What?'

'That we're in it together. I can handle anything as long as you're with me.'

It was Sarah's turn to fall silent. She hadn't intended to drop her guard. But her heart was going out to him and she was tired of resisting.

'Will you come down?'

'I will.'

'Shall I pick you up?'

'No. I'll cycle over in a while.'

'You promise?'

'I promise.'

'We'll sort something out, Sarah. I know we will.'

28

Garda Murray had exhausted his enquiries into John Kilroy's whereabouts, but the possibility of a connection between the boy and the bulls was still nagging at him. He knew that Sarah O'Malley had seen a grey car, and he wanted her to make a closer identification of it. So he drove into Ennis to get some photographs to show her. If she could make a positive identification of the car, it might cast an interesting light on John's sudden disappearance.

It was dry when Sarah set out on the bicycle, but she hadn't gone far along the road when it began to rain. It was a light, soft shower, not remotely unpleasant, but it was surprisingly penetrative. By the time Sarah reached the bungalow, everything she had on was saturated.

Malachy took her jacket and hung it over the back of a chair. 'Do you want to change? I could lend you some dry things.'

'No, thanks.'

'A towel at least.' He pulled a clean one out of the hot press beside the range and handed it to her. She dried her hair, aware that she was rubbing all the tangles back into it, and handed the towel back to Malachy. He hung it over the rail at the front of the range.

'I was so afraid that you'd gone,' he said.

'I couldn't go,' said Sarah. 'Not with all this going on.'

'All what?' said Malachy.

They both knew she was talking about John. They both knew she was talking about something else as well. Malachy laid a hand on her shoulder. Sarah reached for it. She had it in her mind to move it away, but as soon as she touched it she drew it closer instead, and held it against her cheek, and turned her lips towards it. It neither smelled nor tasted of blood.

There was no hay left in the manger, and the concrete was cold and uncomfortable without it. John paced the edges of the box, examining the construction for the hundredth time for any signs of weakness. He played with the idea of a fire, but he couldn't think of any way of starting one. For the only time in his life John regretted that he wasn't a smoker.

He regretted, as well, that he had given up carrying a penknife. There was a time when he had never been without one. If he'd had any kind of tool he could have carved or jemmied away at the wooden partitions. But the only things he had in his pockets were a fine-toothed comb and the last of his money.

The bullock was lying in the driest corner of the box, dozing peacefully. John stepped over it and settled himself on the shavings with his back against the beast's warm side. He could feel the slow, steady beat of its huge heart. It seemed a shame to stop something that functioned so well; had so many years of useful working left in it. If the bullock had been a car, he would have bought it.

The heartbeat reminded him of his first day in the slaughter hall. He had been put to work near the start of the line, where the carcasses left the blood bath and began their long, slow journey towards the cold rooms. His job was to cut off the forelegs at the knee joint. He had been shown how to do it, but it wasn't always easy to get the knife in at the right point in the joint, and it was requiring all his concentration to keep up with the work.

He remembered the surprising keenness of his blade as it sliced through skin and sinew, the hot, heavy tumble of the spilling guts at the next station, the quick skill of the lads loosening the hide as it was dragged clear. Beneath, the stripped carcass was pristine, the covering of fat still warm and translucent and glistening. It was dead, he knew, but it seemed to him more like something newborn.

He was struggling with a particularly awkward knee joint when something hot and wet hit him hard on the side of the head and dropped on to the concrete beside him. It was a bullock's heart.

He looked around. Further along the line each of the men was working at a particular task; taking out the liver or the lungs or the kidneys, but John couldn't see which one of them was doing what. There was no way, without going down there, to see who had thrown the heart.

A few minutes later another one hit him on the shoulder. He stopped what he was doing. 'Who the fuck keeps doing that?'

A snigger rippled around the slaughter hall, then one of the lads said, 'You'd want to watch yourself. It looks as if you're prone to heart attacks.'

Sarah and Malachy made it to the bedroom at last and made love again, at a less urgent pace. For each of them it was the breaking of a fast that had gone on for too long. And they made a fine meal of each other, blotting out all the uncomfortable things that were outstanding in their lives, perfectly engrossed in the moment.

Afterwards, as they lay in tangled silence, Sarah understood that she was, after all those years, finally ready to let Duncan go. The sadness that she had never allowed herself to experience now began to emerge, and she cried silently on Malachy's shoulder. He didn't ask her why. The hour belonged to the heart, and not to the mind.

The bullock at John's back sighed. The expansion of its ribcage pushed his torso upright. Its contraction allowed him to slump back again. He laughed.

Malachy nursed my mother through her grief. As her heart began to lift again, she propped herself up on her elbow and looked into his eyes.

'Hello, stranger.'

He pushed her hair out of her face. 'I'm no stranger than you are.'

'I can't understand how this has happened,' said Sarah. 'We have nothing in common at all.'

'We do, though,' said my father. 'That's what I've been trying to explain to you all along. We have a lot in common. Far more than you think.'

'I guess it's time to listen, then.'

Malachy opened his mouth to speak, but was forestalled by the phone. He got up to answer it, walking naked into the kitchen. When he came back he began to get dressed.

'It's Oliver,' he said. 'He's got practically nothing left to sell.'

'Can't it wait?'

'He says if I don't bring some meat to the shop he'll close it up and come down here and get some.'

He pulled on his shirt, and Sarah watched with regret as he buttoned the delectable warmth of his body away inside it.

'It won't take long,' he said. 'I'll be back in no time.'

'What are we going to do about John?'

Malachy said nothing, but the lover's softness dropped

away from his face and was replaced by the more familiar hang-dog look.

'Let's not worry about him now.'

'We have to worry about him, Malachy. We have to come to a decision.'

'But not now, all right? We can talk about it later. We'll sort him out.'

He went back into the kitchen. Sarah heard the outside door close behind him, and the van start up. A few minutes later it returned from the buildings, passed the bungalow and moved away along the drive. Sarah was still listening to it receding into the distance when the phone rang again.

She answered it without thinking. 'Hello?'

'Is that you, Sarah?'

'Mairead? How did you know I was here?'

'I guessed. Are you in some kind of trouble, Sal?'

'No. Why?'

'It's just that Raymond Murray was here again, looking for you.'

'Who's Raymond Murray?'

'The guard, remember?'

My mother's skin crawled. 'What did he want?'

'He didn't say. I said I had no idea where you were. Was that the right thing to do?'

'Of course. But I don't know what they could want.'

'Sarah?' said Mairead.

'Yes?'

'Are you and Malachy . . . You know.'

Sarah found herself grinning. 'I suppose you could say we are.'

But as soon as she rang off the grin fell away from her face. She began to get dressed. The appearance of the guard again worried her. She knew that Eileen Kilroy had been looking for him that morning. Was there any chance that he had begun to put two and two together?

Without warning, a whole series of sinister connections began to click into place in her mind. She had given them her name, and the same London address that she had given the English police. What if someone had looked up her file? Found that she had a criminal record, for malicious damage to farm property. What if they had matched her fingerprints with some found on Tom Deverix's cattle crush. Or Micky Mac's gate. The possibilities were bad enough, but a worse one abruptly presented itself, in the form of a vivid memory. Malachy was struggling with John beside the inch. John was trying to get at his knife. And she grabbed it from his belt. Grabbed it and flung it aside. She knew the guards had found it. Her prints would be all over it.

They were sure to come down here looking for her. She had been seen drinking with Malachy in the pub. She had been heard making outrageous statements about farmers. Mairead O'Malley's mad sister. They were going to come down here and find her; find John locked up; find John's concealed car.

Anxiety was piling upon anxiety, and she was close to panic. Whatever her feelings for Malachy, she would be a fool to stay around and wait for the whole lot to come tumbling down around her ears. She had to get out, and fast.

She was already running towards the yard before she had fully worked out what she was going to do. She still didn't trust John, but in a choice between him and the police he was winning hands down.

John and the bullock leaped to their feet at the sound of Sarah's feet in the yard.

'I knew you'd come back!' said John, as she ran down the passageway and into the tack room. 'Fair play to you, woman.'

There was no bolt-cutter or crowbar in the toolbox, but there was a heavy steel rod which might work. She took it and set about trying to wrench the padlock open. John craned his neck, but couldn't see. He tried to supervise anyway.

'Get some leverage. It ought to pop.'

Sarah swore, put her foot up against the door frame and threw her full weight against the bar. The padlock sprang open.

'We have to get out of here quick,' she said. 'He'll be back any minute now.'

They tore at the bales around the car and flung them, bent and breaking, across the coach-house floor. As he cleared the driver's window, John said, 'Fuck. There's no keys.'

'Can you start it without them?'

'No way.' He opened the car and hunted around on the floor and in the door pockets. 'Fuck.' He was about to stand back when he thought of one last place to look and reached up to the folded sun visor above the driver's seat. There was a gratifying jangle, and the keys fell on to the seat.

'Yesss!' said John.

He was about to get into the car when the bullock gave a mournful call from its dark, lonely cell. The weanlings, crowded against the furthest wall of the coach-house, replied. John hesitated and looked back.

'You want one more day, Ferdie?' he said.

'What?' said Sarah.

John ran back along the passage and slid the door open again. The bullock wandered out into the passageway and stood watching him as he jumped into the car and started it up.

Sarah moved to the passenger side, then hesitated. John leaned across and opened the door for her.

'What are you waiting for?'

Still she didn't get in. She was remembering the darkness, the blood, the dead bulls.

'Come on!'

Sarah looked down. Some instinct for self-preservation had made her keep hold of the steel rod. She swung it once to test its weight, then got into the car.

29

Malachy called through the empty house. He knew that Sarah
couldn't be far away because Mairead's bike was still leaning
against the wall outside. But apart from the damp towel and
the smell of her body, still clinging to the deserted bed, there
was no evidence at all that she had ever been there.

Malachy went out into the rain and called again. He
walked beneath the sycamores; saw the fresh tyre-tracks
in the soft ground, began to run before the tide of anxiety
that was rising in his heart.

The coach-house was full of bellowing. Malachy saw the
stain of leaked oil in the vacant space and the strewn bales,
which Goggles was contentedly eating.

'Sarah?'

Only the calves answered.

'Sarah!'

Malachy's legs wouldn't support him. He leaned against
the wall and slid down it on to the cold, flagged floor. The
troubled voices of the weanlings reflected his own misery.
Their worlds, and his, had been torn apart by sudden and
unexpected separation.

'Where are you headed?' asked John.

He had instinctively taken the minor roads out of town,
travelling towards the Burren on the safest route to Athlone.

'Dublin.'

'You're travelling light.'

'I don't approve of possessions.'

There were things that Sarah regretted leaving behind, but it wasn't worth the risk of going back for them.

John took a right turn, heading east. 'Dublin it is, then.'

'You're going to take me there?'

'Why not? One good turn deserves another.'

He knew how to bypass Ennis and Limerick. For the rest of the way, he would just have to trust to luck.

Sarah was relieved to discover that he drove proficiently and carefully. Her own nerves were fragile, though she wasn't sure whether she was expecting to be apprehended by the police or turned on by John. She kept a good grip on the steel bar, which rested across her thigh. But as the distance increased between themselves and Kilbracken, she began to relax. Her clothes were still soaking wet, and she reached for the heater.

'It doesn't work,' said John. He put on the poncy voice again. 'It's just my summer runabout. Sorry about that.'

Sarah let her guard down and laughed.

Malachy knew that there was only one way that he could deal with his own condition, but it was a long, long time before he mustered the necessary energy to get himself up on his feet again. The first thing he did was to return Goggles to his box. He had a bellyful of hay, now, and Malachy wouldn't be able to kill him before tomorrow. It didn't matter. If anything, he was relieved.

Mechanically, he restacked the scattered bales, straightening the bent ones, throwing the broken ones into a corner, to be used first. When he had finished he returned to his previous routine, letting out the bullocks, all except Goggles, giving them their bait in the slaughterhouse.

Afterwards he went into the cold room, prepared the

Galway order and set out to deliver it. He didn't feel safe on the roads, but he didn't turn back. He knew that it had nothing to do with the traffic. He wouldn't have felt safe anywhere, that day.

Sarah and John met the Dublin road at Birdhill. John concentrated on keeping within the speed limit, and for a while they travelled in silence. Sarah's thoughts returned to Malachy. Leaving him like that was painful for her. She knew that she would never have found happiness with him; she would never have been able to come to terms with what he did, even though she had an instinctive faith in his integrity. Their paths were destined to cross, she believed, but not to merge. But no amount of reasoning could eradicate her regret. It was like Duncan all over again. She had anchored her heart to her past.

John intruded upon her thoughts.

'Are you going to hit me with that thing?'

Sarah looked down at the rod.

'I'm not going to jump you or anything,' John went on. 'You needn't worry.'

Sarah didn't answer. John turned on the radio, then turned it off again. 'You still think I did it, don't you?'

'I know you did,' said Sarah.

John sighed. They passed a white car parked in a gateway. It had no markings, but John kept an eye on it in his rear-view mirror until he was sure that it was innocent.

'And what if I did?' he said.

Sarah looked up at him, and he glanced at her with a shrug. 'I didn't. But what if I did? I mean, what's the difference between killing a bullock in a slaughterhouse and killing a bull in a field?'

'I can't see any virtue in either of them,' said Sarah. 'I'm a vegetarian.'

'That's beside the point,' said John. 'What's the difference?'

Sarah was stumped. There were all kinds of things she could say about farmers' rights of ownership, but not with any kind of conviction.

'Do you think it makes any odds to the beast?' John went on. 'If you were a prisoner would you rather be driven to the slaughter or given a fighting chance?'

'Jesus, John! It's hardly the same thing!'

'Isn't it?'

They stopped to get petrol. Sarah insisted on paying for it, and John seemed to lighten up a bit afterwards. As they joined the traffic again, he said, 'You living in Dublin, then?'

She had no desire to tell John where she was going. 'I might stay there for a bit,' she said. 'What about you?'

'Oh, back to Athlone. If my job's still there.'

But he wasn't as sure as he sounded. The idea of stepping back into that carnage was repugnant to him. And not only that. Although he said nothing to Sarah, he was haunted by Malachy. A whole raft of conflicting emotions were centred around the butcher. John wasn't entirely sure of its nature yet, but he was in no doubt that he and Malachy had unfinished business to attend to.

Malachy called in on Mairead on his way back from Galway. Between them they worked out that Sarah had gone, and why, but neither of them knew where.

'Is she likely to come back, would you say?' said Malachy.

'It's possible,' said Mairead. 'But somehow I doubt it.'

She and Malachy had been nodding acquaintances for years. It was rumoured in town that he suffered from depression, but until now, Mairead had never seen any evidence to confirm it. She saw it now, though. Several times she tried to engage him in conversation, and though he responded in a moribund sort of way, he spent most of the time in a brooding silence, looking down into his lap, rubbing his thumb against his palm with compulsive regularity. The coffee she had made for him grew cold.

Mairead felt vaguely responsible for his misery, since his distress appeared to be centred around her sister. But nothing she said seemed to help, and on the one occasion when she spoke dismissively about Sarah, Malachy gave his only display of animation in coming to her defence.

As time went on and Malachy showed no sign of going home, Mairead began to get worried. She was solicitous, but she didn't feel equipped to deal with the enormity of his despair.

'Have you ever thought of going to a homeopath?' she said.

'A homeopath? What's a homeopath?'

Mairead explained. 'They have remedies for all sorts of things that doctors can't cure.'

'What do I need to be cured of?' said Malachy.

Mairead shrugged defensively. 'I wasn't suggesting—'

'Sarah,' said Malachy. 'Do they have a cure for Sarah?' He laughed for the first time, and stood up. 'Thanks for the coffee, Mairead. Will you let me know if you hear from her?'

'I will,' said Mairead.

John dropped Sarah on the outskirts of Dublin. She watched as he drove away, and her spirits soared. In the end it had all been so simple. He hadn't attacked her or abused her in any way. He had even seemed quite normal, in the end. As she stood on the kerb, wondering which direction to take, she realised that she was still holding on to the steel bar. It seemed absurd. She laughed at herself, and dropped it into the gutter.

She began to walk along the street, looking out for road

signs. She had nothing except for the few pounds in her pocket. She was striding towards her next adventure; safe and free and totally without baggage of any kind.

Or so she thought. She had no intimations yet of the small encumbrance that she was carrying.

In a little over an hour, John was back in Athlone. The other lads in the house were gloomy. The farmers were still picketing the plant. There was no work, and no work meant no money. Brian, the one John liked best, had already packed up and left for Dublin.

'Maybe we should all go,' said Kevin. 'This is the age of the Celtic tiger, after all. There's plenty of jobs.'

But John's mind was focused on the west, not the east. When the others went out for a pint he declined to join them.

'I have to go back to Clare.'

'Got something on the go, have you?' said Kevin.

'I might have,' said John. 'But come here. If anyone asks you, I've been here all week, okay? Since Monday night.'

'Why? What have you been up to?'

'Nothing. Just sitting around here with you lot. Waiting for the factory to open.'

''Course you have, John. Bored out of your brains with the rest of us.'

As soon as they were gone he raided the small stash of savings which he kept inside a pair of socks in his bedside locker, and left the house.

He stopped first at the filling station and then at the nearby chipper. Back in the car, he drove on past the processing plant where the farmers were still picketing, sheltering from the wind behind their banners. Outside the town he pulled in and sat in the car at the side of the road, eating the greasy chips and thinking.

He had, he knew, only one chance at this. If he didn't do

it now, he never would. A deal would soon be struck, the factory would open again, and he would be back inside its grim grey walls for ever. But tonight he could change all that. If he had the courage to go through with it he could restore his injured pride, embark upon a different kind of future, finish, in the most unexpected way, what he had begun.

The tree people were gone, their struggle abandoned, their houses heaps of rotting lumber and tin among the doomed oaks. Sarah would have found it impossible to believe that the end had come about so suddenly, if the evidence had not been there before her eyes. She walked past the triumphant machinery and in among the trees, until a guard spotted her and ordered her to leave.

Sarah decided not to put up a fight. She wandered back to the road and sat on her heels, watching the speeding traffic. She was waiting, she thought, for spirit guidance, but the truth was that there was only one place that she could go. When the guard appeared again, strolling along the green border of the road, she approached him.

'Which way should I go for Carlow?'

Night was falling by the time John set out for Clare. He drove slowly and steadily, an exemplary motorist, courteous and careful. He had made mistakes in the past and he knew, now, what the results of recklessness could be. This time everything would be perfect.

He arrived in Kilbracken before dawn, and drove on through the silent town. He parked the car beneath the trees at the entrance to Malachy's avenue and got out. The wind was tossing the branches, masking the sound of his footsteps as he walked through the darkness. He was glad that Malachy had no dog.

The bungalow was dark. That was good. He wanted to

check out a few things. He wanted to be prepared when
Malachy brought the spectacled bullock to the slaughterhouse. That way, there would be no doubts in his mind.
There would be no dissuading him from what he intended
to do.

The slaughterhouse wasn't locked. John found the humane
killer in a cavity block at the head of the crush. It was already
loaded. He couldn't believe his luck.

Malachy went to bed early. He slept like the dead, dreamed
of the dead, woke feeling like the dead warmed up. Death
awaited him as well, in the slaughterhouse, but he didn't
allow himself to stay in bed. The dreams had frightened
him. If he kept still for too long, he might never get up.

It was best to get the killing over and done with. The
bullock ran ahead of him, out of the coach-house and
along the concrete road to the holding pen. Malachy slid
the heavy door across and it went in, heading straight for
the crush. But something moved in the shadowy interior
of the building, and it hesitated.

Malachy saw the movement as well, and hung back as
John stepped forward into the light.

'Hello, Malachy,' he said. 'Hello, Ferdinand.'

The bullock, reassured, went on into the crush. Malachy
stayed where he was.

'What's wrong, Malachy?' said John. 'Your nerves giving
you a hard time?'

The bullock watched him, then returned its attention to
the empty manger. The humane killer was in John's hand,
and Malachy cursed himself for leaving it in a place where
it could so easily be found. It was bad practice, he knew.

John came around the side of the crush. Malachy was
certain that his hour had come at last. There was time for
him to turn and make a run for it, but he didn't. He was
afraid, but some drifting part of his being was watching

dispassionately, and he was aware of some elegant kind of logic acting itself out. It seemed to him that he had been trying to dig his own grave for years. Perhaps he had finally succeeded?

He took a step back, but John didn't follow. Instead, he passed him by and closed the rear gate of the crush. The bullock was beginning to get restless. John walked to its head and laid a calming hand between its ears. It glanced up at him and its hot, inquisitive huffing ballooned his shirt-front. As Malachy watched, John lifted the bolt-gun, positioned it quickly and carefully, and fired.

The bullock collapsed like a dropped puppet. Malachy hesitated for a moment, then found himself moving forward instinctively, to hoist the beast and bleed it before it could recover consciousness. The two men worked in silence, united by the familiar procedure. They had been engaged with the carcass for some time before Malachy came to a realisation that astonished him. Imprisoning John had been the craziest and most dangerous thing he had ever done. But it had worked an effect that was above and beyond his wildest expectations.

30

The guards questioned John at length about the bulls. He told them that he had returned to Athlone to watch the picketing of the meat plant and see what transpired. He had plenty of witnesses to confirm that. He expressed amazement that his mother had reported him missing.

The knife taken from Seanie Walsh's bull had revealed no fingerprints, and the one from inside Micky Mac's gate had been too muddy to test. Since the only person who had seen the car had vanished without trace, there was not enough evidence to go on. Raymond kept an eye on John over the days and weeks that followed, but his behaviour gave him no reason for suspicion. There were no more attacks on bulls. As time went by the file sank to the bottom of the pile and was eventually lodged with the rest of the unsolved cases.

Malachy had expected Sarah to rescue him, but it was John who did it. By returning to him, by understanding what he was doing and why, John affirmed him in his life's undertaking. Malachy still yearned after Sarah, but without the suicidal desperation that had haunted his thoughts in the past. With John's help, he was able to start putting the farm back in order; running things the way they ought to be run. He spent more of his time with the younger bullocks, moving among them, making friends with them, teaching them a trust that their species had all but forgotten.

John's confinement was never mentioned, even when he took over the management of the coach-house and its residents. He and Malachy rarely talked about anything beyond practical matters. But they understood each other perfectly. There were times, in fact, when Malachy believed that John had an even better grasp of the business's underlying principles than he had himself.

My mother had only intended to pay a visit to Theresa. But Theresa, without Mike, was having a hard time of it, both emotionally and practically. A few days turned into a month, and the month was in the process of becoming a season, when Sarah came to the realisation that she was pregnant.

The bottom fell out of her new world. She was perpetually nauseous and light-headed, and although she continued to work as well as she could, it cost her considerably more effort. Her dreams were populated by the gaping jaws of garden pests and newly born infants. She began to lose her weed battles.

She might have considered an abortion, if it hadn't meant that she would have to get it through the despised medical system. The herbal alternative that she tried was an assault on both our constitutions, but it didn't have the faintest chance of dislodging me.

Theresa noticed that Sarah was off-colour, and asked if there was anything she could do to help. Sarah made excuses and carried on as usual, but she found the burden of deception intolerable. Eventually, one morning, she bit the bullet.

'I'm going to have to move on,' she told Theresa. 'Things aren't working out the way I planned.'

'Why?' said Theresa. 'What's gone wrong?'

My mother couldn't look her in the eye. 'I'm pregnant,' she said.

Theresa jumped up and danced around the cottage kitchen. 'Don't move on!' she said. 'That's the best news I've heard all century! I thought there would never be any children here!'

She came around to Sarah's side of the table and, bending double, addressed me in my mother's womb.

'Welcome to our little enterprise, young traveller.'

As time went on, John gradually took over all the killing. He was up at dawn every day, not groggy and haggard as Malachy was, but fresh and energetic; ready for the work. In Malachy's hands, the bolt-gun would never be more or less than a murder weapon, reluctantly wielded. Every time he killed he waged a battle with his own heart, resisting the executioner role, acting under self-imposed duress.

But when John took a beast to the slaughter he walked tall and his back was straight. Effortlessly, and with perfect dignity, he succeeded where Malachy had perpetually failed.

In his capable hands, each bullock's death was an act of worship.

Epilogue ∫

In my mother's room, stacked behind the door, are piles of jotters and newspaper cuttings. She did begin to write that book, but she never finished it. In the end, she didn't have to.

She kept her pregnancy a secret, even from her parents and Mairead. But her feelings for my father ran deeper than she would have expected them to, and when I was six months old she took me on a bus to visit Kilbracken. She had planned what she would say to Malachy. 'He will not be a butcher, even though his father was.' But Malachy wasn't there to hear her say it.

John was running the place, with the help of his new, young wife. Everything was ship-shape; the yards were clean and the bullocks were healthy and happy. John paid a regular share of the profits into Malachy's bank account, but where he had gone, no one could say.

The farm here is running well, too. We earn a basic living from it, and during the busiest seasons we employ an extra gardener. I'm already big enough to help with a lot of the work. I can handle the cob who pulls the plough and the produce cart, and I can run the market stall on my own for a while, if it's not too busy.

Theresa says that since I'm old enough to work, I'm old

enough to sit in on the planning discussions. So I do, if they're not too late or too boring. Yesterday we discussed whether or not we should start keeping our own chickens.

My mother was against it. We buy good organic eggs in the market and keeping our own flock would just be an extra responsibility. Theresa said they would cost us nothing – they'd eat the small potatoes and the scraps from the house. In return we'd get not only the eggs, but some good manure, which is getting hard to come by.

My mother was pressed into revealing her deeper reservations. The hens would have chicks. We would have more cockerels than we needed. We would be faced with the necessity of disposing of them.

'I'll kill them,' I said. 'I won't mind.'

My mother looked at me as though I had turned into a werewolf in front of her eyes.

'No,' she said. 'I vote no. No chickens.'

I won't be a butcher, though. It isn't in my bones or my blood, any more than it was in my father's. Besides, it is a declining trade. The CAP has turned its coat again. The planet is overheating. It can't support so many cattle, and the beef industry is being quietly strangled by the new slaughter taxes. Not before time, says my mother.

But there may still be a future for the bullock in Ireland. We have heard rumours of a man in County Meath who is training them to the yoke. The demand for horses is exceeding supply, now that diesel prices are putting lorries off the roads, and prices have gone through the roof. My mother says she likes cattle; always has. She says that our old cob is nearly ready for retirement and she's thinking that some day, maybe in the autumn, she might take a trip to Meath to check out those bullocks.

And there's no doubt at all that when she goes, she'll be taking me along with her.